Raven Heights Manor

Raven Heights Manor

Sharol Louise

FIVE STAR
A part of Gale, Cengage Learning

Farmington Hills, Mich • San Francisco • New York • Waterville, Maine
Meriden, Conn • Mason, Ohio • Chicago

Five Star™ Publishing, a part of Cengage Learning, Inc.

LIBRARY OF CONGRESS CATALOGING-IN-PUBLICATION DATA

Louise, Sharol.
Raven Heights Manor / Sharol Louise. — First edition.
pages ; cm
ISBN 978-1-4328-2940-7 (hardcover) — ISBN 1-4328-2940-8 (hardcover)
1. Orphans—Fiction. 2. Cornwall (England : County)—History—19th century—Fiction. I. Title.
PS3612.O82R39 2015
813'.6—dc23 2014026878

First Edition. First Printing: December 2014
Find us on Facebook– https://www.facebook.com/FiveStarCengage
Visit our website– http://www.gale.cengage.com/fivestar/
Contact Five Star™ Publishing at FiveStar@cengage.com

Printed in the United States of America
1 2 3 4 5 6 7 18 17 16 15 14

Lovingly dedicated to my three amazing granddaughters:
Kaitlyn Elizabeth,
Megan Nicole,
and Violet
and to Tomás, life partner *extraordinaire*

ACKNOWLEDGMENTS

I gratefully acknowledge my comrades who supported the adventure by reading my first draft, rescuing me as I began my usual cycle of self-doubt:

Pat Mack
Lynette Schell
Linda Hoversland

We recently adopted a nomadic lifestyle while exploring North America. Much of this novel was written on the serene decks and lanais of our gracious hosts:

Patty & Al Smith, Washington
Carolyn & Charlie Francis
Jennifer Endsley, Florida
Sherri Diesing

A special thank you to Wolfgang Marquardt, for his gracious help with German translations.

Finally, an indebted acknowledgment to my friend and patient editor, Alice Duncan.

Prologue

Claire trailed her right hand along the damp tunnel wall, afraid to miss the next turn in the dark. The winnowing candle in her left hand barely illuminated the confining trail.

Two right turns, and then the second left, Vitus had said. She remembered how he'd repeated the instructions, waiting sternly for her to nod her acknowledgment. As if he knew her life depended upon escaping the underground maze.

When first she came to Raven Heights Manor, she believed the mansion on its cragged perch above the sea to be as forbidding as its name. Now, trapped in the earth beneath its solid weight, she no longer held the heavy stones to blame. As her right hand brushed across an open space, she stopped and turned to face the opening. Both arms stretched straight as a sleepwalker's, she waved the candle as she groped the air to determine whether it was a false turn into a dead end of stone.

Finding no rock wall to block her path, her feet shuffled slowly forward, her fingers stretched ahead. The junction was true to the specific directions she'd been given, yet she hesitated, looking over her shoulder. She disliked leaving the main tunnel behind.

But the faint light she carried was enough to give a slight illumination to this branch. Or perhaps her eyes were becoming better accustomed to the dimness. Placing her hand again on the wall to her right, she continued forward, the ground now sloping upward ever so slightly. *One more right turn,* she said to herself, and then the second left.

She could hear her father's voice from years ago, challenging her with the riddle of the two men: one of these men always tells the truth. One of these men always lies. Do you know which is which, Claire? he would ask.

Vitus had told her the path she must follow through the tunnels. Which man was Vitus? The liar or the truth-teller? She no longer knew.

Chapter One

North Coast, Cornwall, England, late 18th century

"You're not to speak in your uncle's presence unless he asks you a direct question. Is that clear?"

Claire watched the countryside blur by the window of the coach, answering without turning her head. "Yes, ma'am," she mumbled.

"And for goodness sake, if and when he *should* deign to speak to you, do not mumble so."

The young lady, not quite sixteen years of age, did not bother to mumble a reply. She hoped the rumbling of the carriage hid the rumbling of her stomach. She hadn't been able to eat the previous night, nor sleep, and had barely touched the soft goat cheese and crusty bread on the sideboard this morning, before her uncle's carriage had arrived. Her neglecting to eat would be another excuse for Mrs. Cunliffe to scold.

Perhaps it was best she had not eaten, as Mrs. Cunliffe's potent ambergris perfume mixed with the hot air in the stuffy carriage. Claire sniffed surreptitiously at her own sleeve, wondering if the nauseating odor permeated her own body like a stain that would never wash out. She slanted her eyes to the side to sneak a peek at her guardian.

Mrs. Cunliffe had returned her gaze to the window at her side, her lips pursed as she determined whether this countryside near the coast met with her approval. The woman's dark, heavy taffeta skirts swished noisily as the coach swayed. Claire was grateful her own traveling outfit was a simple light-colored muslin dress suitable for a young lady. She remained comfortable in the sunlit coach, rather than wallowing in yards of dark purple, which brought an unseemly sheen to Mrs. Cunliffe's face, and in particular her upper lip.

Claire noted the slowing of the rhythmic harness jangles. Just in time, she put her hand on the carriage wall to steady herself as they took a turn too sharply. Her companion slid across the opposite banquette, bumping the window sash with her traveling bonnet, which now tipped ludicrously low upon her forehead, nearly covering her eyes. The older woman screeched her indignation. If she hadn't been leaning and blinded by plumes, she would surely have banged her cane on the roof, admonishing the driver.

The narrow entry tunnel they now funneled through must have caught their driver unawares. The high-ceilinged tunnel exited through an open gate into a wide avenue aimed straight as an arrow shaft at a massive stone structure.

Claire leaned forward, pressing her face against the carriage window, straining for a better glimpse of the towering walls in the distance.

This, then, was Raven Heights Manor, rising from a sea of cobbled stones at the end of the long lane. Claire shuddered involuntarily, and her stomach capsized in its wake. Shrinking back from the window, she glanced over to see if Mrs. Cunliffe witnessed her fear. But her escort was busy rearranging the crushed plumes of her bonnet.

Their heels echoed across the stone floor in the entry hall and continued loudly as they followed the crisply uniformed maid into the first parlor on the right. Heavy wine-colored damasks draped the windows and sturdy armchairs graced the room, formally lined up in two facing rows with a walnut table in their center. The richly hued Aubusson carpet beneath the furniture added to the darkness of the interior, except for the relief of a few pale roses scattered along its burgundy border. The armchairs were tapestried with the same dusky roses among pea-green twining leaves.

Claire's companion immediately plunked her ample frame in a central chair, with a long-suffering sigh. Intimidated by the formal arrangement, Claire sat tentatively on the forward edge of the chair closest to the door.

"Tea, mum?" asked the parlor maid.

"Yes. With extra cream." The young servant turned to leave. "And extra sugar," ordered Mrs. Cunliffe.

Claire assumed she needn't respond, as the maid departed straightaway.

Almost as soon as the heavy door closed, it opened again. Dwarfed by the tall door, a small woman in grey bombazine came briskly forward. "I am Mrs. Dawson."

Claire rose instantly, but Mrs. Cunliffe's eyelids narrowed as she watched Mrs. Dawson come forward. She apparently assumed the woman to be another staff member, as she did not bother to budge her large hips from the deep-cushioned armchair.

"And you must be Claire." Mrs. Dawson approached Claire directly, taking both Claire's hands in hers. "Of course. I can see you have your uncle's hazel eyes and the same lovely arched brows." Mrs. Dawson's gentle voice was welcoming, and she finally released Claire's hands. "Have you been offered tea?"

"Yes, ma'am, the maid—"

"I beg your pardon," said Mrs. Cunliffe in frosty tones, making it obvious she never begged, and pardon would not be on her list of needs, should she ever choose to do so.

Claire and Mrs. Dawson both stepped apart and turned to the seated woman.

"I am Mrs. Cunliffe, of Whiteworth's Boarding School. I have been authorized to escort Miss Temple to Raven Heights Manor. And you are?"

"Oh, did I not say? I am Mrs. Dawson."

Claire noticed the serene Mrs. Dawson did not elaborate, simply folded her hands upon her skirt, tilting her head to study the frowning Mrs. Cunliffe.

Mrs. Cunliffe's eyes briskly raked the smaller woman from the tip of her grey head to her sensible shoes. "I should like to speak to Sir Rudyard. Please inform him at once that his niece and I have arrived."

"Would that I could! However, Sir Rudyard is not in residence."

"Then I shall take tea, and I shall await his return." She turned her bored gaze to the door, already having dismissed Mrs. Dawson.

"Of course. Though that may be a lot of tea," said Mrs. Dawson with a slight smile. "We do not anticipate his return any time soon. Perhaps as much as a month or two."

"But—" Mrs. Cunliffe's stare returned, her mouth wide open. She closed it, then sputtered, "But he sent an urgent request to the school, asking that his niece be delivered immediately. Here. To Raven Heights Manor. Why would he do that, if he planned on being away?"

"When he returns, that is the first thing we shall ask him! Shall we send the answer to you at the school? Or perhaps that will not be necessary, if you plan to await his return." Mrs. Dawson spoke in a voice so sweet it should not have surprised Claire to see nearby butterflies flutter in through the arched windows. She wondered if the tiny, grey-haired woman was being facetious, or whether she was a bit slow-witted.

Mrs. Cunliffe's annoyance was punctuated with disbelief. "He wrote, giving us the impression he had only recently learned of the existence of his estranged brother's child. He was most adamant that we should send Miss Temple to him without delay. He sent the carriage for us."

"Yes, yes, he made that clear to us as well. It is his explicit wish that his niece should be brought here."

"But surely you realize I cannot leave her here if he is not in residence." It was not stated as a question.

Claire watched the two women as the words volleyed between them. In spite of her instant dislike of the ancient manor house, the thought of returning to the school rolled a stone of defeat to the pit of her stomach.

"She shall be well looked after until he returns." Mrs. Dawson's voice remained serene and confident.

"Who is in charge during his absence?" demanded her escort.

"That would be I."

"And you are?" Mrs. Cunliffe raised a pudgy arm, her open palm facing the older woman. "And *please,* do not again tell me you are Mrs. Dawson," she added in obvious exasperation.

"I am Sir Rudyard's second cousin. Will that do?" Mrs. Dawson squared her shoulders, raised her head pridefully. "Or would you prefer to take the child back with you, and explain to Sir Rudyard why his niece was . . . detained?" She did not pause for an answer. "By *your* command. Upon the sole authority of Mrs. Cunliffe, Headmistress of Whiteworth's Boarding School." Her eyebrows lifted, seeking contradiction. "Do I have that correct?"

Mrs. Cunliffe—overworked staff member, never headmistress—did not answer right away. She looked speculatively at Claire.

"Sir Rudyard does not tolerate having his wishes thwarted," prodded Mrs. Dawson. "He shall not be happy if he returns to find she is not here."

This did not make Claire any less nervous, hearing her guardian was an intolerant man; perhaps a short-tempered man as well. She was beginning to appreciate Mrs. Cunliffe's suggestion that they return to the school together.

Before Claire could mumble her agreement, however, her escort arose abruptly and moved toward the door, not inviting the young lady to accompany her.

Without turning, she called out, "Good day, madam. Goodbye, Miss Temple."

The heavy door closed behind her.

"Oh, dear," said Mrs. Dawson, under her breath, "that was a close miscalculation on my part." She turned her large blue eyes upon Claire. "I should *not* have said I was Sir Rudyard's cousin. Did you see how she hesitated? I should have insisted I was his sister."

"Are you? His sister?" asked Claire with curiosity.

"Heavens, no." This was accompanied by a tiny tinkling laugh. "I am more akin to housekeeper."

Claire considered this, wondering once more if the woman were a bit daft. "And if Mrs. Cunliffe had said 'no'?"

"Easily rectified, dear. I would have brought Sir Rudyard's brother Myles in to confront her."

"Ah. Then I have another uncle to meet—Uncle Myles?" This made Claire doubly apprehensive.

"I am afraid not." Mrs. Dawson patted her hand sympathetically. "No, Myles is long dead. I'm sorry, as he would have loved meeting you. Reggie, our butler, however, is a marvelous actor! He was always impersonating Myles when Myles was alive. But we needn't let your uncle—the live one, that is—know that, need we, dear?"

Claire did not need to answer, as tea arrived at that moment. With extra cream and extra sugar.

Chapter Two

From a far distance, the manor could be seen in silhouette on the jutting point high above the thundering waves. Raven Heights Manor perched like its namesake, its claws buried tenuously in the crags of the cliff.

Tiers of ancient stone the color of the surrounding rock balanced upon one another, wedding cake layers supported by tall columns and floor-to-ceiling windows, pinnacled by numerous steep gables. Gothic icing of gargoyles and weathered quoins made it more appropriate to a funereal celebration, perhaps.

A small figure stood on the bedroom balcony overhanging the sea. Still in her travelling dress, Claire stood facing the turbulent waters, feeling unsettled and alone.

As the sun dipped below the horizon, everything became drenched in its amber light, reminding her of a piece of honeycomb she'd held as a young girl. Not wanting to violate its perfect translucency, she'd held it toward the sun until the temptation to bite into the earthy wax could no longer be resisted. How long ago were those sweet, safe days?

A gull with angled wings came close by, eyeing her, then floated away soundlessly as a spirit. She willed her eyes to stay dry as she listened to its piercing call joined in answering chorus. Even seagulls had friends, no matter how they scolded and cried at one another. But she had no one to confide in.

Clouds moved menacingly nearer, their yellow underbellies ready to burst. As they sent a few errant drops, she felt tears she could no longer elude mixing with the rain, tasting salty as sea spray. She should move inside. Listless, she stayed rooted, resembling the trees on the grounds below, waving helplessly as they bent to another's will.

Long ago—a fairy tale age ago—when it thundered, her mother would allow her to hide under the covers in the safety of their huge four-poster bed.

The rain stirred her from her reverie as an icy sheet swept sideways upon her, and she backed into the room. Lightning lit the cliffs along the hill, holding her transfixed as the imprinted light faded from her vision.

As the faraway growl grew frighteningly close, she retreated farther inside, drawing the tall windows closed. Night clothes had been thoughtfully laid out upon her bed; she hadn't been aware of a maid's movements while on the balconied terrace, but someone had efficiently unpacked her few trunks.

From the high mattress of her bed, she could see the sea's horizon. She watched the dark storm's approach through the triple windows spanning floor to ceiling along the balconied wall. At the first thunderous jolt, Claire imagined the house speared by a lightning bolt from a hunter's quiver and dropping into the sea. How would it be to lie here while it creaked and groaned and fell around her? Would the floor remain intact as it slipped sideways? Would her bed skid along the floors, bumping into the window frame, and tipping her out over the sheer bluff?

Her mind replayed the evening's events following Mrs. Cunliffe's hasty departure. Cook had prepared a simple soup of potatoes, leeks, and cheese. Claire assumed Mrs. Dawson, as housekeeper, must decline to join her in the empty dining hall, however much Claire might wish for company this first night. As if reading her mind, the diminutive woman took the seat across from Claire and flicked a napkin across her own lap.

Regardless of whether the woman was a relative or a

delusional servant, Claire was relieved to have company at the large oak table. As they talked companionably, Mrs. Dawson admitted to truly being a cousin to Sir Rudyard. Though hardly destitute, as a spinster cousin she welcomed the opportunity to oversee his household in his absence of a wife.

"Perhaps tomorrow you'd like to walk to town," suggested Mrs. Dawson.

"I thought I might begin by exploring the gardens." Claire remembered the unending flower beds of different shapes and sizes, bordered by paths, which she'd spied from the coach yesterday as they wound their way slowly up the drive. Anxious lest she appear an ungracious guest, she quickly amended with embarrassment, "That is, if I may."

"Absolutely, child. This is your home." Mrs. Dawson dipped her spoon into her soup and raised it to her lips.

"I did not realize Uncle lived so close to the sea." Claire glanced toward the windows as if she could see the coastline, which was not visible from this side of the house. "It will be enjoyable to take brisk walks along the bluff."

Claire jumped as Mrs. Dawson dropped her spoon. It clattered against the fine bone china, splashing yellow puddles on the snowy white tablecloth.

Mrs. Dawson stared at Claire, ignoring the spilled soup. "I—I think it best you avoid the cliffs until your uncle returns."

Claire felt uncomfortable under the woman's intense gaze. Mrs. Dawson retrieved her spoon the moment Claire mumbled, "Of course. If you say so."

Claire's dinner companion delicately sponged the stain and continued, without making eye contact. "I don't mean to frighten you, dear. But I really would prefer you stay away from the trail on the bluffs."

"Yes, ma'am." Claire picked up her own spoon and kept her eyes on her bowl, eating her soup in silence.

"Claire." Mrs. Dawson waited until she held the young woman's attention. "I did not intend to say anything about this matter to you, but perhaps it's best you know. We've had a death in the village, fairly recently. About six months ago. A lovely young woman. She was your age." She shook her grey head, tears touching the corners of her blue eyes.

"How did she die?"

"It was an accident." Mrs. Dawson watched Claire, as if daring Claire to disagree. Leaning forward, she said softly, but firmly, "That is what the inquest determined."

Now, lying in bed, Claire watched wide flashes of lightning light up the middle of the sky, sandwiched between the dark sea below and the low, darker cloud layer above. Involuntarily she jumped as thunder crashed immediately upon its heels, directly above the manor.

Dark clouds confined in a box shape drifted closer to shore, the sparks and bolts colliding inside, like a sinister puppet play on Drury Lane. The hinged window frames protested, jostling and straining to the crescendos of wind. One blew open on a fierce gust of air, and she heard heavy drops pelt the bedroom floor next to the window, where no Aubisson carpet protected the wood. She slipped out of her cocoon, ran to the window, and struggled against the wind to push the pane closed. Just as she reached up to latch it, a fork of lightning struck and she screamed. Forcing herself to secure the clasp, she ran back to bed, afraid a random bolt might follow her inside and across the room.

Claire turned on her side, pulling the down pillows over her ears. The storm was now directly above the manor, she was sure of it. The timbers shook with each—what? Did they shake with the crack of lightning, or was it the thunder that shook the foundation? She couldn't discern, as one fell upon the other in rapid succession.

She shivered, but her room was not cold. She thought of Zillah. Was that the young woman's name; had Mrs. Dawson said? Yes, it was Zillah, an unusual name. She thought of Zillah's lifeless body floating in the cove where they discovered her. Zillah had fallen from the pinnacle of Raven Heights to the chilling water below. Had she died the moment she hit the rocks, or had the foaming water surged and sucked her life under with rabid swallows?

And why had there been an inquest? Was that normal in a violent death?

Burrowing deeper beneath the damask coverlet, Claire wished her existence had never been discovered by her uncle. She wished she'd never been brought to Raven Heights. Even its name frightened her.

She inhaled deeply, then forced herself to exhale slowly. *Things are always simpler in the morning,* she promised herself. *I can make it until the morning.*

Chapter Three

Apricot conquered grey, as the sun scaled the rim of the sea. Claire was surprised to have slept so deeply. She lay in bed and listened to a dog barking somewhere outside and a goose honking intermittently, wondering if one were cause for the other. Closing her eyes for another minute, she took stock of her feelings and was ready to face the day.

Crossing to the center window, she undid the latch she'd so hastily secured the night before. She retraced last night's steps to stand on the balcony facing the sea. A warm breeze swirled the hem of her white muslin nightdress and lifted dark curls that had lain plastered along her neck during the humid night.

She saw in the morning's light that the circular balcony that began at the bedroom wall on her left did not end symmetrically at the corner of the right wall. She approached the corner carefully and peered around the side. A walkway edged along the wall of her bedroom, then ended abruptly approximately where the interior wall of her room ended. Bordered by a marble balustrade, the walkway would be wide enough for a chair, but not much more. A small tea table, perhaps? She strolled to its end, sliding her hand along the decorative railing. From this vantage, she could see a slice of the manicured grounds leading up to the cliff's edge.

All right, she admitted begrudgingly. Uncle's home and grounds *are* beautiful. The portion of lawn she could see from here sloped slightly upward, ending at a wide path that separated the lawns from the sea far below. Her eyes followed the trail as it edged the cliff like a copper-colored ribbon, an occasional remnant of an old stone wall standing sentinel.

She was drawn to the landscape below. If she'd been a painter, she doubted she could ever have dreamt such a palette of contrasting colors and shadows. The quilt of verdant grass was bordered on the sea's edge by the brown path, its bare crushed rock glittering here and there as the clouds shifted. The far edge of lawn was riotously edged by a mixed border of flowering plants. It was too far away for her to distinguish the individual flowers, but here and there was a splattering of ruby red.

Mesmerized, she stared at the colorful scene, until the red flowers soon transformed into blotches of blood, reminding her of Zillah, the young woman who'd fallen to her death. Was this the side of the manor where she'd stood on the last night of her life? Were the cliffs below stained with blossoms of red?

Had anyone seen her fall? she wondered. Surely a guest in this room would have a clear view of the tragedy. Unless it was a dark night; would Zillah have been on the cliffs without a lantern or a candle? Claire rubbed her temples. She must stop thinking of the young woman's death.

Claire pulled her gaze away from the bluffs. Down to the right, past the lawn, she spied a small gamekeeper's cottage, surrounded by a gravel path that continued along the skirts of a forest. She could just make out a small wooden bench next to the cottage door. The gravel path meandered on and ended at several rows of clipped hedges surrounding what must be a summer-house, as only a small roof was visible from here. She pictured a walled garden hiding within the maze of hedges. Here her vista ended from her high perch, unless she were to lean out farther. She involuntarily shuddered and backed away from the balustrade, closer to her wall, as she returned to her room.

With unexpected determination, she looked forward to exploring the grounds today. And the manor itself? Perhaps the manor tomorrow. Or perhaps not at all. Besides her bedroom, the dining room, and the guest parlor she'd arrived in yesterday, she did not care if she never stepped into another room in this entire mansion.

Perhaps, though, she amended with a rueful grin, I shall locate the breakfast room.

Satisfyingly full of smoked kippers, scones with spiced apple jam, and oatmeal with thick cream, Claire was well-pleased to have discovered the breakfast room. The enigmatic Mrs. Dawson had never made an appearance, but it was rather late in the morning when Claire had taken a seat in the welcoming room. Doorways flanked each short wall of the long rectangular breakfast room. One door connected to the kitchen, down three broad stone steps, and the other led out into the hallway, from whence she'd entered. Of the other two longer walls, the first was lined with tall windows overlooking what appeared to be a sizable kitchen garden. The remaining wall was interspersed with small, square windows close to the ceiling, and serpentine mahogany sideboards beneath. The windows were of thick, irregular glass, and while too high to allow a view of anything but the sky, they reflected the early light in stripes of colors on the wooden floor.

She peeked around the arched doorway leading into the kitchen without descending the steps. Other than a darkened fireplace with oven and grills, bare oak tables, and a cavern of hanging pots and ladles, the room was currently empty. Its opposite door framed greenery through wavy glass panels. Claire took the steps in two jumps and darted through the kitchen to the adjoining garden door.

There was no reason she should hurry, other than shyness at meeting more of the staff. But having the quiet rooms to herself gave an imaginary air of mystery, and she pretended she'd come upon a deserted castle in the midst of a fairy-tale forest. She opened the outside door quietly and tiptoed across the threshold, anticipating a magical garden of towering runner beans, giant squash, and secret witch's seedlings.

It was a tidy, ordinary garden at first glance, until the pungent herbs and floral scents greeted her. She took a few steps into the aroma of rain-soaked earth now steaming in the sun like damp sheets pressed by a giant flat iron.

Strolling along well-tilled rows, she stopped and bent to smell each new flower she spied; there weren't many blooms among the pews of green on each side of her. She was surprised that many of the plant groupings had a pleasing smell, though no flowers were visible. A branch or two might make a welcome potpourri in her bedroom. She reached out and explored many of the leaves, some as curly as parsley, others narrow like rosemary needles, and some waxy. Pinching a leaf or two, she would gently rub the leaf between her fingers, then bring her hand to her nose. She recognized many of the herbal scents, though she did not know most of their names.

"Stop!"

Claire jerked upright and spun around. She'd been about to touch another of the plants in the next row, with attractive alternating leaves, considering it for a vase in her room.

Confronting her was a tall young man, about her own age. All she noticed at first impression was how dark his hair was, and that it was unfashionably long.

"What do you think you're doing?" He continued striding toward her.

"I—" Claire blushed. "I thought I might gather a few flowers." She met his serious gaze. His grey eyes appeared even lighter against his sun-browned skin. "And a little greenery. For a vase." At his continued silent stare, she added lamely, "For my room."

"These are not the cutting beds." He looked down at the plant she'd been about to pluck. "This is an herbal garden, for medicinals and for cooking."

"Yet I see flowers here as well." Claire's face was still hot, but she didn't care for his didactic tone. "And I do know the difference between a kitchen garden and a cutting garden."

There was a hint of a smile as he replied, raising his glance to hers, "My apologies. I'm sure you do." But the dryness of his tone implied otherwise. After an uncomfortable silence, Claire was the first to break eye contact.

He looked back down at the plant she'd been about to pull, as if inventorying to determine how many leaves she'd already picked. "Nevertheless, I would not recommend pulling that plant to fill your lady's vase." The smile tucked away, his serious gaze moved from the plant to hers.

"I wasn't going to gather a large bouquet. Just a few sprigs." She found herself becoming more defensive. Without realizing it she put her hands on her hips.

"That's not the point." He looked at the carefully tended plants. "Regardless of how many or how few you desire, you should not be pulling these herbs without asking."

This is getting tedious, she thought. *I have a right to stroll in my uncle's garden, and one missing herbal stem will surely not put my uncle into debtors' prison.* This man was too young to be the gardener. An assistant, then?

"Are you one of the under-gardeners?" She enjoyed the discomfited look on his face.

"No. And what does that have to do with anything?" He moved a step closer, his tone still too aggressive for her liking.

He put his own fists on his hips.

The thought that he might be intentionally mimicking made her purse her lips in further annoyance. "Then, sir, since you are not employed to patrol the parsnips, I suggest you go about your business. And I shall pick any plant I choose, for this is my uncle's garden. His *herbal* garden. You see? I am not totally ignorant." And with that statement, she returned to the plant and spied a single stalk heavily laden with tiny clustered flowers. She grasped it decisively.

"Ow!" She pulled her empty hand back and turned it over, studying her painful palm.

"I was about to warn you that the nettle's sting can be quite painful. Which is why it is best harvested while one is wearing leather gloves." He bit back the tiniest of grins. Turning to leave, he said, "I shall now go about my business, as you suggested. And, by the way—" He turned to face her. "Do feel free to collect any plants you choose, including the parsnips." His shoes crunched on the gravel path as he strolled away.

Claire tried massaging her hand, but that only made the stinging worse. The plant must have left tiny barbs in her palm.

"What a horrid man," she muttered, eyeing the curve of the path where he had disappeared.

"Yes, he is horrid," said a voice behind her.

Once again, Claire jumped. How had he circled back behind her so quickly? No, she now realized, this young man's hair was not as dark, nor as long.

"I'm sorry to startle you. My name is Roman. But I shan't take your hand in mine, as I believe you should not press any further upon those nettles in your palm."

Claire cupped her right hand in her left, the palm up. "I don't know what to do. Shall I wash it?"

"I'm not sure. Vitus is more knowledgeable about all of that than I am. But I believe a little mud will help alleviate the sting.

There is a small pond in the middle of the maze, and we could mix a small batch of mud. Even if you were to do nothing, however, the pain will slowly dissipate on its own."

"Then I shall ignore it the best I can, though I thank you for the offer." She dropped her hand to her side. "I wonder why that painful plant is allowed to be grown in the garden at all."

Roman looked to the garden, then spied the plant she referred to. "I may not have Vitus's passion for plants, but I've been told that the juice extracted from the leaf is effective for arthritis. Did you know your uncle suffers mildly?"

"No, I'm afraid I don't know my uncle well." She smiled at Roman. "That isn't true. I don't know my uncle at all, as I only arrived last night, and he is not in residence. I am told he may be gone a month or two. How did you know I am his niece?"

"I was just up to the manor to see Mrs. Dawson about an errand. She mentioned you were in residence."

"And you mentioned the name Vitus. Is that how my uncle is known?"

He laughed. "I would not know how his peers address him, as I've only ever respectfully known your uncle as Sir Rudyard. No, the Vitus I mention is my younger brother. The 'horrid' man?" he reminded her.

"Oh! My apologies." Claire looked down, embarrassed. "I should not have voiced my opinion aloud. I fear it is one of my faults."

"It happens I share the same opinion." Roman smiled. "And the same fault. So please don't apologize." His stare was bold, appraising. "How long shall you be visiting Raven Heights?"

"I am not sure." Claire chose not to elaborate, as she did not know her uncle's plans.

"May I know your name?"

She hesitated briefly. "Claire. Miss Claire Temple. Do you live nearby?"

Roman turned and pointed past the gamekeeper's cottage. "Through those woods. We border upon your uncle's property. Our families have lived near one another for generations. I know all of the shopkeepers in the village, and would be happy to make introductions for you."

"That is terribly kind of you."

They strolled forward at a leisurely pace, walking between the rows of herbs.

"It would be my pleasure," offered Roman. "If there is anything else I can help you with, anything you need, please just let me know."

"I do have one question." Claire paused on the gravel path.

"Yes?" He waited.

"Did you know Zillah?" Claire thought she saw the young man stiffen, but his face remained carefully neutral as he replied.

"Of course. Everyone knew Zillah." He turned his head toward the manor, as if he could see the long drop to the sea through its thick stone. "A careless accident, that. She had no business being on the cliff edge in that weather."

"Why do you say that? How was the weather?"

"Similar to last night, as I recall. Dark. Thunderous. She is lucky she was not first hit by a lightning bolt." Realizing what he said, he added, "Though perhaps it would not have mattered, as she fell, regardless."

"Then you believe it was an accident?"

His head turned quickly back, his eyes seeking hers. This time there was no mistaking his displeasure. "Of course it was. What did my brother tell you?"

"Nothing! We never spoke of it. It was Mrs. Dawson who mentioned it to me last night. I've barely spoken five words with your brother Vitus." Claire retreated a step, feeling somehow threatened, though Roman had not moved.

But now he did, taking a step backward also, to take his leave.

With a slight laugh, he said, "Well, my brother is odd, so see that you don't mind his fantasies." He paused, apparently deciding whether he should say anything more. "Listen, I don't know what Mrs. Dawson told you, but the villagers are always ready with gossip, and you'd be best to ignore it. There are those who will tell you she committed suicide. But I knew Zillah well, and those are lies."

Not wanting to antagonize him further, she nodded her acceptance, remaining mute.

He touched his hand to his forehead and said, "Good day then, Miss Claire Temple. I look forward to seeing you again." With a quick bow, he excused himself and followed Vitus's footsteps down the gravel path.

Chapter Four

In the following days, Claire gradually perceived a measure of peace. The overcast skies that had mirrored her melancholy on the night of her arrival had dispersed. There was always a variant wind accompanying her daily walks, but she welcomed the taste of saltiness carried by the breeze from the sea. She realized she could find contentment here. Inhaling deeply, she held a breath of cool, clear air, her eyes closed. She listened to the calming music of the gulls and the hedge birds. She did not expect contentment to equal happiness, as her parents were no longer somewhere she could find them, so happiness might elude her for the remainder of her life. But for the first time since she lost her parents, she could touch peace with all her senses.

Would her uncle allow her to stay? She had stopped inquiring of Mrs. Dawson whether her uncle had returned. The answer was always a gentle smile and a small shake of the head. It had been a week since she'd arrived, and no one seemed to know his plans, other than parroting he was certain to return within the next few months. That suited Claire, to be honest. She was in no hurry to meet her obscure uncle. The disquiet she'd felt in her breast upon her arrival was lessening, had become something she could hold apart from her spirit and observe, as a dream one awakens from.

She still avoided most of the rooms in the manor, though she was uncertain why. It didn't matter, as she preferred to explore outdoors.

Beginning at the kitchen doorstep each morning, she would peruse the ornamental and edible plants organized by rows in the kitchen garden. She learned to distinguish the leaves of the broccoli from the cauliflower and the cabbage. She could almost believe that she could see a difference in the number of buds on a certain plant, or in the height of the beet greens. The nettle was now easily avoided.

Her daily path followed one of gravel, as it meandered down the slope of lawn toward the gamekeeper's cottage. She still took Mrs. Dawson's advice and circumvented the cliff, but it beckoned to her each day now. She knew it was only a matter of time until she ventured closer to the views of the pounding sea below. Even this close to the manor she could hear the distinct crash of surf against the rock walls and the cry of a sea bird. Why should it matter if Claire walked along the path? There appeared to be adequate width protecting the safety of any who strolled along the viewpoints of the trail. It was not likely Claire would throw herself into the turbulence below, if that is what Zillah had done. Nor would Claire line her toes along the slippery stones that might accidentally crumble beneath one's footing, if Zillah had done that as the inquest suggested. Thinking of Mrs. Dawson's point of view, it seemed most probable to Claire that the woman wished to avoid Sir Rudyard's displeasure should he return home to discover his niece had arrived and had met her demise due to neglect on the staff's part.

"Yes, Sir Rudyard, she certainly did arrive, per your instructions. Where is she, you ask? Unfortunately, milord, she strolled along the cliff path and was apparently blown over the edge. It must have been our fault, as we neglected to warn her of the danger." Claire smiled at the thought.

Once past the gamekeeper's cottage, she had a choice: a

considerable flight of shallow steps met the floor of forested wilderness behind and below the cottage. The trails, many of them made by the crisscrossing of deer, were not well defined. According to Roman, he and Vitus lived in that direction.

Or she could continue along the gravel path toward the summer-house. She normally chose this route, as she did this morning. Visible from the corner of her bedroom balcony as a glimpse of eaves, at ground level one could not discern the structure hiding within the clipped hedge maze. It was a treat to turn the final corner of formal yews and then to discover the charming retreat surrounded by a tiled courtyard. The door hadn't been locked during any of her excursions, so she hadn't hesitated to explore the softly lit interior. Within the open room, large enough to hold a small garden party, the walls were ringed by a row of arched windows draped loosely with silky yellow curtains. Large potted ferns absorbed the softened rays of the summer heat, while allowing filtered buttercup light within.

Outside the summer-house, a round pond was adorned with a splashing fountain. Claire preferred the soothing outdoor room to the formal seatings within the summer-house. Somehow a soft sea breeze wound its way over and around the tall maze hedges.

She sat upon one of the marble benches now, watching three pearl-grey fish lazily circling the confines of the pool. Yesterday, as she sat by the fountain, she'd been visited by Roman and his brother Vitus. It had been only the second time she'd seen them, and she found herself looking forward to their company again this morning. Or at least to Roman's company. She still barely knew the silent Vitus. When she pictured his unsmiling grey eyes and sober countenance, it gave her a brief chill. The dark-skinned brother brought to mind her first night at Raven Heights, watching the dark storm approach. To be honest, she recalled she *had* seen the barest glimpse of a smile when he'd found humor at her expense that first morning in the herbal garden. Yesterday, however, he'd been quite serious, as prickly as the nettle.

Whereas one could not help but enjoy the garrulous Roman, who'd been full of village gossip. He made her laugh with silly anecdotes, often at his own expense, which she found appealing. And he also made her blush with his charming comments and his flirting blue-eyed stares.

Hoping to learn a little more about the residents of Raven Heights, Claire had inquired openly for any information the brothers were willing to share about her family or the staff. Vitus hardly spoke, usually allowing his talkative brother to drive the conversation. Claire made a point of directing a question to Vitus now and then. He answered without hesitation, so it wasn't that he was reticent or surly.

Neither brother could offer much insight on her uncle or the residents of Raven Heights, other than the facts she already knew: Sir Rudyard was well respected; he was often away from the manor; the capable Mrs. Dawson was in charge of the household; and the only servant they knew by name was the head gardener, Jacoby. She was discouraged. She had never known anything of her own father's family, had never asked him about his siblings. She scanned her memory for any mention by her father of his having two brothers. She couldn't recall. In fact, she could not recall his ever mentioning what his life had been like as a boy, or where he had lived. Why hadn't she thought to ask her parents their family stories? Probably because most young children do not comprehend—probably wouldn't even believe—that their parents had ever been young children. It was assumed that one's parents were born old.

Had her mother any sisters or brothers? Was it possible she had grandparents who were still alive? She'd never met any, at least at an age that she would have been old enough to remember. Straining to remember any conversations with her parents was emotionally painful. She decided not to pursue this desire for family knowledge, at least until she was in the presence of her uncle. And if he did not wish to answer any of her questions? If Sir Rudyard had not even known of Claire's existence, then there must have been a severe breakdown of relationship between the two siblings. Why did he bring her to his home now? His brother was dead. Had time brought healing? Or remorseful regrets?

And what of Uncle Myles? Roman and Vitus had no recollection of her other uncle, Myles; thus Claire assumed he had died when the neighboring boys were young. Or perhaps he had left long before they were born. Had Uncle Myles been in touch with her father? If so, surely he would have known of her parents' deaths almost nine years ago . . . unless he had died first. If Mrs. Dawson had known her other uncle, then he must have been on speaking terms with Sir Rudyard. Had Uncle Myles also despised Claire's father, to the point that he neither knew nor cared that her father had married her mother, and that they'd had a daughter fifteen years ago?

Claire sighed. She knew no more about Raven Heights Manor or her family than she did before she'd asked, other than the gardener's name. She supposed it must be Jacoby she'd seen working the grounds, but had never asked his name, nor had it been offered to her by the kindly older man who was always quick to tip his hat with a broad smile. With a little stoop to his shoulders and a tool always handy, always pointing as he spoke, he directed about a half dozen younger men, who industriously tilled and weeded in and about the various planting beds, garden pathways, and orchards. Jacoby—if that was his name—was the only worker she'd ever seen tending the kitchen garden, other than the kitchen staff. *He* wouldn't have allowed her to mistakenly touch the nettle, she was sure, which brought her thoughts back to Vitus.

Though Vitus was the younger of the two brothers, he was slightly taller than Roman. Roman was fair-skinned and had hair the color of the baked garden earth, a rich, tawny brown. It seemed fitting that Vitus's skin was dark, to match his scowls. His hair was also darker than Roman's, almost as black as a raven's. She smiled at the comparison—Raven Heights.

Twice she'd caught Vitus studying her idly. If she suddenly looked up, he would look away. Roman appeared not to notice as he chatted companionably. She wondered why Vitus bothered to accompany his brother, if he did not choose to join in their conversation.

While contemplating the pond, Claire sensed movement at the corner of her eye. Hoping for the brothers' return visit, she glanced toward the maze entrance. The stone path was bare. Movement again caught her notice. It was a tall fern, rustling at one of the windows inside the summer-house. No one stood at the accompanying window frame, however. *Perhaps a cat?* she wondered. There did not appear to be a gap at the entrance door; it looked solidly closed. It was possible an animal, most likely an inquisitive cat, had been shut inside the building unintentionally.

Claire crossed the terrace and quietly put her hand upon the curved brass door handle. Slowly she pressed down, peering through the glass-panes into the shadowed room. The well-oiled door opened silently. No cats darted by her feet, and Claire took a tentative step across the threshold.

It took a moment for her vision to adjust to the room's lighting, which was a bit dimmer than the bright reflections of the sunlit pond she'd been staring at. Squinting, she remained motionless as her gaze brushed across the room.

By the farthest fern-hidden window, she spied a small figure standing, likely a child. As she moved farther into the room, her steps on the hard tiles echoed in the empty space.

"Who's there?" said a young girl's voice across the room. "I didn't hear the door open." The speaker turned only her head partway, her body still facing the ferns and the sunny window.

"Hello," Claire answered softly, yet the child froze.

"Zillah!" She whispered, and in an even quieter voice—so breathy Claire wasn't even sure she heard her right—she said, "I promise, I never said anything."

Claire froze. With her silence, so did the young girl.

"I'm not Zillah. My name is Claire."

She saw the young girl inhale quickly. "You—you sound so like her. Your voice. And the echo in the room." She twisted her hands together. "But, of course, I knew it wasn't her. She died."

Claire wondered why the little girl spoke to the sunbeams falling upon her wispy silver-blond hair, wondered why she did not turn to face the doorway. Moving slowly toward the tables and chairs clustered near the windows, Claire explained, "Sir Rudyard is my uncle. I am visiting Raven Heights."

"Oh. My name is Alice."

"Where do you live, Alice?"

"At Pelican Inn." Alice still hadn't turned. "With Miss Bethany."

"Would you care to sit down?" Claire didn't bother pointing to one of the several tables, as Alice wasn't looking her way. "I'd like very much to visit with you." With that, Claire pulled out a chair from the closest wrought iron table in front of Alice. The chair's iron legs scraped loudly across the bone-colored tiles, and Claire seated herself as invitation to the young girl.

Alice did move now, taking one step backward. "No. I cannot." She reached for a long, sturdy hiking stick lying across the table behind her. "That is, I don't think I can stay today. Miss Bethany is probably already looking for me." She glanced toward Claire, then back to the window, as if determining the time of day by the length of the fern's shadows upon her face. "I have to go now." The branch was clasped close to her side, similar to a shepherd's hook.

"Wait. Just a few minutes more?" She watched Alice hesitate and added, "I'd love to have a friend." Most young girls would identify with that simple request, if Claire's childhood hung true in her memory.

Alice moved the tip of the stick forward a couple of feet. Turning to face Claire, she said, "I can't stay today, but I promise I'll come back."

Claire noticed the girl's eyes were the softest blue, like the irises bordering the nearby pond. The color was as faint as the wintry color of her hair.

As Alice moved toward the door, the stick slid back and forth in front of her, and Claire suddenly realized the little girl was blind.

"Maybe I could come to visit you, Alice. At Pelican Inn?" Claire was rewarded with a halt and a smile.

"And you could meet Miss Bethany. You'll like her. She's my best friend." As Alice's small hand found the door handle, she paused and turned around. "And you could be, too, if you wish." She smiled again, shyly, and slipped quickly out the door.

Chapter Five

Claire found Mrs. Dawson in the teal parlor. Unlike the visitors' parlor she'd been escorted into on her arrival at Raven Heights Manor, this salon was designed for a lady's relaxation. Lemon-yellow pillow squares were tucked neatly in the nooks where chair arms and cushions met, a pleasant contrast to the soft teal walls and white wainscoting.

Claire appreciated the comfort of this room she'd never before entered. Why, she wondered, was she hesitant to explore the entire manor? Her thoughts were interrupted when Mrs. Dawson looked up from her knitting and spied her.

"Claire," greeted the older woman cordially. "How are you doing, dear?"

"I am doing well, thank you." Claire noticed Mrs. Dawson had set aside the steel wire needles. "Please, continue. Don't let me interrupt your knitting."

Mrs. Dawson smiled and returned her attention to the fine silk yarn in her lap. "Thank you. Though I am sure this could wait. And once I finish these stockings, they'll soon need darning again. Like the dust falling on the furniture and the picture frames. I'm afraid it's a never-ending cycle." She picked up the needles, the stocking still dangling, and began expertly crossing the ends back and forth. "And what brings you indoors? I normally never see you inside on such a nice day."

Claire took a seat in a nearby chair. "I have a question I wish to—What beautiful paintings!"

Bowers of gardens hung on every wall. The paintings, while distinct, all portrayed the same theme: leafy shelters, beckoning the viewer to stroll among overhanging branches and trailing vines.

"They make me want to walk along each parterre." Claire had risen and now stood facing the largest painting.

"My grandmother had such a painting," said Mrs. Dawson behind her. "I can still see every brushstroke. A small cottage by the sea. I would stand and stare at the painting. I asked my grandmother if we might visit that cottage and she laughed, exclaiming she had no idea where it was. 'Perhaps it does not even exist,' she told me. 'But you may visit it whenever you are here.' Do you know," continued Mrs. Dawson, "she whispered confidentially to me that if I watched carefully, and silently, I might see a young woman come out of the cottage to fetch water at the nearby stream?"

Claire turned to look at Mrs. Dawson in amazement. "And?"

Mrs. Dawson looked up from her handwork. "And what a clever way to keep a young child busy! I would stand staring at that painting, determined not to miss the opening of the cottage door."

They both laughed.

"And several times when my grandmother would ask, 'Did you see her, Little One?'—that was what she called me—I would confide that I was quite sure I had *almost* seen someone, as there had been quick movement at the corner of my eye. 'I think she saw me, Grandmother, and closed the door quickly.' And she would smile knowingly." Mrs. Dawson smiled her own private smile. "Isn't it silly, what we believe as a child?"

Claire did not respond, as she could not well remember childhood games and dreams. She strolled around the room, pausing to examine the paintings on each wall. "Are these painted by different artists? Do you know?"

"Your Uncle Myles painted those." Mrs. Dawson looked fondly at the walls. "They used to be scattered in several rooms. Some in the attic even, if you can believe that. I've gathered them in here, where I can enjoy them."

"Why in the attic?"

"Your uncle was a modest man. I would even say a shy man. He loved to paint, but he would only display one or two at a time."

"He was remarkably talented. But I'm not convinced he is my uncle. At least not by blood." At Mrs. Dawson's look of shock, she laughed. "Neither would you be, if you'd seen my pitiable efforts at sketching. These are wondrous."

Mrs. Dawson's needles tick-ticked agreeably, as Claire continued to study the artwork.

With her back to Mrs. Dawson, Claire swallowed and ventured to ask, "Did Uncle Myles know my mother?"

"What a question! Why do you ask?"

Claire turned her head to look briefly over her shoulder toward Mrs. Dawson. "Because I don't understand why I never knew that I had uncles. And I heard Mrs. Cunliffe say to you that Sir Rudyard and my father were estranged. I suspect I know what that means, though I'm not entirely confident."

Mrs. Dawson sighed. "Meddlesome old busybody of a teacher." She eyed Claire speculatively. "Claire, your uncle is an exceedingly generous man. He's shown much charitableness toward me." She waited until Claire turned to face her, waited until Claire nodded in acknowledgment. "And to you."

"Yes, ma'am." Claire waited, as it took several moments for Mrs. Dawson to speak again.

"This makes me hesitant to discuss anything with you. Surely it is not my business, nor my responsibility, to be telling family tales." Again she stalled indecisively. "I am not comfortable speaking to you of your uncle behind his back, as it were.

Perhaps we should wait for your uncle to return, and you may ask these questions of him yourself."

Claire did not breathe, hoping the woman's tide of inner hesitancy would not recede, but would spill into decision.

Mrs. Dawson pursed her lips, looked down at her knitting, then set all aside with another sigh. "You must promise not to repeat anything I say to you. I am trusting you with this confidence. I shall summarize what I know, and then we shall not speak of this again."

Claire tiptoed to take a seat in a chair facing Mrs. Dawson.

"There was a falling-out."

Claire wanted to ask what it was about, but suspected she should not interrupt.

Mrs. Dawson answered her unspoken question. "I don't really know why, or what it was about. I'm not sure most people ever remember what starts these silly feuds. All I know is that before I came to Raven Heights, an argument occurred between the brothers."

Claire waited soundlessly.

"Your father was the middle of three sons, Myles being the youngest brother." She paused in thought. "How unlikely that Sir Rudyard should have outlived his younger siblings, but this is the lesson that life teaches us. Death plays no favorites, has no rules, no logic.

"I never met your father. I only know what Myles told me. So I cannot be accused of making up gossipy stories, I am telling you the facts as I was told them. Whether they are true I cannot say. So you must keep in mind that I am only repeating what Myles said. He said his brothers were both excessively stubborn, prideful men. Evidently there was some sort of dispute over your grandfather's will. I never learned further details. Normally everything goes to the eldest son, so I cannot even begin to guess what caused the ruction. In addition, Sir

Rudyard had begun drinking heavily. That may or may not have contributed. I'm certain it did not help, though he has remained sober these many years I've lived here. Regardless, Myles said they stopped speaking to one another."

"Was it before my father married my mother?"

"I would assume so, as Myles never mentioned your mother to me. And your grandfather would have died when your father was away at school, a very young man."

"Did Uncle Myles fight with his two brothers about this as well?"

"No. At least, he says he did not ever take sides. Your uncle Myles is—dear me, *was*—a gentle soul, rather a timid man. He left school, came to live here with Sir Rudyard. I don't believe he mentioned ever corresponding with your father, but your father may have severed all fraternal ties, and left without informing Myles of his whereabouts."

Mrs. Dawson looked again to the walls full of paintings. "No, Myles would be content to paint, and would have shied from any conflict." Looking at Claire, she said, "That is all I can tell you. Perhaps your uncle will share more family insight. He is older now, Claire. He has lost both his brothers, and I know he regrets past choices. But you shall have to ask him if you wish to know more."

"Thank you for telling me this story, Mrs. Dawson. I shan't repeat it, not even to my uncle."

"And I trust you, my dear." She picked up her needles. "And was this the question you came in to ask me, Claire? About your uncles?"

"No, I'd forgotten! The paintings distracted me."

"So, then . . . ?"

"I met Alice this morning, in the summer-house."

"Ah, Alice! A delightful child, don't you think?" She glanced up, but was able to continue knitting. "I find it inspiring that she manages so well. Blind, and at such a young age. We have always ensured she is made welcome to visit here. Like you, she enjoys the gardens and the pond at Raven Heights. Probably because she can sit and listen to the fountain music. Of course, the ocean waves would also be soothing, but I shouldn't like to think of a sightless child wandering too close to the cliffs."

"Has she always been blind?"

Mrs. Dawson paused to consider. "As long as I can remember. Of course, she only came to stay at Pelican Inn a few years ago. Bethany Coulter, bless her, has a reputation for sheltering those who need shelter." She moved her gaze to her stitches. "How old would you guess little Alice is?"

"About six? Though she sounds older."

Mrs. Dawson nodded. "I believe she's closer to eight, but she's a wee thing."

The two ladies sat in silence, with only the clacking needles accompanying the ticking of the clock on the mantle.

"Alice said something today. Something about Zillah."

Immediately the needles stopped in midair, though the clock kept its steady beat.

Mrs. Dawson began knitting slowly, focusing intently on her handwork, not glancing up. "I see. And what did she say?"

Claire replayed the scene in her mind. "I had no idea she was there, until I entered the atrium and said hello. She didn't know my voice, of course. And . . . she thought I was Zillah."

"But surely she knows Zillah is dead."

"Well, you would have thought she'd seen a ghost." Realizing the little girl could not see anything, Claire was embarrassed. "Anyway, I'm sure I frightened her. She told me our voices—mine and Zillah's—are alike."

"Yes, now that you mention it, that is true." Mrs. Dawson studied Claire for an uncomfortable length of time. "And? You were saying she said something to you? About Zillah?"

"I could have misunderstood." Claire was beginning to think she should not be repeating what the child said. She wasn't sure why, but had learned since young to rely on her instincts. "In fact, I wasn't sure of anything, except that she called me by the name Zillah. That's probably all she said. I really couldn't hear. Her voice is so soft."

"Nothing else? You are quite certain?" Mrs. Dawson pierced Claire with her intensive gaze.

Claire wondered where the gentle-voiced woman was, the one who had taken her hands in welcome on that first day, the woman who had recently shared fond recollections of Uncle Myles. This woman who now sat across from her was visibly upset, her hands shaking. Claire noticed the sharp needles happened to be pointed in her direction.

"I am certain, yes." Claire watched Mrs. Dawson's hands relax her grip on the knitting needles. "I do recall she mentioned our voices sounded similar, but nothing else was said."

Mrs. Dawson metamorphosed into the soothing soul again. "Of course. I'm sure she simply misses Zillah." The needles began steadily clacking. "Did you know Zillah also lived at Pelican Inn?"

The conversation was redirected to another topic, and when Clair took her leave, she'd made one decision: she needed to visit Pelican Inn.

Chapter Six

"Hello," Claire called out tentatively toward the open half-door.

She waited on the footpath, behind a low wooden gate facing the kitchen side of the building. If no one answered here, she would continue along the path to where it joined the main road, and she would approach the inn via its formally porched entry.

That was not necessary, as a woman with shoulder-length auburn hair soon stepped into the dark opening, peering out. Her face lit with a welcoming smile.

"You must be Sir Rudyard's niece! Come in. Welcome." She unlatched the lower kitchen half-door, swinging it inward to match its upper mate.

Claire unhooked the gate and followed the tidy stone path to the door.

Stepping aside, the woman said, "I'm so pleased you took the time to visit. Alice told us you were staying at Raven Heights."

"Mrs. Dawson asked me to bring this quince jelly," Claire said, holding out a wicker basket. She judged the young woman to be in her mid- to late-twenties. "And are you Miss Coulter?"

Taking the basket, the young woman said, "I'd prefer you call me Bethany. And do thank dear Mrs. Dawson for me. I always enjoy her jams and preserves." Bethany reached into the basket, then held the jar up to the light. "What a beautiful rose color. It's too pretty to keep in the cupboard, don't you think? Please come in, Miss . . . I apologize, but Alice did not know your last name."

"Temple. But please, it's Claire for me as well." She crossed the threshold and stepped just inside the door, admiring the tall-ceilinged kitchen. Polished brass cooking pots and kettles hung within reach near the open hearth.

"This is wonderful. It's the largest kitchen I've ever seen. It's so massive, you must be able to feed a hundred guests."

"I'd be happy to have simply a full house of guests to feed. However, I'm sure that hasn't happened since the turnpike arrived." Bethany untied her apron and asked, "Cream or sugar with your tea?"

"If I'm not interrupting your schedule, I should love that. With a tiny bit of cream, please."

"Then pull up a stool, and we'll get to know one another." Hanging her apron on a nearby hook, Bethany turned and moved across the kitchen toward the hearth.

Claire could not help but stare at Bethany's retreating back, noting the slightest of limps as the young woman crossed the tiled floor. It was more of a graceful roll to her gait. Claire hastily averted her eyes to the closest stool as Bethany reached the hearth, afraid she would be caught gaping. But Bethany did not turn around. Instead, she swung a spouted kettle nearer the hearth flames and whisked two cups off the sideboard.

Claire took a seat, looking around at the rows of colorful plates displayed on the nearest wall. "This is a most inviting room." She turned round to notice the end wall where she'd entered was covered by copper molds and decorative iron trivets, all in meticulous rows. "How long have you lived at Pelican Inn?"

"I was born in this very house." Bethany loaded a handled tray with the cups and a matching teapot, cream pitcher, and sugar bowl. Setting them on the table in front of Claire, she said, "When I was young, I dreamed I would leave and go far away." She arranged a dozen iced biscuits on a lavender-colored plate. Claire noticed that Bethany stacked the biscuits quite precisely, in a pleasing pattern, like the kitchenware covering the walls.

"I did love my parents, mind you." Bethany rearranged two cookies that appeared out of balance. "I think it's just the typical dream of every young man and woman, a craving for adventure, for the unknown. Did you dream the same?" she asked, glancing over her shoulder at Claire as she went to retrieve the kettle.

Claire shook her head in the negative, choosing not to elaborate.

Bethany continued, "And then, when Mother died so young, I knew I would stay here and mind the inn with Father."

Claire didn't know what to say. She waited silently until Bethany returned to add the tea leaves and the heated water to the teapot.

"We began as an inn at the crossroads," said Bethany. "That was why my grandparents settled here, seeing an opportunity to build a stopping post for travellers. My father assisted as a young man, and his new bride—my mother," she explained with a smile, "was eager to help as well. But the new turnpikes were established, and carriage traffic along these roads declined."

She sat down across from Claire and settled the flower-topped lid upon the teapot. She lifted the lid, allowing a gasp of steam to escape, and gave the lid a quarter turn, reseating it so that one of the twining vines on the teapot lined up with the painted vine stem on the lid.

Claire watched in fascination as Bethany straightened their spoons, each equidistant from the saucer. Bethany raised her eyes and realized Claire was studying her movements. "I can't help it," she sighed with mortification, pulling her hands away and folding them upon her lap. "Father says when I'm nervous

I'm constantly tidying. He calls me his fidgeter," she added in a rueful tone.

"Do I make you nervous?" Claire had never been on the other side of nervousness.

"Oh, no! It's just me." She poured tea into each of their cups. "I've been anxious for several days now. But it's nothing." She focused on stirring a spoonful of sugar into her tea.

Claire wondered briefly if Bethany's anxiety had something to do with the unevenness of her walk, perhaps the pain of a recent leg injury. But she would not ask.

"And I expect things shall clear up very soon. But—listen to me, doing all the talking. Please, tell me about yourself. And have some cream."

For some inexplicable reason, Claire always felt a little ashamed when she talked about her past. Though it wasn't her fault she'd been left orphaned. Regardless, she decided to be as honest as possible with her new friend. She instinctively knew she could become close friends with Bethany. If Bethany chose to disapprove of Claire's past, however, then so be it. Best to know now if the young woman looked down upon Claire's status as an orphan, something she'd perceived in many adults she met. While they might not raise a genteel nose and sniff openly, she'd learned to watch their eyelids for a hooded shuttering.

"I was orphaned at about seven years of age, when the pox hit our small village." At Bethany's sigh of sympathy, she felt safe to continue. "My parents had enough money—I was one of the lucky orphans—that I was placed in a good school. I lived there," she said, pausing to reckon, "over eight years, until just now. I have no siblings, and I didn't even know I had an uncle." She laughed. "And then Mrs. Dawson informs me I have—that is I had—two."

"Ah! Of course," said Bethany. "I'd forgotten about Sir Rudyard's brother Myles. What a loss, such a nice gentleman. Very much like Sir Rudyard. He's a good man, your uncle. And I don't believe he knew about you, either, or I know he would never have seen you go to an orphanage or a distant school. Not even for a day."

Claire added cream and didn't bother to stir, as was her habit. There was something relaxing about watching the swirl of cream uncoil and dissipate in the brown liquid. "I am sure he must be a good man, to do this for me. But I've yet to meet him." At Bethany's surprised look, she explained. "I arrived last week, but he has not been in residence. And the staff is uninformed about his schedule. Or they do not bother to pass it on to me."

Bethany huffed. "Ah! Just like my father! Those two men so much alike. Adventurers, not bothering to let anyone know their specific whereabouts, or what they are up to." She took a sip of her tea and patted Claire's hand. "Well, you can believe me that Sir Rudyard *is* a wonderful person. You'll love him when you meet him."

"Did I hear you mention adventures, dear?" A tall, white-haired woman shuffled into the room. Even though slightly stooped, she was taller than either Bethany or Claire.

"Good morning, Aunt Amelia. Would you care for some tea?"

"No, thank you, dearest. I had tea and scones in my sitting room." Aunt Amelia turned her gaze upon Claire. "Do you know my brother Bertie? He is always on one adventure after another."

"No, I haven't had the pleasure."

"Oh, it wouldn't have been a pleasure. Bertie is an annoying man. That is why we encourage him to leave. As often as possible." She turned and tottered back out the door.

"Is Miss Amelia a guest of the inn?" asked Claire.

Bethany waited until the woman was out of earshot. "Yes, you could say so. She's a permanent guest, and we all love her."

"Even though she speaks disparagingly of your father?"

"Oh! No, Bertie is not my father. This may be a bit complicated to explain, but Aunt Amelia is a bit complex herself. You see, Uncle Bertie and my grandfather were Amelia's brothers. She is in truth my great-aunt, but we all call her Aunt Amelia. She's a darling, and while some days she is perfectly lucid, there are other days she does get a bit confused with her timeline. The fact is, Great-Uncle Bertie died before you were even born. But she sometimes still thinks he's on another one of his trips. I think she often confuses him with Calden, my father. Who is not annoying," Bethany added with a soft smile.

Claire recalled Mrs. Dawson's words, about Bethany Coulter being a compassionate soul. "Do you have many permanent guests? Like Aunt Amelia?"

"You've already met Alice. Have you met Grace?"

Claire shook her head no.

"She's a bit older than Alice, but younger than you. She is so kind to Alice, and I know she'll enjoy meeting another young woman closer to her age."

"And Mrs. Dawson mentioned that Zillah had also lived here?" Claire immediately regretted her question, seeing the sorrowful look on Bethany's face.

"Yes. She did. Poor Zillah." Bethany's hands were wrapped around her teacup as if seeking warmth. She stared at the clear brown liquid.

Claire felt uncomfortable, seeing Bethany momentarily lost in somber introspection. Certain that she'd overstayed her welcome, Claire rose. "I'm sorry for asking, Bethany. I . . . I think I should go now. It was nice visiting, thank you for the tea."

Bethany looked up, as if she just realized Claire was talking to her. "What?"

"I said I should be getting back to the manor." Claire took a step away from the table. "It's been nice visiting you."

"Oh, of course. I enjoyed our visit as well." Bethany stood up and accompanied Claire to the door.

"I'm sorry if I made you sad," said Claire as she looked down in remorse. Feeling Bethany's touch on her sleeve, she glanced up at the other woman.

"Claire, it's fine." Bethany smiled and gave Claire's arm a friendly squeeze. "We *must* talk about those we love who are no longer with us. It keeps the good people alive in our memories. Else, what is the purpose of our short lives? And I want you to promise you'll come back to see me. Soon. Promise?"

Claire promised.

CHAPTER SEVEN

The continually splashing water in the limestone fountain enticed her to the summer-house courtyard. Within the larger circle of the pool was an inner tier, set higher, and adorned with bronze spouts whose arcs of water gently jetted from the mouths of arching—fish? Claire realized she did not know what type of animal spewed the crystal water. It had a piscine tail, though, split and delicately curved.

She stared, hypnotically transfixed by the consonance of sight and sounds. Unlike the unceasing beat of the waves below the cliffs, the fountain sounds varied enchantingly. Sometimes she would sit on the hot masonry circling the pool, a book on her lap. But usually she preferred one of the scattered benches, from whence she could watch the play of rainbow prisms within the errant spray. Where the rivulets of spewed water met the clear surface, white foam endlessly piled bubbles atop one another. Clear bubble hemispheres routinely escaped the mass, and individually skated across the clear surface, only to burst into nonexistence before reaching the fountain's rim.

She listened, tried to match a sound to the splashing water. How could one describe it? There was a *whirr* sound where the upper pool burbled over the rounded edge of hot masonry into the lower pool. And where the water from the fountain hit the surface, it sounded like it said *lub, lub.* Or *lud, lud.* Soon, however, all she heard was *blood.* Claire turned her attention elsewhere.

The tiled terrace, anchored by the fountain in its center, was bounded by oversized Italianate pots outlining its perimeter. She studied the heavy pots that cast fat, squat shadows in the morning sun. Each clay pot's exterior was pierced, slightly below its curved lip, and a large iron ring dangled from a stud. What could be the purpose of the black ring, other than ornamental? Once potted with heavy soil and small trees, one would not think the pot easily moved by pulling on its ring, as if it were a stubborn bull.

She turned to the large book on her lap, letting the weighty covers split apart and expose her marker, when she heard a new sound. The tap-tapping of Alice's wooden staff was barely discernible above the water's music, but Claire recognized it and turned.

"Hello, Alice." She closed the book, setting it by her side. "Come and join me?"

Alice carefully sat on the neighboring bench, whose curved arm aligned with that of Claire's bench. "You love it here, too. The fountain, I mean. I enjoy listening to the different sounds the water makes."

"Most certainly the fountain." Claire considered. "*And* the herb garden as well. And even the path to the gamekeeper's cottage." She smiled. "I guess I've come to love all of this estate. I'll miss it if I have to leave. Though I haven't yet explored inside the manor. Or the cliff walk."

"But why would you?" asked Alice.

"Explore the manor? Or, why haven't I explored the cliff walk?"

"No." Alice drew the single syllable into a keening lament. "Why would you have to leave?"

"I shouldn't make that assumption. In truth, I don't know what the future holds for me. But I haven't even met my uncle yet, so it's difficult to have any sense of security. Is that silly?"

"No, I understand. When I first arrived at Pelican Inn, I waited for Miss Bethany to change her mind, to send me away. And the more I wanted to stay, the more I worried. Even when I was happy, it made me feel like crying." Alice beamed a wide smile. "But not anymore. Now I know that Miss Bethany will let me stay forever. She told me." Alice swung her feet, which dangled just above the tiled ground.

She scrunched up her brow. "But why haven't you explored all of the manor? Or the cliff walk? If I could see, I would want to go look at both."

Claire thought about the question. "I've wondered myself why I haven't explored the rooms of Raven Heights. I suppose because I feel I'm a guest still, and I don't want to go peeking into rooms that aren't mine. As if I'll be asked to leave if I'm nosy. I'm afraid to chance that. Though Mrs. Dawson did say I might explore anywhere I wish."

"And the sea path?"

"Now, that's easier to answer. Mrs. Dawson explicitly asked me not to go there until Uncle returns. Because of . . ." Claire thought better of explaining in detail. "Anyway, I guess my reasoning is the same as for the manor. I don't want to risk violating any rules that will end my visit here."

Alice nodded in understanding. "I can hear the water crashing when I'm walking over here. And I can smell salt, and . . . and something else. I'm not sure how to describe it."

"Fishy?"

"Maybe." Alice considered. "I don't know. But why does Mrs. Dawson want you to wait for Sir Rudyard?"

"I suspect it has to do with Zillah." *Zillah's death,* she finished silently in her mind.

"Ah." Alice tipped her face toward the sunlight, changed the subject. "I like how the sun feels on my skin, and at the same time, how the water feels in my ears."

"I admire you, Alice. In spite of not being able to see, you treasure other sensations. You're a wise young lady."

"I like to smell, too. If I'm—Did you hear that?" Alice turned her face toward the maze. "I think someone's coming."

Claire peered toward the maze. "No, I didn't hear any—Oh! Hello, Roman." Claire reached over to touch Alice's arm. "Very impressive!" She watched the young girl beam with pride.

"Greetings, lovely ladies." Roman strolled across the paved courtyard and took a seat facing them, upon the fountain's edge. Vitus soon followed via the hedge maze opening. He did not acknowledge them, but came and sat on the fountain's wide rim as well, turning sideways to study the play of water spilling musically into the pool.

Claire stared at Vitus, amazed by his silence. And annoyed at herself that she should care whether he bothered to acknowledge her. Was he sullen? Or simply rude? The bronze spouting figurines behind him reminded her of her earlier thoughts. "Roman, what kind of fish is that?"

"Where?" asked Roman, turning to look down and peruse the few lazily swimming fish in the shallow depths of the pool.

He was interrupted by his brother, who hadn't even glanced their way as he studied the fountain. "It's not a fish. It's a dolphin. Have you never seen one?" asked Vitus, finally turning his dark gaze curiously toward Alice and Claire.

"No," said Claire. "How do they taste?"

Vitus laughed without malice. "I wouldn't know, and I hope you shan't either. The dolphin is a mammal, not a fish, and they are . . . sacred. Magical. Beautiful."

"Why, brother," said Roman, "I've never heard this poetic side of you."

Vitus ignored his brother's sarcasm. "They are sometimes seen along this coast, in the summer."

Claire ignored Roman as well, addressing Vitus directly. "I'm not familiar with this area, and I'd never been to the coast before."

"But surely you've seen images of them, on artifacts from the past?" When she shook her head in the negative, Vitus continued. "The Greeks revered them. There are lots of carvings and paintings of dolphins on early pottery. And on coins or jewelry."

Claire blushed. "No, I hadn't known of that." She suspected her paltry education was obvious.

"You see, Vitus? You've embarrassed her," said Roman, looking only at Claire as he spoke to his brother. "Young ladies are to be admired for their accomplishments." He smiled warmly, his eyes holding hers. "And their beauty. Not for their scholarship. Anyway, not everyone is interested in the obscurities like you, wasting time with their wrists manacled to books."

Claire didn't agree with Roman, as books and learning were part of her values. Before she could argue, she caught Vitus looking at her speculatively, as if embarrassment could be measured. "Did I embarrass you, Miss Temple?" It was not an apology.

"No. Not at all." The attention brought a further blush; she felt the heat beneath her skin. "I should like to know more about these dolphins." She studied the arching bronze statues. "Have you yourself seen one? In the water, I mean, not on an antiquity in a museum."

"Yes, from this very coastline. And to see one is to fall in love with it." He too looked up at the dolphins rising from the center of the fountain. "They play as children do during the day. See how they are jumping? That is exactly how they break from the sea's surface. And I think I once saw one in the moonlight. Not jumping, but resting, shimmering just below the surface."

Claire's eyebrows rose as she studied the back of his long hair. This was the most she'd ever heard Vitus say in one visit. She remembered that she'd heard there were those who were more comfortable around animals than people. Perhaps Vitus was one of those persons.

"If you saw it here . . . Can one walk along the cliff at night?" She shuddered. Zillah must have done so, at least upon that one night. "Is the moonlight truly bright enough to show the path?"

Roman answered for his brother. "Quite so. I often walk at night, when the waves can be heard more strongly. They echo up from the base of the cliff. I don't know if they crash more violently with the pull of the moon at night, or if it's because all else has quieted down. Regardless, it's easy to follow the path, even at midnight. As long as it's not a smuggler's moon."

Claire wondered why someone would be about at midnight. Instead, she asked, "What is a smuggler's moon?"

"A dark night," said Roman. "When smugglers patrol the coastline. Not only is it dangerous to lose one's footing on a path that can't be seen without light, it's critical to avoid discovery during the unloading of the contraband." He laughed. "Critical for the smuggler, and especially for the unlucky observer."

"Smugglers?" asked Alice in awe. "I heard Miss Bethany's father speaking of smugglers. Here on this very spot?" Before he had a chance to reply, she hastily added, "And what is contraband?"

He smirked. "Contraband, my young lady, is whatever illegal goods you are willing to pay for. Could be tea, or tobacco. Sometimes silk or sugar. But mostly alcohol. Anything to avoid paying duty."

"Is a smuggler like a pirate?" Alice turned her eager face toward Roman, though she tended to look too high in the air when excited.

"Now, that depends upon your point of view. Yes, they most likely have weapons, like pirates. But is stealing from the excise man the same as stealing from innocent citizens?" He didn't wait for an answer. "And they do usually arrive by water, similar to pirates. But the smuggler's boat is usually a small fishing vessel, not a massive pirate galleon."

"Fishing boats!" One could see Alice was enthralled. "Mr. Coulter never mentioned they were fishermen. But what do they fish for? The dolphins that should be sacred?"

Claire had to smile, as Alice was quick to make associations.

"No, it's not food they seek. They fish for treasure. Buried treasure. Often, they are retrieving barrels they hid somewhere on the beach, deep beneath the sand. But if there are caves in the area, they will save them the work of digging and marking their burial sites. They can stash their contraband in caves, where it will stay as cool as it would beneath the damp sand."

"But why are they hiding their treasures?"

"They hide their goods until the time is ripe to sell them."

Alice digested this seriously. "What if they use a cave, and the cave is too high to reach, because of the tides going up and down? How do they get to the cave, if it's up high?"

"It often *is* up high. That would help to keep their treasures dry. Sometimes they'll dig their own caves, for that exact reason. And tunnels to reach the caves." Roman shrugged. Alice couldn't see the shrug, but his voice conveyed he was finished with questions. "But they probably hauled the barrels—or whatever—up the cliffs."

"Ohmygoodness." Alice had no further questions. She'd been enraptured with this fairy-tale gift.

"Picture a dark night," said Roman, slowly rising from the bench. "You are a smuggler, and you have to listen for the excise man. He could be hiding round the corner." He tiptoed across the courtyard, toward the two ladies. "But you have your knife. And maybe a gun tucked away as well." He came up silently behind Alice.

If Claire had realized what he was up to, she would have

protested. Before she could call out a warning, Roman tapped Alice in the shoulder blades as he called out "Smuggler!"

Alice squealed and jumped upright, arching her back. She almost slid off the front edge of the bench.

"Roman!" Claire hollered at the gentleman. "That was cruel. Alice can't see you coming. Are you all right, Alice?" She saw small tears of fright in Alice's eyes.

"What is the difference whether she has sight or not?" Roman was not pleased at being chastised. "The whole idea of surprising someone is their not being able to see you. You enjoyed being frightened, didn't you, Alice?"

"I'm fine, Claire." Alice looked only in Claire's direction. Claire assumed she was embarrassed to have the gentlemen notice her moist eyes.

But Vitus apparently noticed. "There are no smugglers in this area, Alice." He gave his brother a look of disgust. "Roman, it's time we were home to help Father." He stood, and saying, "Ladies," he took his leave.

"I shall leave when I am ready, and not because you say, *younger* brother." Regardless, Roman left as well, without an apology or a backward glance.

Chapter Eight

"You can't be serious, Randall."

Claire overheard a snippet of conversation as she entered the apothecary's shop, just after the jangling of the bell above the door.

"And why not?"

"It's not a gentlemanly pursuit."

"Bah! You sound like my family," said the younger man in good-natured disgust.

The gentleman named Randall, packet in hand, bade the shopkeeper good day and headed out the door, tipping his hat to Claire as he left.

"Who was that, Mr. Tulley?" she asked, holding out the list Mrs. Dawson had prepared. "I don't believe I've seen him in the village before."

Mr. Tulley reached across the counter for the list, and halfway through his perusal of it he peeked up through bushy eyebrows to cast a brief look out the bow window at his customer's retreating back. "Malcolm Randall. His aunt is the Widow Perkins. He's visiting her from London. Often does, eh? You recall who she is, Miss Temple?" His glance bounced from the lane outside the shop to Claire, and then back to Mrs. Dawson's precise handwriting.

"Widow Perkins? No, at least I cannot put a face and a name together. But there are still so many neighbors I've yet to meet." Claire set her basket upon the counter. "Where does she live?"

She listened and nodded at his back as Mr. Tulley waddled away toward some hinged boxes along the wall, basket over one arm, and waving the paper in a northerly direction with the other, all the time describing, in short snippets, the yellow home with honey-colored limestone near the creek that ran along the edge of town.

Claire had volunteered to run errands in the village, as she typically did. Getting to know the shopkeepers, and occasionally their customers, was another pleasurable after-breakfast routine. She wasn't sure when it had become a pleasure, rather than an intimidating effort. Naturally shy, Claire was sure if she forced herself to become a bit more outgoing, she'd increase her odds of remaining at Raven Heights. How silly; as if the townspeople would rise up with pitchforks and storm the manor should her uncle decide to send her away in the coming months. Still, it did in fact become easier to socialize each day, as faces became more familiar.

At Whiteworth's, Claire had often been criticized for being too somber. "Your face will freeze in a frown, Miss Temple," intoned the headmistress, rolling her *r*'s. But it wasn't Claire's fault; she no longer knew how to smile. Her parents had taken all the happy memories away with them, lowered and locked too far beneath the ground. And the memories that used to make her smile soon forced her lips into a grim frown, lest her lips should tremble for others to see. Perhaps the headmistress was right.

Never naturally outgoing, Claire preferred to listen to others' conversation in the village, and forced her lips into a small (what she hoped appeared natural and pleasant) smile. To her surprise, the shopkeepers returned her smile, becoming chattier themselves at the incentive of an interested listener.

The apothecary shop was an especial favorite, with its myriad of scents: herbs, tinctures, dried flowers, and an underlying fresh soapy smell she couldn't place. It was a magic cave of tiny cedar chests, bottles, and miniature drawers lining each wall. In awe, she would watch Mr. Tulley duck and dart as he navigated the vast inventory, directly putting his hand upon the tiniest item in an instant. Plus, there was the bonus of Mr. Tulley's enjoyable staccato banter.

As she waited for the portly shopkeeper to fill her order, Claire couldn't help but attend his gossip. Mr. Tulley knew everything about everybody, and considered it his job to educate those who did not.

"He's a disconcerted young man." He put the first item in the basket. "His parents are well-to-do. Sent him on the grand tour. At his request." He grunted as he bent over to grab an item from the lowest shelf. "And then what happens?" His voice rose at the end of the query, challenging Claire to guess the answer.

"Did something happen to him while on the Continent? Highway robbers?" She knew nothing about the remainder of Europe, but tried to imagine what must surely be the worst crisis to befall a traveller. Murderers with knives would be worse, of course, but the man who had passed her upon his exit looked to be perfectly healthy. He was tall, and quite a bit older than she.

"Worse than that! Quite a hugger mugger," Mr. Tulley said.

Claire bit her lip and thought. "Did he become ill?"

"Ill in the head, if you ask me." Mr. Tulley's voice echoed, muffled as he reached to the rear of a deep cupboard. "He learned how to cook."

"Excuse me?" Claire was sure she misunderstood. She waited until the grizzled head popped back out of the cupboard.

"Cook! Bake! Sauté." He shook his head in consternation. "You name it, them foreigners did it to him, them and their fancy kitchens, and their fancy ways of eatin'. Leaves here a perfectly masculine young man. And comes back wanting to wear an apron. Silliest thing I ever did hear." He stood on a small stepstool to reach the final item, and looked somberly at Claire over his shoulder. "It's no wonder his parents are not happy."

She made an effort to match his gravity, had to hide a smile. "But he's home now. I don't see that it matters."

Mr. Tulley set the basket solidly upon the wooden counter. "I agree. It shouldn't. But instead of continuing with his apprenticeship at the solicitors? He has declared he wants to pursue his *dream*." He curled his lips in humour around the word. "And he wants to go back to the Continent. *And* become a chef!" His beefy hand was still upon her basket.

Afraid he would not relinquish her goods if she didn't agree with him, she raised her eyebrows in amazement and shook her head sadly.

It worked. He released the basket and shook his head as well. Claire snaked an arm through the basket and wished him good day as she headed out of the shop.

She'd finished this morning's errands, and with ashen clouds threatening, there was no reason to linger in the village. She retraced her steps along the cobbled street, her thoughts wandering as usual, with almost no awareness of her steps upon the stones, or of the return path to Raven Heights. Eventually she replayed conversations with the various shopkeepers and customers today, and she thought about this Mr. Randall.

He was lucky to have parents who afforded him the opportunity to see other countries. She'd heard about many young men of means taking the time, while young, to explore other cities, other countries. Were their sisters given this same choice? She couldn't remember ever hearing of an unmarried young lady doing a grand tour, or even a short tour. It must be part of a young man's education, to visit ancient antiquities, exotic museums, European works of art. If a family had wealth, would the daughters be given an equivalent education? Most likely not. But wouldn't a father perhaps indulge his daughter's wish, if she was as enthusiastic as her brother to explore? With a companion, of course. Claire would offer to be that companion. She would be the most attentive, helpful, hard-working companion, if only she could explore just one foreign country. Even her own country; she'd hardly seen anything of it. Why would one go to other countries? She knew the answer. It was the word *explore.* It was one of those magical words. To say it was to enter the imagination of another world, mimicking Mrs. Dawson's childhood fantasy of stepping through her grandmother's picture frame to visit the cottage by the sea.

Was this Mr. Randall a bad son, if he wanted to pursue a living other than what his parents had planned for him? As long as he was not destitute—and it did not sound so—shouldn't he be able to make his own choices? Ah, but perhaps his family would disown him. Would he succumb to parental pressure then? What would she do in the same position? She had no idea, as she had no wealthy parents, and she would never be independent. She knew she would not cross Uncle. She didn't even know her relative, but he'd given her this opportunity, and she would be foolish to go against his wishes, to end this fragile happiness.

The realization struck her, and she stumbled to a stop. *She was happy.* It had been a long time since she'd been buoyed by the lightness that floated along with happiness. Claire continued along the path, admiring the wildflowers along the edges of the open fields, and the clematis climbing the fences. She appreciated the clean village, with its happy children and friendly residents.

Claire came around the bend and saw Raven Heights on its pinnacle across the yellow meadows, contrasted against a pearl-grey sky. When had it become home? She looked forward each morning to strolling in the gardens, watching the butterflies near the summer-house. When she'd arrived in the spring, the tears she had shed those first nights seemed so far away; surely they belonged to another lonely young woman.

But it wasn't just the buildings and the gardens. She had come to care for the manor's welcoming staff and neighboring friends. Mrs. Dawson, Bethany and Alice, Aunt Amelia—memory of the older woman's disjointed observations brought a smile—and Roman and Vitus.

Roman was now a good friend, though she'd learned to be wary of his moods. She'd glimpsed a petty and defensive Roman on those rare occasions that his smiling, charming mask had slipped askew. As long as he was not crossed, he was an entertaining flirt, and she could not help but look forward to his company.

This connected her thoughts to his brother Vitus, and she flushed. She wasn't sure how she felt about Vitus. Sometimes he seemed gentle and solicitous, and other times he frightened her. Perhaps fright was the wrong word; more an inner nervousness when she caught his stare. The silent, dark man was so intense, she often suspected he disapproved of her. She'd tried drawing out his monosyllabic answers, but could only engage the man in discussions of any length if his brother Roman was not present, and if the topic interested Vitus enough to overcome his reticence. He was fair in his opinions, though, and thoughtful in his responses, and she savored that depth, the lack of shallow glibness his brother possessed. He'd lent three books to her the other day, and she'd been surprised to see a volume of poetry in amongst the fiction. She remembered he'd waited until Roman had left before handing the books to her. As if he worried his brother would ridicule him for reading poetry, or that Roman might display his open scorn of Vitus's love of reading. She was being fanciful; Vitus was his own man, and usually dismissed or disregarded his older brother's barbs.

Was this what it meant to have a sibling? She'd always envied those who did. Must it mean a rivalry, a constant dueling with words at ten paces? She suspected that might be a male trait. She imagined Bethany as a sister, and knew they would share secrets and simple pleasures of the day, not mean barbs.

Bethany has a secret pain, thought Claire, recalling their first meeting when Bethany had admitted to some anxiety. They hadn't broached it since, but Claire had seen the tension that underlay her friend's brightness, that sometimes threatened to crack her gentle facade, like a piece of brittle candy. Her limp was more pronounced with the dampness of her spirits, but Claire still did not know if there was a connection. Would it help her friend to talk about it? Claire felt she now knew Bethany well enough to believe the salve of friendship might be of aid, and if not . . . She didn't fear a rebuff, knowing Bethany's gentle ways, yet would respect her friend's privacy.

She decided to drop off the basket at Raven Heights and pay a visit to Pelican Inn before the grim clouds above the sea pulled anchor and advanced inland.

Claire had never been in any of the rooms at Pelican Inn other than the kitchen. She usually arrived for visits at the same time of the day, when Bethany would be in the grand kitchen, often baking the day's bread. They'd chat before having refreshments, if Bethany was in the middle of kneading, and would relax with tea and conversation, their friendship gradually growing, similar to the fragrant yeasty dough.

Often, Aunt Amelia would drift into the kitchen and out again, sometimes more than once on the same day. Depending upon what decade the elderly woman was living in at the moment, she might recognize Claire or she might not. Claire and

Bethany always listened respectfully, even if Aunt Amelia repeated stories of her brothers for the dozenth time. She predictably spoke of her older brother Bertie with disgusted tolerance, and could recite any one of his adventures in Egypt and Greece with repetitious precision. Her stories were always consistent, mused Claire. How does a brain retain details such as the color of the tassels and the shape of the bells upon a camel's blanketed hump, but not the current date? And when Aunt Amelia spoke of Bethany's grandfather Frederick, Amelia's younger brother, she always chuckled affectionately. Always.

On other visits, Grace would come skidding into the kitchen to say hello. The young girl spoke with the same quickness and energy to match her motion. Grace was a whirlwind, with wild red hair to match, compared to little Alice's measured blind pace.

When Alice entered the kitchen, her soft tapping of cane would precede her soft greeting. It was a wonder, thought Claire, she'd never witnessed a Grace collision.

This parlor she and Bethany now entered was a mix of formal and cozy, with overstuffed chairs, a rainbow of scattered pillows, and doily-covered side tables. The gloomy light of the northern windows was further diffused by thin gauzy panels with embroidered cutouts, as if stamped by a tinsmith's cookie cutter.

The polished floorboards squeaked in greeting as Claire followed Bethany across the room to two chairs in intimate juxtaposition, the bulgingly stuffed arms touching like two gossiping dowagers. At times Claire supposed she'd imagined the difference in Bethany's walk, but this morning the uneven gait was unmistakable.

"This weather." Bethany sighed, lowering herself gently into a chair.

Claire smiled to herself as Bethany at once straightened

several doilies within reach, shifting each a barely discernable difference. She knew by now that her friend tidied and fidgeted when anxious. "It is a bit dampening," said Claire. "To the spirit, and I suspect in another hour or two, to the pathway."

"It seeps into my very bones. I don't know if it's my mood that affects this old injury"—here Bethany waved her hand over her leg, the motion of swatting at a pesky fly—"it's really nothing. A childhood accident. But I could swear it is noticeably worse on these wet days, so whether it's the weather, or my mood's reaction to the weather, I suppose it's all the same."

They caught up on the village news, and the health and happenings of the staff at Raven Heights, and the guests of Pelican Inn. Even the antics of annoying transient guests became humorous anecdotes in Bethany's retelling. The more ludicrous the situation, the more she would relish the telling of it to Claire.

But now and then Claire would catch an expression of distracted bleakness when Bethany glanced out the window. Whether it was caused by pain in her leg, or pain in her heart, was not visible. *There is such an aura of peace and stillness in this home,* thought Claire, wishing it for her friend as well.

After a sip of hot tea, Claire took a deep breath, then exhaled before plunging in to a place where she might not be welcome.

"What?" Bethany smiled. "Why such a big sigh? Are you all right, dear?"

"Bethany, I—" Claire set down her teacup with exaggerated care. "There's a reason for my visit."

"Oh, dear." Bethany leaned forward, emoting gentle empathy. "This sounds ominous. Is all well at Raven Heights?"

"I realize it's none of my business, but . . . Bethany, everything *is* fine at Raven Heights. However, is the same true of Pelican Inn?"

Bethany's hand, holding her teacup, stilled in midair. Claire noticed the delicate hand shook just a tiny bit.

Bethany looked down at the table for a length of seconds before meeting Claire's eyes. "It's my father." Bethany's voice faltered, and she cleared her throat, took a sip of hot tea.

"Is he ill?"

Bethany shook her head. Claire noted the moisture that rimmed her friend's eyes, knew the other woman waited until her tight throat would allow the words to pass.

Bethany swallowed, cleared her throat a second time. "Ill?" she repeated. "I don't know. I hope not." She set down her cup and pulled a delicate handkerchief from her sleeve. She dabbed her eyes. "I have not heard from him for too many weeks. This is not like Father, to stay out of touch. Nor to be gone for such a long time."

"I'm sorry to have upset you. It's none of my busi—"

"No. Don't apologize, Claire. It's not a secret, after all. The entire village knows. I am only surprised that you had not heard this from others already." She reached out to the closest doily. With a splayed hand she again nudged it minutely, then realized what she was doing and snatched her hand back with a quick, sad grin. Folding her hands on her lap, she began twisting her handkerchief. "He left, you see, on a plant-gathering expedition. To Africa. He's done that before, it is nothing new. Such trips are usually quite profitable. Exotic plants are his hobby, and the additional income is, of course, welcome." The handkerchief was now tighter than a sailor's knot.

Claire could see Bethany struggled for composure. She waited as her friend traced a slim finger around the rim of the steaming cup.

"That was a little over five months ago." Bethany ignored the tea without having taken a drink and unfolded her handkerchief, smoothing it out on her lap as if ironing out the matching wrinkles of her brow. "Or maybe it's been longer. I am afraid to tally the number of days. As I said, he's never stayed away this long. And he's always kept me informed of his whereabouts, with letters dated at least twice a week, even if the mail has been sporadic in its arrival."

"When was the last time you received a letter from him?"

Bethany held Claire's gaze, then clutched the handkerchief to her mouth as she whispered in a choked voicc, "I havcn't. Not yet. Not once since he left." To hide her tears, she turned her head to look toward the window, as if she could see her father's ship.

Claire felt awful. There was nothing she could say or do to help, and now she felt like an intrusive busybody, sifting through the ashes of another person's hurt, looking for warm embers of gossip. She wanted to reach across to squeeze her friend's hand. Instead, she did what she'd learned to do over the years when discomfited: she sat silently, uselessly.

Chapter Nine

After three quick knocks, Claire reached for the curved handle of the summer-house door. Opening the door slowly, she called out in a songlike voice. "Alice, it's me, Claire."

"Hello, Claire!" Alice directed her eyes above Claire's head, where the half-round fanlight over the door let in the most light. "Are you going to come in and visit?"

"That is exactly what I was wishing to do." Claire crossed the room and took a seat at the same table where Alice sat petting a small kitten on her lap. Its tawny flanks were striped with caramel streaks. Standing on furry white paws, it mewed at Claire, watching her with wide-eyed circles of blue. Once again, Claire was reminded of another of life's visual pleasures invisible to persons without sight.

"I love this kitten." Alice continued to stroke its fur soothingly, from between its ears to the start of its tail, and was rewarded with a humming purr. "It's my favorite of Miss Molly's litter."

This surprised Claire. "Can you tell them apart?"

"Yes, by the collar." Alice moved her hand to finger a small braid of blue yarn. "Do you like it? Vitus made it for me. For her, that is."

A further surprise. "Vitus?" She tried to imagine the serious young man carefully weaving strands of fine yarn. As an act of kindness for a child? "Are you sure it wasn't Roman who made the collar?"

Alice laughed, as if the idea of Roman spending time on handiworks of craft could not be any more ludicrous. "Oh, no. It was certainly Vitus who made this for me. He told me it was a gift." She traced a small finger across the top of the collar, outlining each vee of the braid. "Besides, Roman and Vitus do not sound at all alike. I listen to voices carefully." She moved her hand to smooth the kitten's spine.

"Of course. You are right, they do not talk like one another. Not just the pitch of their voices—Vitus's is so much deeper—but the cadence and the tone are also different." Claire leaned forward to touch the collar. Multiple skeins of soft yarn were twisted with obvious precision. "It's a beautiful braid, woven very carefully. And he chose a beautiful bright blue yarn." Embarrassed to be explaining colors to Alice, who might not have the concept of blue versus yellow versus red, she rushed on. "That was exceedingly nice of Vitus to do that for you."

"Yes. He always offers to help me. He's the nicest man I know. But I can do almost everything by myself."

Claire digested this. She hadn't yet seen this gentle side to Vitus. With a brief start, she had an awful realization. Perhaps Vitus was pretending to befriend Alice, knowing that she might have more information about Zillah. Hadn't Alice blurted something to Claire about Zillah that first day they met? Something Alice said she hadn't told anyone yet. And that could be dangerous for the unsuspecting child.

"Alice," she said, waiting until she was sure she had the little girl's full attention, "do you and Vitus ever talk about Zillah?"

"Nobody ever talks about Zillah." Alice shrugged and returned her sightless gaze down to the kitten.

Claire thought she detected a sheen of tears in Alice's eyes. *Do blind persons cry?* she wondered. "Would you like to? To talk about Zillah with me?"

Alice looked in the direction of the door and asked in a

hushed tone, "Are we alone, Claire?"

Cold pimples washed along her arms, and Claire rubbed her hands over her forearms as she turned around to confirm. Turning back, she said, "Yes. There is no one else here. Just the two of us."

"I've wanted to talk to someone about Zillah. But I've been afraid to." Alice sucked in her breath, as if she regretted sharing secrets.

Alice's world is even more solitary than I realized, thought Claire, wanting to cry in pity. "Why haven't you talked to Miss Bethany about it? She's a good friend to you, I know."

"I did talk to her about it, one time. A long time ago. But she gets sad when she remembers Zillah. And Miss Bethany is already so sad about her father. I don't want to make her more sadder than she already is."

"More sad?" Claire gently corrected the little girl.

"Yes. More sadder," Alice responded.

Claire smiled and reached for Alice's hand where it lay on the tiny kitten. Alice put her hand in Claire's.

"You can trust me." She squeezed the young girl's fingers. "You know that, don't you?"

The child clenched Claire's hand in return as she nodded her head to the affirmative.

"If there is anything you'd like to tell me . . ." Her voice trailed off. She would leave the hint, should it comfort Alice to share her lonely secrets, but had no interest in intruding.

Alice pulled her hand away so suddenly the kitten jumped to the floor and scampered away. Leaning forward, Alice grasped the table's edge with both hands and lay her forehead on top of her hands. "I don't know where the note is." Alice's soft wail echoed in the empty sun-room. "I've tried and tried and tried to find it."

Claire held her breath while choosing her words. "Perhaps I

could help you find the note." She watched Alice carefully and asked, "Was this note from Zillah?"

Alice lifted her head, angled it toward the entry door again. Claire could see her straining to listen for other sounds.

"Zillah told me about the secret note. She let me touch the folded paper, but she didn't read it to me. She said she simply wanted me to know where it would be."

"I wonder why she did not read it to you first, at least tell you what it was about."

"I thought maybe it was a map for buried treasure, with some directions, and she was worried that the pirates might torture me, to reveal its secret. I asked her if it was a pirate's map, but all she said was, the less I knew about what was in that note, the better. Except for where it could be found."

"Did she say why? Why she wanted you to know where this note would be?"

"Because she said I was the only one she could trust." Alice's expression was dreamy. "We liked to pretend we were sisters. She was my big sister, and I was her little sister." Close to tears, Alice moaned softly, "But I tried to find it, and I can't. We hid it together. It was exactly two days before she—And now it's gone. Maybe it blew away."

"The note was hidden outdoors, then?"

Alice nodded. "There was two notes."

"There *were*—" Claire interrupted herself, not believing she should think about Alice's grammar at a time like this. "Why was the note hidden outdoors? Why not somewhere safe indoors?"

"We couldn't hide it in my room at Pelican Inn. Zillah told me the note had to be hidden where *nobody* could ever find it. She told me it could not be hidden in a drawer in my room, or under the mattress, because those are easy hiding places where somebody might look for it. Unless I had a loose floorboard that I knew about, she said we could not hide it in my room." She looked toward Claire with a woeful face. "I didn't know where there were any loose floorboards."

"That's all right, that was not your fault." Claire's voice was soft, soothing, as she prompted, "And so . . . ?"

"So then Zillah said we would find a safe place outdoors, and we would hide it together. She said she would make sure no one was watching us when we hid it. I promised Zillah I wouldn't tell anybody about the note. And then . . . I was supposed to return and find it, if . . ."

Claire was thinking that Alice should have told all of this to Bethany—immediately, after the accidental death—when Alice surprised her. "That was when I told Miss Bethany. After . . . you know. After it happened." It was as if the young girl read her mind.

Claire nodded approvingly, though the gesture was lost on Alice. "And did Miss Bethany help you look for the note?"

"The next afternoon—as soon as the rain stopped—she did. I took her to where me and Zillah hid it. She listened to my directions, and she looked oh-so-carefully. We looked for a long, long time. But when we couldn't find it together, where I was sure it would be, she said to me, 'Alice, do you remember how Zillah was always pretending, and making up stories and secrets?' And I said, 'Yes,' and then Miss Bethany said, 'I'm not convinced this note is real. I mean, think about it, Alice. Maybe Zillah had you touch a blank piece of paper.' And I did think about it. But I told Miss Bethany I don't know. She said, 'Do you know what I think? I think Zillah was inventing a fairy tale, Alice. We both looked *precisely* where she told you it would be, where you yourself helped her hide it, and now we both know there is no note. So let's go home, and let's not speak of this note again.' She said she didn't want to hear about it, and she said it might not be safe for me to tell anybody else about it. Ever."

Claire believed she knew Bethany, but she hadn't known Zillah. If Bethany—who was both intelligent and practical—had spent time meticulously searching, and had concluded there had never been a note, then that was probably that.

Alice continued, "On the walk back to Pelican Inn, we both told Zillah stories. Miss Bethany told me it would make my heart feel better." She wrinkled her forehead, as if recalling Bethany's words. "So it could start to heal."

"Did it? Help?"

Alice shrugged. "We talked about some of Zillah's pranks, but I didn't feel like laughing." She looked in Claire's direction. "Zillah loved to play pranks on all of us. Like the very first note."

Claire stilled. "The first note?" It came to her then that Alice had mentioned there were two notes. "Did Miss Bethany also see the first note?"

"Yes. I showed it to her just before we went to look for the second one. I remember it was rainy and cold and we were in the kitchen, where it was warm. We were waiting for the rain to stop, so we could go look for the outside note."

"I'm not sure I understand. Where was this first note? Was it not outdoors with the second?"

"No. I hid the first one in my room, all by myself." The pride in her voice was evident. "I noticed my doll had a tear on its bonnet. And Grace said I should ask Aunt Amelia to help darn it for me, but then I thought about the note. I folded it up and put it in my doll's bonnet, and I pretended she swallowed it." Her sudden smile was fleeting. "But when I showed it to Miss Bethany, she said it was nothing more than gibber . . ." Alice frowned.

"Gibberish?"

"Yes. Gibberish."

"Do you still have that first note?"

Alice ducked her chin toward her chest, seemingly ashamed. "Miss Bethany told me to throw it away." She swung her legs back and forth, scuffing the floor. Half a minute later, she said in a small voice, "But it's the only thing I have that Zillah ever gave me. So I keep it safe. In my doll. And I hide her, too, way down deep inside my sock drawer." She looked toward Claire. "Because, you know, I couldn't find a loose floorboard."

"Could you show it to me?"

"Yes. I have to go get it, and I could bring—What's that?" Alice snapped her head toward the door, her sightless eyes wide with fright.

Claire and Alice froze.

Just there, on the wall near the door, came a small scraping. Claire squinted in the bright afternoon light. The door was still closed. Claire saw no one else inside the empty room, though she scanned each potted palm carefully. Surely they would have heard the door open.

She recalled how quietly the well-oiled hinges had responded when she'd entered the room that first day to visit with Alice. It was why she had called out after she had knocked. Her heart beat painfully now, wildly looking into corners shadowed by the waning afternoon.

A small patch of color caught her eye, on the floor near the door.

It was only the kitten, scratching to get out.

After Alice left with the kitten, Claire remained seated, staring out the window through the silky yellow curtains. She thought about the tale Alice had revealed, thought about Zillah.

If the first note contained only gibberish, could the second note have been blank? Why would Zillah lie to a friend—a blind friend—about words written on a blank sheet of paper? That seemed too mischievous for a prank. And to go outdoors to pretend to hide a note, secretively, hinting at danger. It was too coincidental, especially as it foreshadowed Zillah's death two days later.

She pictured her busy friend Bethany carefully searching with Alice. Claire could not help a sense of foreboding relief that Bethany had warned Alice to tell no one else.

And suddenly—Claire didn't know why the thought should enter her mind, but she couldn't help but realize one fact: if Bethany had actually found the piece of paper, Alice would have had no way of knowing that. She would not have seen the discovered paper, would not have known Bethany was reading it, would never have seen it slipped surreptitiously into a pocket. She had only Bethany's word that the hiding place was empty.

As she had only Bethany's pronouncement that the first note contained gibberish.

I'm letting my imagination spin away, she admonished herself. *Bethany is as trustworthy as I.*

Chapter Ten

The trail to Pelican Inn was *not* worn down to bare earth, Claire noted, contrary to what Roman swore to her. She knew he was teasing. Sometimes, though, she suspected Roman was petulant about the time she spent with her friend Bethany.

It began when they were visiting at the fountain the other day, their usual meeting place—Roman, Vitus, Alice, and Claire. Claire asked Alice if she would like accompaniment on Alice's return stroll to Pelican Inn. Of course, Alice was quick to welcome Claire's company. At first, Claire thought she imagined Roman's displeasure. It was his own fault, though. For, as attentive as Roman was, he wore Claire down with the intensity of his banter. And the more Roman flirted, the more his brother scowled.

The undercurrents between the two siblings baffled her.

When she'd ask Bethany her opinion, Bethany said it was normal rivalry.

"For what would they compete in rivalry?" She remembered Bethany had turned quickly from the sideboard to study Claire's face.

"Why, can you not guess?" When Claire shook her head, Bethany said, "I'm sure they vie for your favors."

This embarrassed Claire terribly. She frowned in consternation and changed the subject as quickly as she could. Since that brief discussion with Bethany, Claire spent less time in the brothers' company.

This morning, as she and Alice approached the inn, Alice split off to join Grace, who called out for company on her way to feed the ducks in the pond. Claire continued up the path to the kitchen, since that was where she most often found her friend. The upper half-door was wide open, the kitchen unoccupied. When Claire leaned across the lower door and called out, it was Aunt Amelia who responded, shuffling into the kitchen.

"Claire! I'm so glad you are here." She sounded agitated, not glad at all. "Please, come in at once."

Claire unlatched the lower kitchen half-door, swinging it inward. "Is something wrong, Aunt Amelia?" Claire had grown used to addressing Bethany's great-aunt by the name she insisted upon.

The tall woman beckoned her in, her hands fluttering swiftly. "Hurry, hurry."

Claire's heart pounded. "What is it? Is it Bethany?"

Aunt Amelia might not have heard, as she'd already turned and was hastening, with her small mincing steps, out the kitchen into the hallway.

They hurried down the hallway to the spacious office on the left; that is, they hurried at Aunt Amelia's pace.

"Claire is here," heralded Aunt Amelia once she entered the office. "Claire is here." Claire caught Bethany quickly wiping her eyes with a limp handkerchief that Claire suspected was already wetted with tears.

Bethany, sitting at the desk, appeared embarrassed. "Oh, Aunt Amelia, it's nothing. I didn't realize I'd upset you, dear. Good day, Claire," she said with a sheepish grin.

Aunt Amelia *tsk-tsk*ed. "Don't tell me it is naught, dear. I heard you sniffling the moment I came downstairs."

Claire felt horribly uncomfortable. "I'm so sorry. I . . . I thought maybe you were sick. Or hurt. I don't mean to intrude."

Claire took a step back to recross the threshold.

"No, don't. Please stay. Truly, I'd like you to stay," said Bethany.

Aunt Amelia turned to Claire, and with a stern shake of the finger said, "You will most certainly not leave, young lady. You must stay here with Bethany, and I shall see to some soothing chamomile tea." With that, she scurried past Claire and left the office.

"Chamomile tea is Aunt Amelia's cure for life." Bethany chuckled, but Claire thought it half-hearted, as her friend's downturned lips quivered slightly.

Claire willed positive thoughts toward her friend, but was still unsure whether she should stay or go.

"Sit, Claire. I'm glad to have a friend here, as I'm in a silly, blue mood." She stuffed the handkerchief in her sleeve with a determined smile.

"Is it your father?" asked Claire. It was all she could think of to say, but was instantly annoyed at herself for referring to a painful topic.

"No, for a change it is not about Father. But if that burden weren't enough . . . I also have pressing financial concerns." Bethany shook her head, looking at the disarray of papers on the open shelf of the walnut secretary. "Father always took care of our dealings with creditors, and now—" Her voice broke. Still not raising her gaze from the desk, she took a breath and said, "Well. Now I must decide what to do. I cannot put off matters any longer."

Aunt Amelia and Grace arrived together at the office doorway, each bearing a tray. "Come to the lavender parlor, dears. We will have tea and you will feel better."

"Of course, Aunt." Bethany rallied a smile for the elderly woman. "Thank you, Grace," she said, nodding to the red-haired youngster as she rose. "I think that is an excellent idea."

She held out a hand to Claire and squeezed it. Both women followed Aunt Amelia and Grace along the hallway.

"With fewer visitors—the highway, once by-passed, diverted travellers and their pocketbooks to the tollhouses, not to our inn—we decided to take in boarders. Students, actually." Her slight laugh was more of a rueful sigh. "We meant to take in paying boarders. But . . . it seemed we kept picking up strays whose tuition dried up, and they became part of our family."

Claire listened as Bethany told her tale. After tea, Aunt Amelia and Grace had left the parlor, but Bethany had insisted Claire stay to visit.

As she spoke, Bethany turned her gaze to the doilies on the far table. She rose and crossed the room to straighten a tatted circle.

"Did you make these doilies?" Claire was unsure if it would help to change the subject.

"Yes, when I was first learning to tat." Bethany tugged a crisp white circle an inch toward her, then returned to her seat. "Where was I?"

Claire did not turn the subject again, but let her friend unravel the burdens twisting inside. Bethany told her about Grace's arrival, followed quickly by Zillah, and within a few months, Alice.

"Even with Father's extra income acquiring and selling exotic plants, we've always struggled to keep the inn profitable. When it's been difficult, Father's always kept us positive with his ideas and his bargaining. But . . . I find that on my own, I continue to slide further behind."

She was pensive a moment, and then looked directly at Claire. Her expression carefully neutral, she confided, "I am thinking of selling Pelican Inn."

★ ★ ★ ★ ★

Bethany stood at the open double door. She stared at Claire's receding back, but her mind was elsewhere; she did not see the young lady who followed the curved path. Instead, recalling their recent conversation, Bethany was lost in reminiscence.

It had been surprisingly simple to take in the earliest student boarders, once she and her father had made the decision. The most time-consuming effort came before that decision: charting the profitability and appraising the potential pros and cons.

Two young girls arrived within days of one another. Grace came first, accompanied by a woman not many years Bethany's senior. Bethany could barely recall the woman's pale face, with its tiny features buried within a dark, voluminous travelling dress and oversized bonnet.

"Grace is my cousin," the woman explained, giving the young girl a gentle push in the back when she did not immediately advance to curtsy.

Bethany crossed the parlor to meet her new student partway.

"What happened to your leg?" asked the child in fascination as she noticed Bethany's slight limp.

"Grace!" admonished the cousin.

The cousin did not bother to introduce herself. Bethany would soon realize that most relatives wished to anonymously drop off their charges and quickly brush themselves of the responsibility. Any introduction would simply slow the process, would be one more tie to be snipped.

"It's all right." Bethany smiled at Grace, then turned just her head to look at the cousin. "Everyone wonders, but only a child is honest enough to ask." She returned her gaze to Grace, and spoke directly to her. "I was in a carriage accident. I was much younger than you at the time, and one of my legs was crushed. As I grew older, it could never quite catch up, and so is a little bit shorter than the other."

"Does it hurt?"

Bethany looked up to find the cousin waiting for her answer, listening in silent horror, but no longer willing to politely turn the subject.

"Only now and then. If I've done more walking than I should, as I did this morning. But that does not keep me from walking." She smiled. "And what of you, Grace? Do you enjoy walks in the shrubbery?"

"Yes, ma'am."

"Then you shall certainly derive pleasure from our local scenery and pathways. The salt air in this part of the country is most invigorating, and the temperatures moderate. And you may call me Miss Bethany, Grace." Bethany glanced at the cousin. "Shall I ring for tea?"

The woman started, as if remembering a sudden engagement. "Oh, no. I must be off without delay. Grace—come child, and give me a kiss, and say your goodbyes."

Grace returned to where her cousin stood and rose hesitatingly on tiptoes to kiss the dry cheek that was offered as the cousin bent forward. The woman straightened quickly. "She's a good child," she said awkwardly.

"I'm sure she is," said Bethany with a smile toward the young girl. To the nameless cousin, she said, "Please feel free to visit Grace as often as you like."

Grace and her cousin both looked at one another without any enthusiasm at the suggestion.

"Well, goodbye, Grace. Be sure to write."

"Yes, ma'am," Grace chanted obediently, quietly, but the woman was already on her way out the door and might not have heard.

Zillah had been the second to arrive. But within the coming year, Bethany and her father realized that student boarders would not be as lucrative an idea as had appeared on paper.

Alice had been the last to arrive. Bethany *did* still recall the bearded gentleman who dropped her off. He waited until Alice was led to the kitchen by Aunt Amelia for a treat before confiding in Bethany that he was the man of affairs for Alice's wealthy parents.

The affluent socialites did not want the embarrassment of a flawed child. The little girl, already shy, had withdrawn even more as her eyesight became worse. Bethany found it difficult to imagine a world of ever-deepening shadows, waking to a twilight that stretched into a permanent winter, waiting for a dawn that never arrived.

She wondered how much vision remained. Did Alice have enough remaining eyesight to notice when others stared? The adults would not be so bad. They would glance, then look away, but discreetly sneak an additional peek at the clouded eyes.

Children, on the other hand, had no sense of discretion. Or courtesy. They did not care whether Alice noticed them staring her way. They'd turn and crane their necks as their mothers pulled them away.

To the Coulter family's relief, Alice's relatives soothed their consciences by continuing to generously support her residency at Pelican Inn. But it no longer mattered. The small girl would have stayed either way, as she'd become a member of the family. Bethany had a special place in her heart for Alice. As she did for Grace. As she had for Zillah.

Chapter Eleven

Claire heard laughter outside, and crossed the upstairs parlor to peek out the window. The soft gauze panels distorted her view, but she could make out the gardener, Jacoby, on the lawn below. And Vitus and Roman appeared to be running around him, laughing. *How odd,* was her first thought. Claire squinted through the sheer fabric, and could now discern small furry balls circling all three men. She hastened to investigate.

Roman's laughter was intermixed with small barking puppies, as he bent to dangle his hands playfully near two pudgy caramel-colored pups. Vitus was on one knee, a giant next to the tiniest puppy, a darker-colored runt. Its tiny tail whisked side-to-side, and scrunching up its wrinkled body, it barked bravely at him. He scooped the puppy up, cupping it in his palm. "I'll take this one, Jacoby." He walked over to stand next to the gardener.

"It's the runt, as you can see, Vitus." Jacoby looked skeptical. "Don't know that it's as healthy as it should be."

"The younger runt. How fitting!" Roman laughed meanly.

Vitus glanced over at Claire, who had overheard. Roman had not yet realized she was there.

"Morning, Miss Temple." Jacoby touched his cap, then moved off to clip the grass where it met the adjoining terrace.

She had barely greeted Jacoby before Roman was at her side. "Would you like one of the puppies for yourself, Miss Temple?"

Gazing longingly at the roly-poly babies, Claire had a pang of desire for a pet of her own. But she shook her head, regretfully. If Uncle did not invite her to remain at Raven Heights, she knew she would never be allowed to keep a dog at the school, no matter how small.

"No. I cannot," she answered as she strolled over to Vitus and asked, "May I pet him?"

"Of course."

She rubbed the tiny puppy between the ears. "What will you name him?"

Vitus held the puppy up, surveying it. "I don't know yet. I shall have to watch him, and then I'll think of a name." He looked sideways at Claire. "What would you call him?"

She tilted her head, deliberating. "A noble name. Something from mythology, like the dolphins you told me about. Are your names—Roman and yours—from mythology?"

"Mine is." Roman had followed to stand by Claire. As he reached to stroke the puppy, Vitus turned away from his brother, pulling the puppy to his chest.

Roman turned to Claire, ignoring his brother's rebuff. "Latin mythology. Romulus and Remus were the twin founders of Rome. I am named for Romulus." He smirked toward Vitus. "I'm sure father would have named my brother Remus, except that he much preferred to give a hero's name to his favorite dog: Remus."

Vitus held the puppy toward Claire, so she could pet it again. She noticed he never responded to Roman's barbs. "I also was given a Latin name. Vitus means 'life.' " Vitus grinned as he mumbled, "And I suppose I can only be thankful my father's horse was already named Bucephalus."

"Bucephalus was Greek, not Latin," corrected Roman.

Claire was growing tired of the one-sided bickering. "And who was Bucephalus?" she asked in a bored voice, still petting the tiny puppy. "Did he found a city as well?" She spoke to the air, did not bother to soften the edge in her voice.

Roman answered again for both of them. *Of course,* thought Claire. He said, "There *was* a city named Bucephalus, but it was named in honor of a horse, not a hero. Bucephalus was Alexander the Great's horse. Naming a city for a horse! Though, that would have been fitting for my brother, don't you think?"

She refused to be drawn in, nor did she smile, hoping Roman would perceive her annoyance. As flirtatious as Roman was, he lacked a depth of awareness. It irritated Claire that he assumed she would side with him against his brother, even if Vitus was more withdrawn than his glib brother.

Claire decided to take her leave of the gentlemen and, dropping her hand from the warm, wrinkled puppy, she moved slightly away from Vitus and the pup, when Vitus surprised her by stating quietly, "We have not seen you of late." Vitus spoke without making eye contact. His dark lashes were all she saw as he looked down at the puppy nuzzled against his chest.

"I've been spending time with Miss Bethany Coulter. At Pelican Inn, where Alice lives. I'm sure you know of Pelican Inn, on the outskirts, near the highway."

Vitus hadn't looked up at her reply, but the ubiquitous Roman moved closer. "Of course. Everyone knows of Pelican Inn." He picked up a nearby stick and threw it toward the circle of puppies, who were too busy frolicking to notice. "It's a shame Coulter left his daughter on her own, to run the inn." Ignored by the pups, he turned back to address Claire. "That was too irresponsible of him."

This further irked Claire. She did not even know Calden Coulter, but felt defensive for her friend's sake. "And how do you know it was intentional? He is on another continent. Perhaps he has been injured, or fallen sick, or—"

Roman snorted as he dropped down to sit on the marble balustrade outlining the terrace. "Fallen sick with too much whiskey is more like it."

"Roman," warned Vitus. He must have noticed the florid tint to her cheeks. "Miss Bethany Coulter is an especial friend of Miss Temple's." Roman had the grace to desist, when he saw Claire look her thanks toward his brother.

"If only her financial worries could be staved off until her father returns from Africa," wished Claire aloud.

"What sort of financial worries?" asked Roman.

"Oh. I . . . Forgive me. I have no right to speak of that. It is none of my business." Claire wished, as she often wished during her life, that she would think before speaking.

"Well, if her father doesn't return soon," said Roman with a scowl, "it's her own fault if she does not wash her hands of that inn."

"But it's been in the family for generations," Claire argued.

"Be that as it may, she cannot oversee it on her own." He sounded bored. He leaned back on an elbow, pontificating to the sky.

"That's not so." Vitus disagreed with his brother, as was to be expected. "Miss Coulter has always made most of the day-to-day decisions, even when Mr. Coulter was—When he was here."

"Regardless," pressed Roman, "it is unnatural for a woman to take on that role."

Vitus had a slight smile on his face, as he closely monitored Claire's expressions. "Let's ask Miss Temple how she feels about that, Brother."

From his relaxed slouch on the balustrade, Roman angled his body toward her. "Come, tell us your thoughts, then," he invited, his voice confident of her reply. "A woman running a business, conjuring up figures and attempting to tally. Don't you agree it goes against the natural order of society?"

"Unnatural?" Claire asked incredulously, her eyebrows raised. She found herself becoming angrier. Miss Bethany worked harder in any one day than she'd seen Roman work in the weeks she had known him. It was unfathomable to her at this moment that she'd ever been attracted to the pompous young man.

"Miss Temple?" prodded Roman, oblivious to her surprise.

"I thought they repealed the witchcraft law in seventeen thirty-six," Claire said with no inflection.

Roman frowned, evidently uncertain of her meaning.

She found her fists had tightened. She placed them on her hips. "And where do you suppose she would live?" asked Claire. "If she 'washed her hands of the inn,' as you blithely suggest, if she sold it and had to move out? She's lived in that house her entire life. She was born in that inn."

Roman shrugged. "She must have relatives somewhere, I am sure, besides that doting old woman she calls her aunt."

Claire threw her hands in the air, in supplication for patience. Now he disparaged sweet Aunt Amelia. *It is my own fault if I stay and listen to this drivel.* As she turned to depart, his next words stabbed her motionless with icy precision.

"Where do other women live, when their fathers are dead?"

"Don't say that!" Claire spun back to face him, shocked to hear the words finally spoken aloud by someone. She thought only of her friend as she repeated, "Don't you dare say so! We don't know that."

"I apologize." He held up his hands toward her in mock surrender. "But if the ship he left on is still in one piece—and no one has heard otherwise, I admit—why has he not returned? I believe you are an optimist, Miss Temple." Roman smiled warmly. "Personally, I find that charming. But it is time to be a realist."

"A realist, Roman?" asked his brother. "Or a cynic?"

That was it. Claire was weary of this topic, and she'd had enough of bickering brothers. Gathering her skirts, she thought perhaps she would head to Pelican Inn to see Bethany and Alice.

She heard Vitus's next remark, meant only for her ears. "What if Miss Coulter were to find an investor? Perhaps a partner," said Vitus quietly as she moved past him. "Do you think she could then survive financially?"

"That's absurd, Vitus." Roman had overheard.

Claire noticed he was always nastiest when responding to his younger brother. It was no wonder Vitus was withdrawn, if he'd grown up holding silent counsel.

"Who would put good money into a failing venture?" continued Roman. "And if one owner cannot make it profitable, how could it support two?"

Claire hardly listened as the brothers continued arguing. Vitus had given her an idea.

Chapter Twelve

"Good afternoon. We've never met formally, my name is Claire Temple." She curtsied to the elderly woman who stood skeptically in the doorway of the trim cottage.

"I live with my uncle, Sir Rudyard." When the woman did not respond, Claire added, "At Raven Heights." She raised her voice at the end, making it a question.

This did earn a flicker of a friendlier reaction from the sober matron. Barely.

"Yes?" The woman's voice was dry, hollow.

"I was in Mr. Tulley's apothecary the other day, and—Would it be possible to speak to your nephew? To Mr. Malcolm Randall, that is?"

Eudora Perkins stared at her a moment, as if deaf. Just as Claire wondered if she should repeat, enunciate more clearly and at a higher volume, the woman turned and disappeared into the dark room. She did not close the door. Nor did she invite Claire into the cottage.

Perhaps she is senile, thought Claire, wondering if she should turn about and leave. Claire did not even know for certain that she was at the correct cottage. Mr. Tulley had been busy reaching and bending as he'd waved the general directions with his arm. Though she was positive he'd mentioned honey-colored limestone. She leaned back to survey the front of the house. The wooden window casings on both floors were unmistakably a bright, crisp white, the cottage door itself an inviting ivy green.

The stones surrounding the windows and covering the remainder of the wall were more of an ochered, earthy color. She recalled his mention of a yellow house, but there was not one speck of yellow paint to be seen. Even the trim along the roof was the same snowy white color as the door.

She glanced over her shoulder at the apricot-edged roses she'd admired on her approach. They climbed and spilled along the rail fence edging the front of the property. Those *could* be considered yellow. Creamy yellow, anyway. If someone were passing in a carriage, she could imagine their overall perception might be soft, buttery leather tints.

Turning back with a mental shrug, she waited for one more uncomfortable minute, averting her eyes so as not to peer into the parlor. She studied instead the tendrils of sweet pea climbing up the porch lattice, not seeing any buds yet.

Now she deliberated. Should she call out in a louder voice, or should she reach out to pull the door shut and take her leave? She leaned in toward the doorframe, still unresolved as to which she would do, when a man appeared in the doorway, startling her.

"Oh, my! Please forgive me," she apologized. "I didn't know if . . ."

"You didn't know whether my aunt would be returning? She does that to everyone, so don't think you are special." His smile belied the harsh words.

"Mr. Randall?" She recognized the young man from the apothecary, but waited for his affirmative nod. "My name is Claire Temple. I apologize for this intrusion, but I was in Mr. Tulley's apothecary the other morning." She didn't see any recognition on his face and said, "I was coming into the shop. As you were leaving."

"Oh, yes," he said. But his demeanor spoke otherwise, saying he was still not sure of who she was, and why she was here.

At least, Claire was relieved to note, it was an open, inquisitive expression. She liked that the only discernable creases on his face were from smiling, not those she associated with overused frowns.

"I live at my uncle's home. Sir Rudyard, of Raven Heights Manor."

"I hadn't known he had a niece," he said pleasantly, but still had not invited her in.

"Evidently he did not know either," she said with a rueful grin. "Until recently, that is. I've only come to Raven Heights a few weeks ago."

"Shall I invite you in, Miss Temple?"

"No! I mean, thank you. That is, I wasn't planning on staying very long." Already extremely uncomfortable, Claire was certain that stepping into the cottage could only make her more so. "This is rather rude of me to admit, I realize." She licked her lips. "I overheard part of your conversation, you see. In the apothecary. And then—after you left—Mr. Tulley mentioned that you had an interest in . . . in cooking." She watched to see if he would dismiss her and shut the door, but he did not. Not yet. Claire rushed on, "So I thought maybe you'd be interested in . . . an opportunity?" Her voice rose with the question, and she practically squeaked the last word.

The dimple in his cheek deepened with the twinkle in his eyes. "Ah. And you are looking for a personal chef. You find your uncle's table lacking? Though I am not sure you could afford my services."

Claire was embarrassed, not knowing where to begin her response. "No, it is nothing like that! It's just that I—"

"Forgive me, Miss Temple. I am teasing with you." At her confused look, he added, "My brothers despair of my lack of seriousness. Have you any brothers?"

"No. The only brothers I have observed seem to do nothing

but argue. It is quite tiresome, really—" She remembered why she was here. "But that is not what I came to speak to you about."

He lowered his brows. "I am done with teasing, then. This is my serious face."

Claire had to laugh. Relaxed, she determined to recite the speech she had rehearsed. "I know of an opportunity, a wonderfully unique opportunity, for a person who desires to cook." She rushed on before he had a chance to react. "Are you familiar with Pelican Inn?"

He shook his head. "No, though the name does sound somewhat familiar. I do not live here, you see. I am visiting my aunt."

"Pelican Inn is a busy inn. It belongs to the Coulters. And it's been in their family ever so long, for generations—well, two, at least." She noticed his smile, but proceeded to blurt the most difficult part. What was the term Vitus used? Investor? She decided not to use that; she liked the other term better. "And I believe the owner of Pelican Inn may welcome a partner."

"If the inn is busy, and one would then assume successful, why would they seek a partner?"

"Well. They haven't *quite* said they need a partner. At least, not in those exact words, but . . . With your skills as a chef—"

"I would not call myself an experienced—"

"I heard you talking to Mr. Tulley. And he said you had a passion for cooking. And I was thinking that a partnership would be a marvelous idea. You could be the chef. At an established inn. You would attract customers with your reputation. And when there are guests at the inn, you would have customers already available."

"Miss Temple—"

"You could experiment with menus. I know Miss Bethany, and she would be so very agreeable to any menu suggestions you would have. I know it."

"Who is this Miss Bethany? Is she the housekeeper?"

Claire debated whether to admit that Bethany was running the inn by herself, with her father gone on his expedition. She chose to ignore his question.

"Please, come by and see the inn yourself, Mr. Randall, before you make a decision."

"I shall give it thought, Miss Temple, but—"

"You should visit with them before another investor comes along. And you must mention that I sent you, so that they will understand. Not that they would not be gracious. They are most accommodating and gracious, you will see. Their guests all adore them."

"That is a glowing recommendation. Thank you, young lady. And shall you receive a commission?"

"Oh, no. I just wanted to let you know about this possibility." Her voice trailed off when she saw his eyes crinkle. With a slight blush, she realized he was again teasing her.

Anxious to escape, Claire said her goodbyes. Relieved she'd accomplished her mission, she was mortified at how difficult it had been. But if it helped Bethany, it would have been worth the discomfort.

Mr. Randall watched the young girl let herself out the gate, and he spoke without turning around. "So? What do you think, Aunt Eudora?"

"Me? About what?"

"Oh, I see. Shall we pretend you were not listening near the door?"

The woman harrumphed, rather than deny it. "You know I am hard of hearing, Malcolm."

"I'm teasing you, Aunt. It doesn't matter, however"—he closed the door and looked out the window as Claire receded along the path—"as I cannot imagine that I should ever be interested in pursuing such an opportunity as that. Can you?"

Chapter Thirteen

"This is the paper that Zillah gave me."

Alice did not immediately relinquish the folded sheet. With the note clasped in one hand, the blind girl reached out the other empty hand toward Claire, obviously reluctant to hand the note to anyone else; she would be certain it was Claire who was the recipient. As soon as their fingers touched, Alice felt for Claire's wrist, then turned Claire's palm up and placed the folded piece of parchment there.

They stood in a clearing between the manor and the gardener's cottage. A bonfire crackled nearby, consuming dried twigs and rakings. Alice spoke so softly, Claire could barely hear above the snapping of the dry pile. The blue hazy smoke rising from the hot flames leaned toward them, as if eager to hear any secrets. Claire said, "Let's move away from the path of the smoke." She put a hand on Alice's shoulder and they moved a few feet to the side, enough to avoid the wisps of smoke and fumes.

"This is the note you showed to Miss Bethany?" Claire hadn't unfolded it yet.

Alice nodded.

"Do you already know what is written in this note?"

Reflecting, Alice did not shake her head, nor did she nod affirmation. "Zillah didn't tell me what it said. But I think I know some of the words in it now." Alice kept her voice low, and Claire had to lean forward to hear above the vigorous popping of the fire. "When she gave it to me, it was already folded. Like it is now. She pressed it into my hand. And she told me that I should not tell anyone about it." Alice's small mouth trembled. "Unless she . . . unless she never came back. Those were her words."

"And? What were you to do then? Did she say?"

"No. But she told me it was important, dangerous news." Alice turned her face toward the heat of the fire.

Perhaps she's listening for other sounds, thought Claire. She'd learned to trust Alice's keen hearing.

Alice stared in the direction of the fire, closed her sightless eyes to its warmth. Without turning, she added, "She made me promise I wouldn't tell Miss Bethany."

"*What?* Why ever not?" Claire was confused. Bethany Coulter had spoken so warmly of Zillah. The first day Claire met Bethany, the woman's distress at the mention of Zillah had been palpable. Claire assumed the affection had been mutual between the young student and the caring innkeeper. "Did Zillah say why you must promise not to tell Bethan—Miss Bethany?"

"Yes." Alice turned back to speak in Claire's direction, a frown of recall on her smooth face. She held up an index finger. "One, she said it was not safe for me *or* Miss Bethany to know what was in the note. Two," she said as a second finger was raised, "she said that Miss Bethany already had too many sorrows. I was not to add to her . . ." Alice's brow wrinkled as she squeezed her eyes shut, then cleared as she opened them. "Her burden." She dropped her hand to her side. "But it doesn't matter. Vitus told me what the note says."

Claire's insides froze. "You showed the note to Vitus?"

Alice nodded, vigorously this time. "Because Zillah told me it was all right to show it to someone if she didn't come back. And if it would make Miss Bethany sad, I decided to show it to Vitus first. We can trust Vitus, Claire, like Zillah trusted me."

"But—Didn't you tell me the other day that Miss Bethany saw it? And thought it was . . . I believe she used the word *gibberish*?"

Alice nodded again. "I didn't tell her that I showed it to Vitus first. Vitus said he recognized the words that Zillah used."

Claire unfolded the ivory paper, took a moment to peruse it. "I don't understand this."

"I remember one of the words is 'rex,' " said Alice. "I tried to memorize two of the words he told me. I remember rex." Panic tinged her voice. "I can't remember the other."

Claire looked up at Alice. There was no word "rex" on the page she held. Either Alice was mistaken, or Vitus had lied.

"Oh, yes I do!" Alice sounded exaggeratedly relieved. "There is also another word that sounds like 'links.' "

"What is this? I still don't understand." Claire stared intently at the page, expecting the words to sort themselves out, the letters to rearrange and suddenly make sense.

"Rex. Links." Raising her voice, Alice repeated each word distinctly. "Those were the words that Vitus said." Her brow was pinched in frustration. "Can't you see them on the page?" Slowly and loudly, in order to be heard over the escalating bonfire noise, she hollered, "Rex. Links."

"Alice!"

At the sharp command, Alice jerked back a step. Vitus strode up to them.

"What are you doing with that note? I thought you said you were going to destroy it." His voice was loud, stern, as he saw the bone-colored paper in Claire's hand.

Alice turned her face toward the ground and crossed her arms across her body to comfort herself. She started to sniffle.

"Vitus, you've upset Alice." Claire could sound just as stern and loud as he.

Vitus acted as if she'd slapped him. "Alice, I'm sorry. I had no right to upset you." He put a large hand on the young girl's shoulder, ever so gently. "Please don't be upset."

"It's all right. It's just that you startled me." Alice swiped the back of her hand at the corners of her eyes.

"Take this handkerchief, dear." Claire pressed a small linen square into Alice's hand and Alice thanked her as she wiped her nose.

Claire stared at Vitus, and he returned her stare.

When Alice was composed, and the three had stood in silence for a full minute, Vitus asked with gentle solicitation, "Alice, why do you still keep this note?"

She shrugged and turned her face down again.

"Do the words on this note mean anything to you?" Claire watched his face closely, to see what he would give away.

"Yes."

That was not the answer she was expecting. She assumed he would prevaricate, given his displeasure that Alice had kept the confusing scribbles.

"But it's nothing," he told Claire forcefully. "A silly game." He looked in Alice's direction, but the young girl froze like a statue and did not contradict him. In a gentler tone, he said to Claire, "You didn't know Zillah. She was always playing games. She had a passion for riddles and mysteries. Everything had to have a secret meaning in her world."

When Claire didn't say anything in response, Vitus sighed. "My grandmother was German."

"I don't understand what that—" began Claire.

"Hear me out," Vitus interrupted, shaking his head in annoyance. "I told you that Zillah loved secrets and puzzles. She asked if I knew any other languages, and I told her I knew a few words in German, that I had learned from my grandmother. My grandmother is no longer alive, but I was fairly certain that 'links' was left, and 'rechts' was right. One of our games—Zillah's games—was *Links Und Rechts.* The idea of deciphering instructions and directions added an element of . . . I don't know what." He gave a small laugh, shook his head at Zillah's caprice.

Alice tugged on Claire's sleeve. "I need to return to Pelican Inn now."

"Do you want me to accompany you?"

"No, thank you. I've been gone too long, and I didn't tell Miss Bethany where I was going. Goodbye, Vitus."

"Good day." As she started to walk away, he called out, "Alice? I'm sorry."

She turned, leaning on her stick, and smiled shyly in his direction. "I know." With that, she turned and was on her way home.

Claire faced the path, watching Alice's departure, and saw Roman circling toward them. "Greetings, Miss Temple," he called. He nodded at Vitus. "Brother." They waited together, not speaking, until Roman was about to join them. He was a few feet from Claire when he noticed she held the sheet of paper. "What have you there?"

"Nothing," said Vitus curtly.

To Claire's amazement, Vitus grabbed the paper she'd been holding loosely. He walked directly to the high flames of the bonfire and she saw a ball of paper going into the fire.

"Vitus!" She stopped when he turned a warning glance to her. Claire watched with a sinking heart as the paper caught instantly, and was soon unrecognizable among the other ashes.

Roman watched his brother return to their circle from the fire's clearing. "And what are you two discussing today?"

Vitus didn't bother to answer his brother, but he seldom did. Claire felt uncomfortable with the drawn-out silence. "We were discussing Alice," she said lamely, her face red. She was sure she looked as guilty as she felt.

"An odd little child, isn't she?" Roman was now directing his conversation toward Claire, his mood open and friendly.

"She is different," said Claire defensively, "but I do not think her to be odd."

She was rewarded for her honesty with a bright smile. "That is what I enjoy most about you, Miss Temple. You refuse to be swayed by the opinions of others. I think . . ." He glanced in Vitus's direction. "Even were my brother to tell you tales about me, I know you would come to my defense." He approached her too closely. "Would you defend my honor?" He asked his question softly, too close to her ear.

She shivered slightly, her gaze flying to Vitus's. His contempt was open.

Stepping away from Roman, she moved toward the path to the manor. "I must go now. Good day, Roman. Good day, Vitus."

Vitus stared darkly after her, but Roman lifted a hand and waved cheerily. Vitus turned abruptly away from Roman and walked the opposite way along the path.

Claire had decided to seek the solace of the summer-house fountain, to think on what had transpired. She had only just reached the maze when she heard the gravel crunching behind her. She turned, then gasped.

"You startled me."

Vitus held a finger to his lips. Once it was evident she would not speak out loud, he turned to survey the path behind them. It was empty.

"Vitus, you had no right to burn that paper," she whispered angrily. "It belonged to Alice."

"I did it for her own safety. I'm not sure she should be keeping that with her."

"But she kept it because it was her bridge to Zillah. Her last bridge, Vitus. Zillah gave her that paper, so it had sentimental value to Alice. And now she has nothing of Zillah's."

Was that pain she saw in his clear grey eyes? It was gone in a moment.

"It was necessary. Zillah is gone. We need to let this drop." He raised a dark eyebrow, watching her. "And you must mind your own business. Will you leave this mystery alone, Miss Temple?"

She licked her lips, wondering whether to tell this man the truth.

"I know you," he said in light disgust. "Why do I even ask? You are so like her. Like Zillah."

Claire felt a frisson of fear for the first time in Vitus's presence. She chose not to answer.

"Do you know," he said, "there are some who do not believe Zillah died accidentally." When Claire swallowed but remained silent, he said, "Very well, Miss Temple. But be forewarned."

Too frightened to say anything, Claire took a step backward.

"Wait." Vitus moved closer, spoke quickly and softly. "If you plan to pursue this matter—against my recommendation—then perhaps you *should* memorize the clue she wrote. I burned the paper so that no one else will see it. But perhaps there is something there that might have saved her life. Do you remember what it said?"

Claire did in fact remember the German words both Alice and Vitus had said aloud. There were a few other words on the paper that meant nothing to her. But she wondered if admitting anything to Vitus might seal her own death warrant. Cautiously, she shook her head no.

He studied her for a long moment before saying, "The note said *'rechts, rechts, zweite links abbiegen.'* A right, and another right. And then the second left. We should both remember that, Miss Temple. It may be important." He didn't bother to wait for an answer, but turned upon his heel and disappeared along the path.

Chapter Fourteen

Claire deliberated. Sitting on a tall stool in Pelican Inn's spacious kitchen, she watched Bethany attending to one of her friend's favorite chores, baking bread.

When Claire had left Raven Heights for her daily stroll, she had convinced herself it was perfect weather for a long walk. And she'd reasoned with herself that she was overdue for a long visit to Pelican Inn.

But as she sat here in the kitchen, a niggling inner voice prodded, *Admit it. You came here to bring up the subject of Zillah's note.* And that was true. But that desire glossed over the fact that Alice had shared information with Claire in confidence. Alice said Bethany had warned her never to speak of the note again.

Yet Claire yearned to confide in Bethany, to discuss the German words on the note; to share her indignation at Vitus's high-handed burning of the note; to empathize with its sentimental value to Alice.

Bethany had told Alice she should throw the note away. Certainly no one who knew the compliant little girl could imagine her to be capable of disobeying. Was this why Claire hesitated?

"You're quiet today." Bethany, kneading and turning the dough rhythmically, still had her back to Claire. She plopped the oval of dough into a wide, shallow delftware bowl and covered it gently with a thin cloth. Her attention next turned to the loaves that were almost finished baking.

Claire picked up her teacup, set it back down after inhaling the soothing rose hip blend. "I was thinking about something." Claire knew that if Bethany prompted, even ever so slightly, she would spill the whole tale.

"Something you wish to talk about?" asked Bethany.

Thank you, thought Claire. If Bethany were her true friend, there should be no secrets between them.

"Yes, I would very much like to discuss it with you. On the one hand, I'd value your thoughts and your insight. On the other, though, I worry about violating a confidence I've been given. You see, it has to do with—Oh! Oh, my! Bethany, there's something we need to talk about. Immediately."

Bethany laughed. "Yes, you already said that." She slid her paddle under a loaf of sweet-smelling bread whose butter-brushed top had browned to perfection in the hearth oven. "I'm listening. Give me a moment to finish these, and I'll join you."

Claire glanced outside again. "No, this is something entirely different. You may have a visitor arriving shortly."

Bethany concentrated on sliding each loaf of bread off the paddle and onto the counter. "What sort of visitor? I wasn't expecting anyone."

Claire, her eyes on the path outside, said, "It's just that . . . The other day I was thinking about you, and your father, and the inn, and—" She was interrupted by the jangle of the bell signaling the front entry.

"Excuse me, Claire." Bethany set the paddle down. "Allow me to go and see who that is."

The insistent jangling competed with Claire's next words. "But, Bethany, we *really* must talk first."

Bethany slipped her apron over her head, hung it on an S-hook next to the kitchen entry, and smiled at Claire from the doorway. "And we will, I promise, as soon as I check the door.

It may be guests needing to register, and I'd like to intercept them before Aunt Amelia does. I'll be right—"

Bethany almost collided with Grace, who raced around the corner to enter the kitchen. "Miss Bethany, there's a gentleman in the green parlor to see you."

"Thank you, Grace." Bethany swirled around the young girl and down the hall.

"No! Wait!" Claire protested, but Bethany had already disappeared around the corner, followed by Grace.

Malcolm Randall stood in the center of the front visitor's parlor, admiring the room. Freshly painted white wainscoting bordered the four mint-green walls.

Prints of exotic orchids beckoned to him, and he moved along each wall, his hands behind his back, admiring the watercolor paintings. There was a marked diversity from one plant to another, yet the illustrations appeared to be grouped somewhat logically, with a predominance of yellows and purples. Small canvases in one corner featured a grouping of waxy, yellow stacking flowers. He moved on to a pastel sketch, elaborately framed, of a garish orchid in shades of rose with maroon veins, sticking out its hairy tongue edged in white.

"Fascinating," he muttered. "I would swear it wears a facial expression."

"Epidendrum."

Malcolm turned to face the young woman in the doorway. "I beg your pardon?"

"That particular orchid is a member of the Epidendrums. And I agree with you about their personifications." She moved to tenderly touch a painting on the wall nearest the door. "I swear to you that this plant has the same drooping, curly ears as my favorite hound." Bethany found it easy to return the gentleman's easy smile. "But the Epidendrums are my favorites.

That picture to the right of yours," she pointed and he turned back to study it, "is in the same category as the purple. But look how it is shaped like a star. With reds and oranges, it reminds me of the sunsets right before a storm sweeps in to the coast."

He nodded. "Since we are being fanciful, look at this one." He retraced his steps to one of the yellow floral images. "I was instantly reminded of a monk in a cowl, with a tiny face peering out at me."

Bethany laughed. "Most perceptive. And I am happy we were able to entertain you while you waited. My name is Bethany Coulter. Welcome to Pelican Inn, sir. Won't you please have a seat, Mr. . . . ?"

"Randall. Malcolm Randall." He moved to a heavy settee with clawed feet, where he remained standing as Bethany crossed the room. "You have an obvious love of orchids, Miss Coulter."

"I seem to have inherited that from my father. This is part of his collection."

"Fascinating." He watched her slight limp, then directed his eyes back to the paintings.

Bethany moved to straighten one of the larger frames. "A friend of my father's was a gardener at Chelsea Physic Garden. One of their visitors was Mr. Linnaeus himself. Are you familiar with the famous gentleman from Sweden, the botanist?" She moved to one of the chairs facing Mr. Randall. "He—my father's friend, that is—was thrilled to have met the man, and later showed my father a monograph on orchids, entitled *Species Orchidum,* in which Mr. Linnaeus describes several species of orchids, whilst classifying within categories." Once seated, she waved her hand about the room, encompassing the many floral prints. "The rest is fate. With a sprinkle of obsession, my father's favorite spice." She smiled. "How may we help you today, Mr. Randall? Are you looking for a room?"

Mr. Randall took a seat and was about to state the purpose of his visit when he spied Claire at the doorway. "Ah, Miss Temple."

Bethany turned to look at Claire, eyebrows raised. "You know one another?"

Claire blushed, and she mumbled, "I did mention, Bethany, that we needed to talk?"

As Mr. Randall and Bethany both sat staring at her, Claire realized they were waiting for her to explain.

All right. She would. "Did you know, Bethany, that Mr. Randall has been on a grand tour?" she asked as she took the seat closest to Bethany's, also facing their visitor. Still they waited. "And that he is a chef?"

Mr. Randall sputtered. "Now, Miss Temple, I never—"

"And so," said Claire, interrupting his protest, "it is quite possible that I happened to mention something to Mr. Randall." She quelled under his icy gaze. "Rather, I am certain that I did mention to Mr. Randall that Pelican Inn might like to have a partner."

"Claire! But I never—" Bethany's eyes were round.

"And just think of it: two partners running the inn. Two investors," Claire said the last word slowly, waiting for Bethany to pick up the implication. "A chef—" As Randall opened his mouth, she amended, "A cook. A very *good* cook." She looked at him, daring him to contradict. "And an established inn with *generations* of experience. Imagine the possibilities!"

Surely they could see this bridge to the future, this rainbow that took each of them where they desired?

Until Mr. Randall asked, "And where is the owner of Pelican Inn?"

"What do you mean?" responded Bethany with steely eyes.

"I mean, who is the gentleman who owns the inn?"

Her brows dropped one notch lower. "And why do you assume it must be a gentleman who owns this inn?"

When he did not immediately respond, Claire realized he must have noted Bethany's peeved tone. *Not,* thought Claire, *that one need be at all perceptive to pick up on that.*

"My apologies, Mrs. Coulter." He stressed her title. "Of course, I should have realized that you and Mr. Coulter own this inn together."

"There is no Mr. Coulter," Bethany said with asperity. "Other than my father, of course. I myself am not married."

"You own this inn by yourself?" He sounded a wee bit incredulous.

Claire moaned inside. This potential partnership was not going as she had envisioned it. The imagined rainbow bridge turned brittle, broke in half, and colorful shards tinkled to the floor.

Bethany's eyelids narrowed. "My father and I run this inn together. Is that so hard to believe, Mr. Randall?"

"Again, my apologies." Malcolm Randall had apologized, but with a shake of his head and a clench of his teeth as he smiled. "When I came here to visit, I was under the impression that the owner—that is, your father—" Quickly he amended, "Or rather, that *you* and your father . . ." He sighed, moved his gaze to Claire, and then back to Bethany. "I was told you might be interested in a business proposition." He stood and gave a slight bow. "I was mistaken. Thank you and good day."

"Wait." Bethany was still seated. Her eyes were closed. When she opened them, Mr. Randall was still standing, watching her. "Please. I am being so rude. And I know it. Won't you please sit, Mr. Randall, and have a cup of tea with us?"

When he hesitated, Bethany glanced at Grace, who nodded and swiftly left the room to fetch the tea service. Claire could imagine Bethany's notion that if tea were on its way, this might help the gentleman make up his mind to linger.

Bethany smiled charmingly, beseeched him gracefully. "Please."

The smile was what made the decision for him, Claire was certain, as Malcolm Randall retook his seat.

Chapter Fifteen

They'd agreed to meet at the gamekeeper's cottage.

Claire sat on the wooden bench, watching a rabbit lope unevenly along the perimeter of the lawn, always within a nervous skitter to the underbrush. Its coat was white with a single line of color along the spine, but its face, as it sniffed the air in her direction, showed nose and eyes circled by matching puddles of cinnamon.

There was something about rabbits that triggered memories from childhood. She pictured her mother placing small infant bunnies on her lap, as she sat with her pudgy legs outstretched on the grass. She could recall the feel of their downy fur. She had to smile, as she had even stronger memories of bubbly rabbit stews. Thankfully, it wasn't until she was much older that she made the connection.

She could smell the stew cooking on the oven, even now. She knew her mother would make a strong-smelling bundle of herbs and set it afloat on the liquid. Claire recognized the smells of bay leaves and garden thyme but didn't know what else went into the thin bouquet. And it was tied; she saw her mother's long fingers binding the pungent stalks together. But she couldn't picture whether it was bound with . . . string? . . . or narrow leaves of some kind.

She knew that turnips always boiled in the pot with the rabbit. And there would be exactly one onion, peeled and studded with small irregular nail-like cloves. Finally, when the delicious smells could be borne no longer, the mix was removed from the heat and piled into a pastry shell. She could salivate now, remembering the blending of hot crusty smells with the rabbit filling. *Odd,* she mused, *how smells can envelop and lock in the strongest memories of our past, just like the sealing of a circle of pastry crust.* She wished the memories of her mother's face could be locked in as securely.

"Claire?"

She jumped at the voice near her elbow. "Good morning, Alice. You startled me."

"Why is that?"

"Because I was daydreaming."

Alice reached out tentative fingers and touched Claire's cheek. "You were crying. I thought your voice sounded like tears." She drew her hand back.

Claire laughed. "You are so perceptive. You're an amazing young lady. But I am fine now, and I am determined that you and I shall be successful this morning."

"I hope so." Alice sounded skeptical.

"Where shall we start?"

"Claire?" Alice hadn't answered her question, even though Claire had risen and was ready to proceed. "What happens if we do find it? If we find Zillah's other clue?"

"I don't know. It depends on what it says." She noticed Alice looked a little sad now. "It won't bring her back, you know. But the memories are still here with you." She touched two fingers to Alice's heart. "And they won't disappear." She waited until Alice nodded, then said, "And that's *if* we find it. So. Where shall we start?"

"I remember that day, hearing the waves and the seagulls." Alice tilted her head slightly, listening. "Like now."

The dirt path they were on was smooth, easy to walk, despite its slight slope. A bank of earth rose knee-high on one side of the trail, and sparse golden-yellow broom bushes were scattered along the other.

"Have you taken this trail often? Were you already familiar with it?"

"No. There are so many paths leading into the woods behind the gamekeeper's cottage, I don't normally walk in that forest. It's too dark. I prefer the sunlight."

"Was it difficult locating this same trail, then?"

"Miss Bethany was familiar with it. She said this was the only path she knew of that was bordered by a rock wall. Somewhere up ahead. And that's where we have to search."

"Ah." Claire wondered if this same path led to the home where Roman and Vitus lived. She was sure Roman had pointed toward these very woods, that first day they'd met.

Alice swept the level trail with her cane. "I remember the path was mostly dirt, with a few small scattered rocks . . . like this." Sheepishly, she added, "I suppose most of the paths are. But you'll have to tell me when you see the split tree."

"Split?" Claire looked around at the trees she could spy from the trail. "Do you know what kind of tree we are looking for?"

"I don't. But Zillah had me touch it, where the trunk went two ways. I remember that. It was as if two branches were arguing, and they both wanted to be the main trunk of the tree."

The analogy made Claire smile. "Sometimes, when lightning strikes a tree, the trunk is charred and stunted, and side branches take over its job of reaching for the sky, similar to church spires. When you touched the tree, do you recall whether it had needles or leaves?"

"No. I only remember touching the bark. Where the split was."

"I don't see any forked trees here, but the trail curves ahead, so let's go farther."

As Claire led the way, she could hear the far-off gulls and a whisper of waves crashing upon the sea cliff. They were not too far from the manor.

The trail wound slightly away from the sea and deeper into the forest. There were several breaks in the yellow broom, and one of the clearings exposed the remains of a single tree, its decaying trunk clefted cleanly.

"It's over there!" She turned to Alice and reached out. "Here, take my hand. We'll see if that's the same tree."

Alice put her hand in Claire's and they moved forward along the path. When they came to the stump, Claire said, "It's not so large in diameter, but feel the fork in the trunk. Here." She guided Alice's hand to the tree.

"This could be it," said Alice. She sounded unsure. "But there has to be a rock wall nearby."

"There is!" Claire stood still, waiting for Alice's next instruction. "The wall is a boundary wall of round stones, piled on one another. Is that what you recall?"

"If I touch the stones, I think I'll remember how high the wall was." Alice moved forward slowly, swinging her stick toward the side of the path.

Claire noted Alice gravitated toward the left side of the path, which was indeed the side with the retaining rock wall, the side toward the sea.

Alice bumped her stick up against the piled rocks, moved the cane's tip up and over the bumpy surface until it reached empty air at the top of the wall, and nodded with satisfaction. "Now we have to count." She moved left, until there was a gap where the wall began. "I have to count up. To five."

Claire watched as Alice spread her small hands and moved them up five rocks, each rock easily a hand's span.

"Five rocks, or five hand spans?" asked Claire.

"Rocks," she answered, her hand on the fifth rock, almost to the top row. "Now, I'm going to count rocks going to the right." As Alice began tracing her hands over the horizontal stones, she said, "They're not level rows, but at least we can get as close as we can to the right place."

Claire watched while Alice moved to the right, counting aloud. "One, two, three, four, five, six, seven, eight." She stopped and held her hand firmly on the chosen stone, saying, "It should be near this one. Very close to this one."

"Let me mark it." Claire took a berry from a nearby bush, and smeared it into a thick paste across the rock's rough surface, avoiding Alice's fingers where they remained frozen. "All right, you may remove your hand now."

Alice stepped back. "It should be stuck into a crevice, around the edge of that rock."

Claire leaned close to the wall, peering. "There aren't many cracks between these rocks."

"Maybe I was not on the exact rock? Maybe you could look at the closest surrounding rocks." Alice stood by helplessly.

Claire moved to neighboring stones on either side, including those above and below. She studied the wall slowly and carefully. "I don't see it yet."

"Maybe I could help, too." Alice moved to the start of the wall and recounted the stones aloud. As she moved toward Claire, she spread her hands on each stone, running her fingers around each rounded edge.

They continued working the wall together for another minute. Claire was focusing on an area of stones to the right, when Alice screamed, a piercing screech.

Claire straightened abruptly. "What is it?"

"Something on my arm!" Alice was shaking her arm, waving it up and down.

"Let me see!" Claire swiped at a small spider, knocking it off Alice's arm. "It was just a small spider." But she noticed Alice still shivered. "Did it bite you?"

"No, but I *hate* spiders." Alice rubbed her arm, still looking upset. "I don't like them. I don't like their webs, either. Sometimes, when I come to sit at the fountain at the manor, I walk through them on the path. I don't think they are full webs, but little lines of web. Like maybe the spiders were fishing during the night."

Claire touched Alice's shoulder gently. "It's gone. And I understand how you feel about spiders. Why don't you let me look for the note, for both of us? I don't mind at all."

"All right." Alice sounded reluctant, but Claire knew there was relief mixed in as well.

Claire continued silently, unwilling to give up. Based on Alice's directions, it was certain they were in the right area.

"Have you seen anything yet, Claire?"

"No. Not yet. Let me look a bit longer."

Claire realized, after another minute of searching, that she was not going to find anything. She'd been over every rock surface at least thrice. Stepping back, she said, "Maybe the wind blew it away. Or a forest creature dislodged it." She looked at nearby bushes, surveyed the path ahead. "I'm looking in the bushes, in case it blew there," she announced, striding along the other side of the path to peek between branches and the brambly shrub hugging the end of the wall. Finally, she straightened. Turning to Alice, she said, "I don't think it's here."

"That was what Miss Bethany said when we tried to find it together." Alice's small shoulders slumped.

"I'm sorry. I know you said you and Miss Bethany had already combed this area without success. I suppose I just was hoping . . ." She didn't complete her thought.

"Me, too," said Alice.

They stood together another minute, neither suggesting they leave, as if willing the rocks to divulge their secret, to release the note trapped within.

"Shall we return now? I'll walk with you back to Pelican Inn, if you like."

Alice nodded, still facing the wall she could not see. Turning to Claire, she said, "Thank you. For trying."

Claire was aware that Alice had recently lost her only memento from Zillah, and now had no hopes of finding the other. She put her arm around Alice's shoulder and gave a small hug.

Upon reaching the warm kitchen, Alice directly left to go upstairs with Grace, who offered to read a story to her, and Claire remained with Bethany. As soon as she judged the two girls to be out of earshot, Claire asked her friend, "Do you remember the first note that Alice had? From Zillah?"

Bethany leaned against the counter, her arms folded across her chest. "You mean the *only* note? I know Alice says there was a second note, but no one has been able to find it."

Claire chose not to mention that she and Alice had been searching for the second note this past hour. "Yes, that note. It's sad, but Alice no longer has it. I wanted to tell you about it, as it was the oddest thing. Vitus burned it."

Bethany's eyebrows shot up, and Claire continued. "Yes, he burned it. After he'd taken it from Alice, and it upset her, since it was the only personal item she had left of Zillah's."

"She should not have still had the note. I assumed she'd destroyed it months ago. At least, that was my advice to her. Perhaps I hadn't stated it as an order, but regardless, I understand now why she didn't. I'd never thought about it that way. Goodness, what a pitiful keepsake! But—Vitus burned it? Why? When?"

Claire listened to the sympathetic reply with relief; Bethany did not sound to be the least miffed by Alice's retaining the note. The risk of disclosing Alice's transgression, without the young girl's leave, had weighed upon Claire's mind the entire distance to the inn.

"The gardener was burning his rakings in a bonfire. Alice showed the note to me, and Vitus came upon us and recognized it. Then, a little later, when Roman arrived to join us, Vitus grabbed it from me and, without Roman knowing what it was, Vitus threw it into the flames. He claimed afterward, in private, that he did it for Alice's own safety, and that the note should no longer be kept around."

Bethany shrugged. "Well, that I agree with. This speculation about Zillah must end."

Claire rushed on, hoping Bethany did not notice her slight blush. *Yes, definitely best not to mention this afternoon's search.* Yet Claire had to know one thing more before she dropped the subject. "Did you know what that first note said?"

Bethany shook her head. "No. I mean, I saw it, of course. But the jumbled letters on it meant nothing to me."

"Vitus knew what it meant." At Bethany's sharp glance, she continued. "He recognized the words as German, or at least a parody of the few words he recalled from his youth. His grandmother was German. He said it gave directions: right, and right, then second left."

Bethany shook her head again. "I still don't understand. And why—"

"Do I remind you of Zillah?"

"No, not at all. Why do you ask?"

Claire grinned at the silly diversion. "It's nothing, just something Vitus said. He said I should leave this mystery alone, but that I most likely would not, because I was like her. Like Zillah, that is." She was stirring her tea and did not notice Bethany's dark look. "And he made sure I should memorize the words on the paper. Well, not the words, but their meaning. He said that it might have helped save Zillah's life, and it may be important to remember. It was almost as if he expected me to follow in Zillah's footsteps."

Claire glanced up and stilled at Bethany's expression. "What is it?"

"Oh, Claire. I'm hesitant to discuss something with you."

Claire smiled because Bethany looked so serious. "Don't be silly. Of course you should discuss whatever you desire."

"It's about Vitus." Bethany uncrossed her arms and reached for the stack of linen napkins close at hand, smoothing them and aligning the edges. When Claire didn't respond, she continued. "I know you are old enough to know your own mind. However, I'm worried that he is not someone you should want to be spending time with."

"I do not spend any more time with him than with Roman. And only when they stroll to my uncle's for a visit. By the fountain," she added lamely. "Truly, I hardly ever see him. Either of them." She felt a bit defensive, but blushed again, because lately she *did* enjoy his company, despite his not being as talkative as his brother.

There was something comforting about Vitus's calmness. He was not classically handsome like his brother, but Claire found his dark looks growing more appealing. His wry observations and intelligent conversation were honest and interesting to her, unlike Roman's trifling flattery and bothersome mood swings.

Bethany interrupted her thoughts. "Alice mentions that he visits both of you quite often in the garden, at least it seems so whenever she is there."

"But not by himself. He is always in Roman's shadow. And besides, even Alice says she trusts Vitus, that he is kind to her."

Her friend pressed her lips together. "Then I shall speak to her."

"Bethany, on what do you found this, your negative impression of the man?"

"There are numerous things I have heard, here and there. And Roman says . . ."

Claire waited. Bethany frowned, evidently trying to recall the exact words. Finally, Claire pressed. "What does he say?"

"Nothing explicit. He always stops himself. Well, he would, wouldn't he? I mean, considering Vitus is his brother, I can tell he's careful never to say too much. However, the fact that he hints, and that I can see he hesitates, gives me concern."

"Concern about what?" Claire resisted the impulse to pull the stack of napkins away from Bethany's reach. The folded edges were as perfectly aligned as they could ever be.

"Mainly about Zillah. What if . . ." Bethany looked up, finally ignoring the linens, and dropped her voice to a whisper. "What if Zillah's death was not an accident?"

Claire rubbed a hand down her arm to warm the chill of goose flesh.

"I was under the impression that Vitus and Zillah were close friends."

"I thought so, too." Once again, Bethany leaned back against the counter, refolded her arms across her chest. "At least, I used to think so."

"Then what exactly does Roman say—or not say?"

"Roman did let slip that he saw Vitus and Zillah together the afternoon of her death. And Roman also admits the two had a disagreement on that day. A heated discussion." Her stare held Claire's eyes. "Actually, he called it a *violent* disagreement."

"Do you know what they argued about?"

She sighed loudly. "I wish I knew. And if he knows, he has chosen not to say."

"Was it only Roman's word on this?" Claire thought about Roman's enmity toward his brother, his fribbling conversation. "Sometimes, I'm not sure Roman is entirely truthful."

"Coincidentally, Alice had also mentioned the same thing to

me, about an argument she overheard that day."

This came as a shock. "Did you say anything at the inquest, about this violent quarrel?"

"No. Roman had not confided to me prior to the inquest. I only knew at the time what Alice told me she overheard. I wondered what to do. Repeat thirdhand gossip from a blind child? They would discount it, would doubt whether she could be sure of whose voices she had eavesdropped upon."

"But Alice has shown that she can easily distinguish voices."

"And you and I both know that. I've witnessed it myself. And we both know she's truthful. She's an amazing little girl. But . . ."

Claire saw the small girl through the eyes of cynical adults. "Ah. Yes, I can see they might doubt testimony from a young blind girl. Then what of Roman? Was that all he said, that he saw them together that day, and that they argued? Though that does seem significant. Did he openly come forward with this information, other than for your ears?"

"No. He did not. Not to my knowledge. And it was only recently that he has mentioned it to me. As I've said, it seemed an accidental slip on his part. I had the feeling he wished he had not said anything at all. I've wondered . . ."

"Yes?"

"They are family. Brothers." Bethany looked at the floor, as if debating with herself. "Would a man incriminate his own brother at a hearing?" Bethany shook her head. "I doubt he would. Families take care of their own." Her arms unfolded, she nervously massaged her hands. "I should have said something to you sooner. Once I realized how much time you were spending in the company of the brothers. I should hate it if . . ." She raised a haunted look to Claire.

"Surely you cannot imagine I am in any danger!"

"Roman must know you've been curious about Zillah. And

what if he's mentioned it to his brother? Or, perhaps Vitus has also become aware of it. He may be taciturn, but I believe there's a very keen intelligence within those observant eyes."

"Are you afraid of Vitus?"

Bethany hesitated. "No. At least, I wasn't in the past. But I now suspect there is more to Vitus's involvement than Roman is willing to reveal. And I believe my instincts, that it may be unwise for you or Alice to be poking about in the cold ashes."

Aunt Amelia entered the kitchen, and they slipped into other topics, normal topics. By the time Claire departed, she had almost forgotten Bethany's warning. Until she took her leave, and Bethany hugged her and said in her ear, "Be careful, Claire. Please keep in mind what we talked about."

Chapter Sixteen

This parlor is quite pleasant, Malcolm Randall reflected. Upon his first visit to Pelican Inn, he remembered thinking the inn was a bit too feminine for his tastes. However, on subsequent tours given him by Miss Bethany Coulter, he'd seen the impressively masculine library and billiards rooms. And his most recent business meeting with the owner's daughter had taken place in the no-nonsense office, he recalled, where they'd perused the inn's books and receipts. The heavy walnut furnishings were dominated by a massive secretary desk and ornately carved bookcases.

This time, he had been escorted to one of the many upstairs parlors where guests could feel at home, settled with a pot of hot tea at hand. Rather than a single grand tour of the inn, he realized he was being given glimpses of each floor. Most likely depending upon which rooms were vacant on which days of his visits.

He'd yet to spy Mr. Calden Coulter; odd that the other partner of the inn was never available for introductions. Malcolm speculated on different scenarios. Perhaps her father was infirm and bedridden. Or perhaps he preferred a residence in London. Curious that would be, to leave his daughter with the huge responsibility of running an inn with this many rooms.

Waiting for Miss Bethany Coulter, he sipped the hot tea and took a moment to study his surroundings. This room was both tastefully and thoughtfully decorated, as every other room had been. And yet unique. He enjoyed the diverse themes of the various rooms; no repetition of identical furnishings and wallpapers from room to room.

While there were several paintings on the walls of this parlor, none dominated, yet each contributed a soothing seaside scene. Most included pelicans—ah!—for the eponymous Pelican Inn. The room smelled of fresh lemon wax. And there was no sense of clutter.

Of course, he thought with a smile. The overly meticulous Miss Bethany Coulter would not allow any disarray into her life. He had to admit that visiting with her was one of the highlights of each of his days in his aunt's village. He wished he'd made her acquaintance sooner. No matter; if he indeed became a partner with her father, he could enjoy many such visits. *Was this a determining factor in his decision?* he wondered.

He could at least admit that it was the reason he had been coming here for several days in a row with additional questions about the inn. Today he would let Miss Coulter know he was ready to sign an agreement with her father. He could delay no longer, particularly because he could think of no more questions. He'd already asked the obvious: how long had the inn been established, how many guests could it accommodate, what was the average occupancy, what types of meals were currently provided, who were the local suppliers, what were the profit margins, and so on.

He had already discussed the business opportunity with Aunt Eudora on the first day he'd visited the inn. And he had already known, before his aunt gave her opinion, that she would support him in his decision. Especially since she knew her stuffy brother would be adamantly against his son going into trade. While Father was stodgily conservative, Aunt Eudora was a modern thinker. Malcolm missed his uncle—her husband—who had been as delightfully open-minded as his wife. They had contributed to Malcolm's views growing up. In fact, as most of Malcolm's friends left to explore the Continent, his own father had resisted, even though they were wealthier than most. It was his aunt who had argued and cajoled. His father might have remained adamant, except that Aunt Eudora insisted if her brother could not afford to send his son on a grand tour, she herself would pay for the trip. This had offended his father, who was adequately wealthy, and he made it immediately clear that *he* would be paying for his son's travels, thank you. Aunt Eudora only murmured that it was about time.

Malcolm was staring, reminiscing, and returned his thoughts and gaze to the parlor. This brought into his line of sight two doilies in the room, each on its own end table flanking the sofa that reclined below the mullioned window. Each was perfectly balanced, equidistant from the table edges. He found a particular delight in watching Miss Coulter, whenever faced with an awkward moment of conversation, spend a half minute fidgeting with each, sliding each circle to a new point of precision, which was invariably exactly where it had already sat, perfectly. He found this nervous habit of hers exceedingly charming.

Malcolm sat forward; he listened for steps in the hall. Not hearing any, he delicately set down his teacup without even a clink, rose and walked to the door, peering around its edge. No one was in sight in the hallway. He moved quickly, softly, to the closest table and moved the doily slightly off-center. Pausing to listen, he tiptoed to the other table and moved its doily decidedly to one end of the table.

He had barely returned to his seat and eased himself quietly onto the cushion before Bethany came through the door with a tray of iced biscuits.

Malcolm jumped up. "Allow me to help you."

His reward was her welcoming smile. She might also have

said, "Thank you." He really didn't notice.

Once she'd poured herself a half cup of tea and handed a small plate of biscuits to her guest, Miss Coulter sat down on the sofa facing his chair. "I am pleased to see you again, Mr. Randall." With an impish grin, she said, "Though I cannot imagine that there is any single question remaining that has not been asked with the one hundred others."

At his look of surprise, she blushed. "Forgive me. That was not a very business-like thing to say. It's just that I feel I can tease you, because you are so easy to talk with. But I know I should not tease you, since you are exploring a serious decision, and . . . and I am rambling." She closed her lips around a rueful grin and picked up her tea.

Glancing sideways, to look anywhere in the room other than at him, Miss Coulter gazed straight at the offending doilies. Malcolm was delighted when she immediately leaned over, balancing her cup in hand, to the closest end table. She shifted the starched crocheted circle to the exact center of the circular surface.

"I do not mind at all, Miss Coulter. I feel the same, that it is enjoyable to converse with you. And, should we and your father complete this arrangement—" He stopped at the look on her face. "What is it?"

"No, it's nothing, I assure you." She had been midway to setting the second doily in its place and had almost spilled her tea. Hastily, she resumed her seat and added, "You were saying? You are interested in concluding our business deal?"

"With you and with your father, yes. I have finished my deliberations, and my studies—of my one hundred questions." His lips quirked. "And I am still quite interested in becoming a partner of this establishment, and in beginning my career as a chef. I am ready to arrange a signing with Mr. Calden Coulter and yourself." He hazarded a guess that her father had been absent these last couple of weeks. "When do you anticipate his return?"

Miss Coulter appeared visibly deflated, Malcolm noticed, though he had not seen the sofa cushions sag any lower. He had anticipated her pleasure at the delivery of his decision. Regardless, she seemed smaller as she took a swallow of tea, more vulnerable of a sudden. It made him want to put an arm around her for support. "Are you feeling faint, Miss Coulter?"

Taking a long moment to contemplate her tea before another sip, it was as if she recovered instantly. "I am feeling fine, Mr. Randall. Just a bit . . . Perhaps I will have a little more tea. May I refresh yours?"

He nodded and Bethany retrieved his cup, refilled it, and returned it to him. He thought she looked agitated, contemplative as she returned to top off her own cup, and he chose not to say anything more until she was seated and ready to talk.

When she did speak, she sat up straight and was professionally brisk. "We may have a slight problem, but I am sure it is nothing of any great consequence. A somewhat trivial point, as you shall see." She cleared her throat. "My father, you see, may still be unavailable for some time." Raising her chin and looking directly into his eyes, she said, as if rehearsing a memorized line, "But he has given me his full authority to sign any and all papers in his absence."

"This is most . . . surprising." *But that explained why Malcolm had never met him.*

Her shoulders stiffened, she sat straighter, if that was possible. "Mr. Randall, I own this inn with my father. Am I to understand you do not trust my signature on the documents?"

"I hadn't given it thought." Doing so now, he said, "I do believe you when you say that you are also an owner. And certainly I would trust your signature. This is not what concerns me. It's that you two are co-owners, so I would also need any papers to be signed by your father, not only by you." Once again he repeated, "When do you anticipate his return?"

"Any day now. Soon." When he said nothing in reply, she added, "Actually, it may be hard to pinpoint. He is on yet another plant expedition, you see. My father collects rare plants, as I'm sure you will recall the orchids you noted in the other room. It is his passion."

"And he leaves the inn to your care on a regular basis?" He had not intended for that one judgmental eyebrow to rise ever so slightly.

"He does." Her eyes were steely. "Because he trusts me, and as his daughter . . . as co-owner . . . I am familiar with all of its operations, accounts, and—"

"Please, I was not chastising the man, I was simply curious." He hoped she did not notice a faint blush accompanying the prevarication. He looked askance, not meeting her eyes.

"My apologies." Nor did her eyes meet his.

After an awkward silence, Malcolm rose. "I hope you will understand, Miss Coulter, but I will need to think about this. Perhaps to contact my solicitor in London, to determine whether one signature will suffice. I am sure we can come to a satisfying conclusion, but we must proceed cautiously."

Miss Coulter rose as well and nodded. "Of course. I understand." But her voice was sad.

"Perhaps—"

"Yes?"

He hated to extinguish the hope in her eyes. "Is it possible— Has your father, by chance, left a letter of empowerment with you? A legal document, recording his share of authority to be vested in you?" He knew by her expression there was no such document.

Unnecessarily, she shook her head.

"Well, as I said, I shall pursue the matter, however I am able."

He put on his hat and moved toward the doorway. He turned as she joined him there. He could not bear to see her so downcast. "Let us shake hands on the successful outcome to our business transaction."

Bethany placed her smaller hand in his. Rather than a businesslike shake, she placed her other hand atop his. Knowing it was too intimate a gesture, she could not help herself. "Thank you. That is all that I can ask. Unless my father should return."

He held her hand in return, a moment longer than proper. "Good day, Miss Coulter."

Chapter Seventeen

Claire never tired of the view from her room. Upon waking, it was a treat to stand at the tall windows, to capture a new memory of Raven Heights to tuck away for the future. A myriad of memories, for each morning was painted by a different artist: the color of the sky, the shape and tints of the clouds, and the various birds that swooped across the canvas. Even the river of flowers in the beds below could change at the whim of the gardeners.

If the day came when she must leave the manor, she would sit and close her eyes and savor these memories that no one could take from her, whether she was in an orphanage, or placed in service, or in a workhouse. She would pull each memory from her imaginary tea canister. It was made of highly polished wood; she hadn't decided what kind of wood. She'd seen one in the window of a fine shop. Her own tea canister was hinged in a similar fashion, complete with brass lock and skeleton key.

As she opened the shutters and spread them wide, she could also add sounds to her memory canister. Bird duets, seagull cries, and distant waves crashing on those days when gusting winds carried sounds this far.

Today was quiet, however, with dark clouds dampening the expanse of sky. The wet grass below attested to last night's rain. Claire's eyes invariably sought out the forbidden path along the cliff. *It will be muddy this morning,* she thought, though she certainly could not be certain of that from here. She had yet to know the feel of the trail beneath her laced half boots, but her eyes walked it longingly each day, as they travelled it now. The few standing remnants of the ancient stone wall looked darker grey this morning, either because they reflected the darkening sky, or because they were still wet without morning sun to dry their—Claire stood rigid, her eyes on the path and the stones. There is more than one stone wall!

Could it be? What if Bethany and Alice had chosen the wrong pathway?

How could Claire have forgotten about this remnant of wall that outlined Uncle's property along the bluff? She'd traced its crumbling boundaries down into the woods below innumerable times from her bedroom balcony.

Alice had admitted she was not familiar with all of the crisscrossing trails in the forest. Was it possible that Zillah had led Alice through the woods and toward the cliff path instead? Her mind raced. Alice had remembered the sounds of the sea. They would be much stronger along the trail that edged the crags.

Was Zillah more familiar with those paths along the crest of the cliff? Claire never had learned exactly where Zillah's body had been discovered, though she often fancied the young woman would have strolled where Claire was forbidden to go, there, silhouetted in the twilight.

Claire recalled Mrs. Dawson had shuddered at the idea of a sightless child wandering too close to the cliffs when they'd first discussed Alice. Claire agreed; she doubted Alice would go too close to the property's edge on her own. That still left the possibility that Zillah had led Alice somewhere unfamiliar to the young girl. With its proximity to Raven Heights, it would not be an area easily known to Bethany, who had led Alice to a wall elsewhere.

When the brothers had explained a smuggler's night to her,

one of the pictures etched in her mind was of Zillah wandering at night along this very bluff . . . But she didn't know that for a fact; it was an image she'd quilted together on her own. Yet, the fact that Zillah was found broken at the foot of the cliff was proof that she'd walked the edge—at least once. Had she also walked it another time, with an unknowing blind child?

Claire dressed quickly and came down the stairs, careful not to trip in her rush. She knew today was Mrs. Dawson's day to shop in the village. Obviously, shopping was a task that could normally be assigned to one of the servants. However, everyone knew Mrs. Dawson chose to regularly make the trek herself, as there would be gossip to attend to and friends to chat with, in that order. A footman would gather packages at every stop, while Mrs. Dawson gathered newsy tidbits.

If Claire were lucky, she could explore the cliff trail and return before Mrs. Dawson should ask anyone of Claire's whereabouts. Not that Mrs. Dawson would necessarily ask, and not that one of the servants would even notice Claire's lone figure on the cliff, but best not to take any chances. In fact, Claire decided she would squander a few precious minutes on a more circuitous route to the trail, beginning at the gamekeeper's cottage, as a further precaution.

And that could well have been where Zillah's footsteps began.

After descending to the ground floor, Claire nonchalantly asked the first staff member she came upon whether Mrs. Dawson had already left for her weekly shopping in the village. The answer was affirmative. Claire knew approximately when Mrs. Dawson would normally be expected back, and she continued on through the manor and through an outside door of an unoccupied room.

Her heart drummed as she hastened, but not from exertion. *What am I doing, to risk all?* If discovered, she could lose the right to stay at her uncle's, the only thing precious to her besides distant memories of her parents. Of course, once her uncle returned to the manor, it was possible he would meet her and no longer desire that his niece reside at Raven Heights. But she would not think about that.

Travelling up the gully that separated the gamekeeper's residence from the upper cliff path, Claire chose her way carefully among the wet, slippery leaves. The trace of a trail—made by sure-footed deer—wound between bushes while angling upward toward the cliff, but she didn't believe she was too close to the edge yet. Still, she chose her steps carefully, shuddering at the idea of overstepping the overgrown crest and sliding down the far side and over the cliff's edge.

There was a vacuum of sound in this hollow. The occasional snap of a twig beneath her boot was as out of proportion as laughter in a graveyard. Twice, Claire looked back over her shoulder, sure she'd heard other footfalls besides her own.

Relief displaced fear as the trail opened up and joined the cliffside path. The sky was still dark, and the wind whipped her hair about her face. Licking dry lips picked up the crystallized tang of salty air. She heard the muted crashing of the grey sea far below. Claire appreciated the irony that finally walking along the forbidden path was not as pleasurable as she had imagined from the cozy safety of her room. The cold gusts billowed her skirts, and she had to continually smooth stinging hairs from her eyes.

She moved along the wide path in the same direction she and Alice had taken on the parallel path a few days ago. Now she began doubting her earlier logic. Wouldn't Alice have noticed the other path was narrower as she swept her cane? Its tip had surely bumped the banked dirt cut into one side; this trail lacked that low wall of packed earth and exposed roots. And she and Alice certainly hadn't struggled against the wind. Unfamiliar with a maritime climate, Claire wondered if the sea's winds were as variable as the changes in the cloudscapes she witnessed from her room.

And shouldn't she have seen a forked tree by now?

Apprehensively, Claire realized she'd taken a risk, and had nothing to show for it. She no longer cared whether she never walked along the silly path again, even should her uncle grant his permission to do so.

The next curve angled even closer to the cliff, possibly the stretch that came into view from her room. The breeze carried a faint smell of wood smoke. Scanning for a blue haze curling above the trees, she almost missed it: the tree with two distinct trunks. She examined it as she approached. It looked like a low branch had been bent or broken at one time, and had stubbornly refused to die. Instead, it usurped the role of the original trunk and reached straight up to the sky, growing and thickening.

Holding her breath, she turned her face, scanning the path ahead for remnants of a stone wall. She breathed gratefully when she saw the familiar pattern of stone stacked upon stone, its crumbling sections hidden under ivy that reached over the top and dragged mortar down with it.

She could hear Alice's voice, counting up five rocks. Hurrying to the start of the surviving wall, Claire's heart beat furiously as she put her hand upon the fifth rock up from the ground. Taking a deep breath, she moved to the right, counting to herself. When her fingers touched the eighth rock on that row, she could not have said whether she was shocked or not surprised at all, for a corner of yellowed paper was visible, packed between stones where time had broken down the ancient masonry filling.

Afraid of tearing the fragile note paper, Claire teased it out patiently, pinching and pulling reverently. Zillah must have stuffed it with a stick, she was sure, for it to be imbedded so well. Finally, it was free of its prison of rock. Claire foresaw herself opening it and it would be blank. Or any words would be gone, washed away by the many months of weather. She took another slow, deep breath.

As she unfolded the paper, she immediately did think it to be blank. Until she realized there were only two words, faintly scrawled, in tiny letters along the bottom edge.

She turned it over to ensure she'd not missed any handwriting on the reverse side. That side was decidedly empty of any markings, so she flipped the note over again, to the minimal scrawling on the front side. She held the paper close, necessitated by the crimped writing style and the overcast light.

Only two words were scratched in ink upon the lowest edge.

Who, she wondered, *is Benjamin Whittaker?*

Chapter Eighteen

"I'd value your opinion."

"Yes?" Aunt Amelia turned, her attention full upon her grand-niece.

Bethany looked down at the table linens she was folding. "What if . . . it's getting harder, you know, to pretend that father is . . . accessible. Mr. Randall is always asking the most probing questions. And the man is uncannily perceptive. Or, at least, he appears to be. His eyes sharpen whenever—"

"Sharpen?"

"Well, he does this pinpoint thing with his pupils, or maybe it's his eyelids narrowing. I feel I'm being pierced, my words measured for truth, at the very slightest exaggeration. It's most unsettling." Bethany debated discussing her dilemma with Aunt Amelia. One never knew whether the woman would be in a lucid period.

"If he unsettles you, dear, then I would have to ask the question: Is this business decision wise? The man may grow worse upon your nerves with time," said the woman, thus settling the question of lucidity, at least for this afternoon. "I find that people put their best foot forward when newly introduced. Thus, if he is already showing traits . . ."

"No, I think were I to be candidly honest, the fault is mine." Bethany sighed. "He is intelligent and agreeably easygoing. I believe he will be an astute partner and an asset to the inn. In truth, I'm not quite sure why he occasionally annoys me."

"Are you attracted to him?"

"Aunt Amelia!" Bethany blushed and stopped folding the napkin in her hand.

Her aunt chuckled. "There is some truth to the adage that we care about the approval of those we care about. And it is my opinion that you make a delightfully handsome couple." She raised her eyebrows at her niece. "Well? You did ask me for my opinion," she added with the tiniest hint of chastisement.

"Actually, that was not the subject I had in mind when I asked for your opinion."

Both women laughed.

"Well! What was it then, that you wished an opinion of?"

Bethany's brow wrinkled. "What would you think . . . if we were to show Mr. Randall a letter from Father?"

Aunt Amelia's eyes lit. "Your father? He's sent a letter, then? Heavens, child, why hadn't you—"

"No! He hasn't. At least, not yet. But suppose he did?"

"Then how would we—where would it—"

"I meant, suppose I were to show Mr. Randall a letter. A letter *I* wrote, that I'll claim was written by Father. And, suppose we were to suggest we had just received it?"

Aunt Amelia frowned. Either she disagreed or the idea confused her. A half minute later, she asked, "Wouldn't that jeopardize an otherwise honest business relationship?"

Bethany considered. "Yes, I suppose that might be possible." Her great-aunt fixed her eyes searchingly on her, and Bethany added, "Yes. You are exactly right, of course it would be patently underhanded on my part. On the other hand, I fear if I *cannot* come up with documentation showing Father's authorization of any financial transactions I may deem to initiate, there may no longer be a business relationship at all. We stand to lose this inn."

"True." Aunt Amelia's tone was serious as she returned Bethany's stare.

Bethany stood outside the breakfast room and took a calming breath. This was an important morning. Malcolm Randall had offered to arrive early, as he wished to demonstrate his culinary skills by planning, cooking, and serving breakfast.

Bethany was embarrassed she hadn't suggested this sooner. The fact that she was more interested in his investment dollars as a co-owner than in his epicurean ability and aspiration caused a slight guilt on her part. Cooking was the man's passion, after all, and he would be responsible for dining room decisions once they merged interests.

Mr. Randall had been in the kitchen since before dawn, baking and preparing. She had to admit that the aromas filling the inn were divine. She looked forward to a gourmet breakfast. And to his company, she added as a second admission that came as a surprise to herself.

The breakfast chimes had rung at precisely the time he had predicted breakfast should be ready. That was already a good sign; that and the smells wafting through the door.

She straightened her shoulders and smoothed her apron, patting the single wide pocket that spanned the apron from left to right. Briskly she entered the room and looked around. Aunt Amelia had not come downstairs yet. Mr. Randall stood close to the table, teapot in hand, a linen towel wrapped around its pearwood handle. Alice and Grace sat on the opposite side of the table from Aunt Amelia's chair. Bethany took a seat at one end of the table, and accepted the tea placed before her. She couldn't help observing Mr. Randall's large hands and clean fingernails as he smoothly set the cup and saucer down and poured the aromatic tea.

She had decided that two minutes of idle conversation prior

to her announcement should be adequate, so she slowly stirred a single lump of sugar into her tea and waited as conversation idled. She preferred to wait for Aunt Amelia's presence and support, but knew the longer she waited, she might lose her resolution.

"Oh, that reminds me." Here she reached into the pocket of her apron. "I received a letter from Father," she said while looking down. "It's here somewhere," she muttered, as if the wide pocket could possibly hold a voluminous array of tools and knickknacks.

Silence. Bethany lifted the folded missive and surveyed the quiet crowd with eyebrows raised. The others sat stunned. Except Mr. Randall, who'd been standing, but now quietly pulled out a chair and sat, mirroring the stunned stare of the others.

"From Father," she repeated, then took a deep breath as she unfolded it. "Shall I read it?"

Everyone nodded mutely.

"He says, 'Dear Ones.' " She looked up at her attentive audience and licked her lips.

"Dear Ones—first, let me assure you I am well and safe."

Bethany choked momentarily. She hadn't meant to become emotional; it was a pretend letter, after all. But the thought of Father sending such a note, the futile hope that he could possibly be somewhere safe, that he could be well . . .

"Would you like to have someone else read it?" Mr. Randall said it very gently, reaching a hand out tentatively. Though whether his hand reached toward her in sympathy, or to retrieve the letter, she wasn't quite sure. She shook her head and continued.

"I realize I have been out of touch, and I regret any worry I may have caused you. Please believe me that unusual circumstances beyond my control have prevented my writing earlier."

Bethany pictured her father writing these words—to her—and the words became so real that she had to swallow, else she would cry.

"I am writing to tell you that all is going well and per plan. Also, Bethany, you will recall that you and I had discussed the possibility of any necessary financial or legal decisions in the event of my being detained longer than originally anticipated. Should you deem it prudent to follow this course, do know that I hereby authorize you to sign any agreements in my absence.

Yr. Loving Father, &c.

Calden Coulter"

Saying his name aloud saddened her, but she could not say why. Bethany realized that Mr. Randall was addressing her. "I beg your pardon?"

"I said," Mr. Randall was frowning, "This letter is indeed from your father?"

"Of course." Her frown matched his, and she tried to duplicate that eye-sharpening thing he did. Distractedly, she wished Aunt Amelia had been in the room to witness. "Else why would he have signed it Calden Coulter?"

"It's amazing, is all. Is there a direction included?"

"Why, that's a good question. Let me look . . ." Bethany turned the sheet over and studied its blank side. Nothing there, of course. Turning it again, she took a long moment to peruse the forged lines, which had been written and rewritten so many times. She picked up the envelope and scrutinized it carefully. "Hmmm . . . no, it does not appear to have included a location." Her eyes challenged his. "Why do you ask?"

"Let us consider." He looked up at the highest shelf of decorative ceramic bowls, but he might as well have been raising his eyes heavenward. "Your father is somewhere on the vast continent of Africa. He manages 'against unusual circumstances' to send a letter, but neglects to tell you where he is."

"And your point? Isn't it enough to know that he is safe, Mr. Randall?" *Drat, why hadn't she made up a location in the header?* Any location. Though all she could come up with in her head was "the equator," or "the desert," et cetera. Still, even to have said, "From the Heart of the Congo." That would have had a nice ring to it.

"Miss Coulter, I don't mean to criticize your father. Even though one *would* expect that his whereabouts might have been a sensible piece of information to insert into a letter . . . Along with a date, of course." He rested his elbows on either side of his empty plate and steepled his fingers. "I don't expect there is a date on the note, and you simply chose not to read it?"

Bethany picked up the letter again. She squinted her eyes and looked at each line, as if the date were hiding midsentence. She looked at Mr. Randall. The man's skeptical look set her teeth on edge. "No, I don't see a date. Isn't that odd," she said crisply. She turned the page over and carefully reviewed the blank back side again. "Hmmm . . . no, it does not appear to have a date, does it? Of course, there are those of us who are surprisingly pleased to have finally heard from my father, regardless of whether the letter contained the date it was written." She tapped the letter with a slender fingernail. "And would that have made it arrive sooner, I wonder?"

"Oh! I'm so glad to see everyone gathered here." Aunt Amelia shuffled into the dining room, her heels dragging and clicking across the wooden floor. A piece of parchment waved like a flag held high in her hand. "I have the most exciting news!"

Bethany spun around, her letter dangling limply from her

wrist. The others were staring at Aunt Amelia.

"I have received a letter in this morning's post. I swear I almost fainted when I read it. For it is from my nephew, Mr. Coulter!" Her announcement was greeted by open mouths, with no sound emitting. "Mr. Calden Coulter." Still no reply, though all heads swiveled as one to Bethany, and then back. Aunt Amelia looked pointedly at Mr. Randall and explained, "Miss Bethany's father."

The cat sneezed. And the clock ticked.

Aunt Amelia didn't appear to notice the silence. She put on her spectacles. "Would anyone like me to read it?" She didn't wait for an answer. " 'My dear Aunt Amelia—' " She peeked at the quiet group in the room over her spectacles. "I've always had a soft spot for my nephew Calden." She turned quickly to Bethany. "I do hope, my dear, that you are not upset that my dearest nephew chose to send this note to me. That is, instead of sending it to you. I'm sure that the next time he writes—"

"He did," she said in clipped tones.

"Yes, he has on past trips. But I'm sure the next time—"

"He did write this trip, Aunt Amelia." Bethany held up her own note. "Just today. I received mine as well."

"Oh," said Amelia, appearing mildly distraught. "Well, that makes sense, doesn't it? I mean, if dear Calden was finally able to send a note . . . it would make sense, wouldn't it?"

The cat sneezed again.

"Miss Bethany! Where are you?"

Everyone turned toward the door in time to see Grace race around the corner. She slid into the room and came to a stop. "I have a letter!"

Bethany laughed falsely, a little too loudly. "Oh, heavens! This is insane, isn't it?" She addressed herself to Mr. Randall's undecipherable countenance. "First he sends no letters. Then, the man can't seem to stop writing letters and notes."

Mr. Randall said nothing, but still he stared.

Bethany rambled. "Did I ever tell you about my father's cousin Lavinia? She became so addle-minded as she aged, poor dear. I would send her a gift for her birthday, and she would promptly send a thank you. Then, the next day, another note would arrive, with almost identical grateful wording. And another on the third day. Finally, the trickle stopped, a week would pass, and we'd receive a fourth acknowledgment. It was quite comical. Truly," she added upon noting his sober expression.

No one in the room laughed. Not even a small chuckle, until finally Aunt Amelia tittered nervously. "My, that is a funny story. And I now see the similarity between Lavinia and your father. Not surprising, is it, that he should shoot off three letters to us, as he and Lavinia are related."

"But they're not!" Grace exclaimed. "I thought you told me, Miss Bethany, that Lavinia was your favorite cousin on your mother's side. And that would mean she and your father are not related at all." She looked at Bethany for confirmation. "So it is simply what one would call a coincidence, and there is no family resemblance at all, is there?"

Bethany looked over at Mr. Randall. "I suppose there is not," she said with a false smile between gritted teeth.

Chapter Nineteen

Claire stood too close to the edge, the sea thundering far below.

She watched it hypnotically as it receded then rushed forth again, pounding against the cliff, covering the sharp rocks at its foot with boiling foam. She heard a roar of words echoed in the curve of a hollowed wave before it slapped the rocks: "Whittaker," the final syllable dragging out, then dissipating into foam. Whittaker. Claire touched her pocket, felt the thin folded layers of Zillah's note within.

Was this where Zillah had stood the last night of her life? Had she jumped, counting in her head, then pushing the tips of her toes away from the rocks that Claire could feel digging through the thin soles of her shoes? Or had she stepped calmly forward like one who walks in her sleep, allowing gravity to lull her? And how had she timed it? Claire wondered as she watched the pendulum of water. Had Zillah chosen to drop onto the rocks at the moment they were most exposed? That would be a quick end; one would never know the force of the next incoming wave throwing one's body against the hard cliff. Or perhaps Zillah timed her fall so that the boiling wave disguised the sharp objects, and mercifully pulled her out to sea.

She imagined Zillah standing next to her, indecisive, reaching her cold hand to take Claire's, willing herself to step off the edge at the determined timing. Or had Zillah been pushed to her young death?

Claire became oblivious of the bird calls in the thickets along the path. There was only the crash of each successive wave, and silence as the swelling sea sucked everything into its possession again, only to throw it at the cliff again and again.

Something intruded in the corner of her vision. She thought she spied a piece of bright cloth retreating with the pull of the sea. Or it might have been snagged on a tooth of rock, undulating beneath the surface at the whim of the tide. Claire leaned forward to better see what peeked through the foamy spray. She squinted against the weak sun; leaned forward the tiniest bit farther.

Claire screamed as a hand clamped round her upper arm. She pulled to the side instinctively, sending pebbles flying down into the waiting surf as her foot slid inches closer to the edge.

Vitus swore, tightening his grip, dragging her farther from the perilous edge.

"What are you doing?" he yelled. *"Are you mad?"* His angry words were whipped away by the wind, competing with the noise of the waves below.

Claire's breath caught in her throat as Vitus clenched her arm too tightly. She glanced nervously toward the cliff's edge. Had he seen whatever it was that the ocean had brought into view? Was it only a piece of seaweed? If he thought Claire had seen something, would he change his pulling grip and shove her instead? She was already unbalanced, and totally at the mercy of his grasp. If he should open his fingers and let go, it would be a simple matter for her body to totter too quickly the other way.

Conscious of the thin paper in her pocket, she was certain he must know of its discovery; was certain he'd seen her in the woods, spied upon her, watched her scrutinize the telltale name upon the page. Even the seagulls were now crying "Whittaker" as they circled and tattled.

Claire was mute with terror, unable to find a voice even to scream. *Had Zillah felt the same,* she wondered, *just before she fell to her death?*

"Miss Temple!" She was called back to the urgency of his voice. It was tattered and sundered by the wind. She did not suppose she'd been unconscious, as she still stood on her own; then why did she feel she was in a tunnel, and his yell came from far away?

He pulled her away from the edge, and her arm was still manacled by his forceful grip. They were back on the path now. Neither one spoke for a full minute.

"You're hurting my arm."

He looked down at his hand as if he did not recognize it, did not immediately remove it.

"Vitus," she insisted.

He finally released her arm as she tugged it away. He did not seem himself, and it made her afraid.

"Forgive me," he said so quietly that she read it upon his lips.

Forgive him? Was he about to do her harm?

"I didn't mean to hurt you. I was worried about you." He looked to where they had stood. "Why were you so close to the edge?"

"I've never seen the cliff. Not from up close. I mean, I've only seen it from my room." Her mouth was rambling and her mind raced. She was not about to tell him why she was really here on this spot, that she had not only searched for Zillah's lost note, she had found it.

"That was foolish, to have left the path."

The cliff path. Could he be trusted to keep her transgression undiscovered? "Please, Vitus. Please do not tell anyone you saw me here."

"Why?" he asked, his face a dark mask. "What were you doing here, Miss Temple, that must be kept secret?"

"Nothing! In truth, nothing." Her throat was dry. "I have been forbidden, until my uncle returns, to walk the trail that edges the cliff."

She could not read his expression, did not know whether he believed her.

"I . . . I don't want to displease him," continued Claire. "I could not bear to be sent away from Raven Heights."

He at least acknowledged this truth with a nod as he looked around. "Are you saying that no other person knows you are here this morning?"

Claire shivered. She deliberated, debating whether it would be safe to admit that her whereabouts were unknown to anyone who would think to look for her.

He did not wait for an answer, nor did he look at her. He was staring at the cliff. "Was this where she fell, do you think?"

Vitus still had not looked at her. She assumed he was talking to himself, not expecting an answer from her.

He answered himself. "I've asked that question so many times." Now he did look at Claire with his serious gaze. "We couldn't tell how far the tide or currents might have carried her. But it was close to here that we found her. We hadn't known she was missing. When we ran for Miss Bethany Coulter, she denied us with a cry. She swore Zillah was sleeping upstairs, safe in her bed. She took the stairs two at a time. We'd found the body floating face-down, and the hair color was Zillah's. It would be the most horrific error to make if it were not her. But in the two minutes it took for Miss Coulter to run up the stairs and return, we knew by her bearing that there was no error."

He turned and his stare pierced Claire. "Why did she come here that night?"

Claire looked into his eyes but remained mute. If she said Benjamin Whittaker aloud, would he push her over the edge?

Chapter Twenty

"Please do not take this personally."

Malcolm Randall watched Bethany Coulter pace from one end of the lavender parlor to the other. "Do not take it personally?" he asked in a quiet voice, leaning forward from where he sat.

It took some effort for the gentleman to keep his expression neutral, to force his eyebrows not to rise with incredulity. "You suddenly decide you no longer desire my partnership in the inn, yet I am not to take it personally. And how is that possible?" He did not mean his voice to rise on that last phrase, but it did.

Miss Coulter stopped pacing. Wringing her delicate hands, she faced him and said, "Please, Mr. Randall. I thought you would be understanding, but you are making this difficult for me."

This time his eyebrows did rise with incredulity. "Difficult for *you*, madam?" He had a thought. "Is there another partner you have in mind, then?"

She blushed as she stuttered her reply. "No. Not at this time, that is. I mean, I—No." Her eyes closed as she shook her head. "Let me begin again. I am not saying I shall never consider another partner in the inn, but I—"

"Simply not me." His voice was flat.

"Miss Bethany! Miss Bethany, I cannot find Captain Henry." Grace skidded to a halt just inside the doorway. "I've looked everywhere in the inn. And in the gardens." She curtsied to Mr.

Randall before turning back to her mistress. "You asked me to locate him, but I cannot. Have you seen him yet?"

"Ah, I see. You *have* decided upon another business partner." Malcolm did not recognize the gentleman's name. Nor did he recognize the bile of jealousy that crept from his stomach to his heart.

"What?" Bethany appeared distracted as she gave him a quick glance. She turned to Grace. "This is so unlike him, to disappear for so long. Can you please see if he is with Aunt Amelia, Grace?"

"Yes, Miss Bethany." She curtsied again, quickly, to Mr. Randall before turning to leave.

"And check with the others," Bethany called as Grace ran around the corner.

Mr. Randall and Bethany looked at one another, each trying to recall which skein they'd been following in the conversation thread.

He spoke first. "If you were considering a different financial partner, you might have made that known to me earlier."

"Another partner?" She looked confused.

"I note you do not deny it."

"This is absurd. I have already said I have no other partner in mind at this time."

"Does that include Captain Henry?" He noted with satisfaction that he'd shocked her speechless.

But then she laughed. "Captain Henry! Now you are being silly. However," she said, scowling, "The point is, I have decided to dissolve our business relationship."

"You still have not given your reasons."

She might not have heard him, so absorbed was she in her contemplation. "I thought about this all night. I slept terribly, as I could think of nothing else. Replaying yesterday's . . . receipt of a letter . . . from my father."

He remembered the awkward moment in the kitchen. And he'd been charmed that everyone was so enthusiastic about welcoming him to the inn that they had pretended to receive a letter to speed up the process—several letters, as it turned out—from Mr. Calden Coulter, who co-owned Pelican Inn with his daughter Bethany.

That is, Miss Coulter *claimed* co-ownership. Now he wondered whether she had any legal ownership of the building after all.

"What did you say?" He realized she'd been talking as he reminisced.

"I said I believe, Mr. Randall, that we can no longer trust one another."

"*What?* I am not the party who lied, if I may remind you." He wished he had not used such a strong word as *lied.* But what were the alternatives? Prevaricated? Pretended? He instantly held up his palms in peace. "Let us amend that and say, rather, that you fibbed."

"No, you were right the first time. I lied. But . . . I have learned over the years that if one party performs an unethical act, it is only acceptable to another party if that other party has the same code of ethics. Logic follows, therefore, that *you* should no longer trust *me.* But, as you have not said you do not trust me, I must infer that your ethics may possibly be inferior as well."

He shook his head in disbelief as he half laughed. "That is the most absurd logic I have ever been subjected to!"

"I believe my logic is quite sound. If you can condone fibs—lies—then you are also at fault. I believe I can no longer trust you."

"And when did this become about *me*?" He was yelling now.

Bethany folded her hands primly upon her skirt. "I have to say I have never seen this side of you. Perhaps it is for the best to learn now that you have a temper."

"Miss Coulter, you are the one who should be under the lens here. I have been frank and forthright in all of our dealings." He knew his face was red, knew exactly when the veins would be standing out upon his neck, knew he was taking his frustration out upon the only young woman he cared about. "Yet you have taken advantage—"

"That's a lie!" she interrupted vehemently, leaning forward on the balls of her feet, like a skier careening down a slope.

"Aha! And, according to your flawless logic, you should know, as it would take a liar to recognize another liar. Plus, may I point out," he added with a triumphant shout, "That you also have a temper, so it's perhaps best I learned that beforehand. You, madam, are also capable of shouting."

"I am not shouting. I never shout!" she shouted.

"Aunt Amelia, have you seen Miss Bethany?" Claire peeked into the kitchen, where the older woman was stirring a kettle of applesauce.

"She is in the parlor, arguing with Mr. Randall." Aunt Amelia looked at Claire over her half-glasses. "One might wish to avoid that room for a bit of time."

Claire smiled. "Excellent advice. Then, is Alice in the inn, do you know?"

"She was in here not five minutes ago, folding the dinner napkins." Aunt Amelia looked around the kitchen, as if she'd overlooked Alice and her cane. "She cannot have gone far."

"Thank you, ma'am." Claire hurried out to check the other rooms.

She wished she'd asked Aunt Amelia precisely which parlor Miss Bethany and Mr. Randall were in, that it might be avoided. But it soon became obvious. She hurried past the door to the lavender parlor, where the muffled voices did not sound in a pleasant tête-à-tête.

He'd never seen her this angry. He returned her stare. They each breathed deeply. He wondered if she were as shocked at this escalated argument as he. Feeling in better control of his emotions, he was unsure how to proceed, when Miss Coulter decided it for both of them.

"I think it would be best if you were to leave now, Mr. Randall." Her voice sounded tired, yet firm.

"But—"

"I've nothing further to say."

"Yet you—"

"Nothing." She folded her hands across her chest, tapped her toe, barely held eye contact.

He stood, picking up his hat where it sat beside him on the sofa. He took a step toward the door, then stopped. "No. I refuse to leave, Miss Coulter." He turned to face her, saw the surprise in her clear green eyes. "Not until you've given me the truth. I deserve that much. We've sat through many, *many* meetings together. We have spent hours discussing this, we've perused the books and the accounts as thoroughly as possible. I have the funds. I've become familiar with the kitchen. In addition, my parents have all but disowned me for pursuing this venture. I already informed them, unwisely it now appears, that I am going into trade against their wishes." *And I've unwisely fallen in love with you,* he said to himself.

Merely working at the inn side by side was no longer an option. He wanted more than a business relationship. He desired to be at her side from the earliest hour of the morning, and he did not envision that being in the kitchen. He wanted to wake up next to her. He'd been confident she would accept his suit.

"Bethany—" He'd known it was a mistake the moment her

name escaped upon his breath, the instant she stiffened. But he'd said her sweet name silently in his head a hundred times since he'd met her.

"I have not given you leave to call me by my first name, Mr. Randall."

Still she stood with arms crossed, but when she sighed delicately, he knew it might be his last chance to sway her, and continued. "My apologies . . . Miss Coulter, I have come to appreciate you as an open, fair person. Please. Be open with me now. Be fair and explain what happened between the last time I saw you and today."

Miss Coulter uncrossed her arms and clasped them at her waist. She looked down at the Aubisson carpet. "Very well." Looking back up, she held her hand toward the sofa. "Sit, Mr. Randall."

"Only if you will sit as well."

When she moved to comply, he sat again, placing his hat on the cushion at his side. Miss Coulter took a seat closer to the hearth. Her hands still clasped, she placed them upon her lap.

"You are right that I owe you the courtesy of an explanation. As I told you, this is rather difficult for me." She took a deep breath. "The truth is that I am embarrassed. I have thought about what happened concerning the letter from my father and, frankly, I can no longer expect you to believe in my honesty. Not following that debacle."

"That is what this sudden change is about?" He laughed in relief. "That was nothing, madam. I quickly realized that you wanted to close the deal, but your father is not available. It was understandable."

Miss Coulter flushed. "It was unacceptable."

"It was charming."

"It was certainly not charming. It was underhanded, dishonest. Mr. Randall, I embarrassed myself by lying to you." Her lips trembled as she said, "And that is why I can no longer do business with you. I can barely face you now to admit this."

The stone in his stomach inflated with relief and took wing. "I took it as flattery that you so desired my partnership, you were willing to speed up the process. Fine. We shall go back as we were, and we shall wait out the arrival of your father. When he returns—"

"I do not know when he is to return."

"Understood. I am enthusiastic about proceeding, but I am in no hurry."

She could not disguise the wonder in her voice, shaking her head in bemusement. "I cannot fathom that you would wish to proceed."

"Shouldn't it be my decision whether I am still interested in pursuing this partnership? After the *debacle,* I believe you called it?"

She shook her head in the negative again, gently. "Of course. Yet I could not help but ponder, as I played the day's events over and over in my mind last night, why you yourself did not sever the relationship immediately." At his look of surprise, she said, "Don't you see? You should no longer have been interested in the partnership." Tiptoeing verbally, she explained in a friendly tone, "You must admit that does not bode well for your business acumen, to be so easily duped."

His emotions shifted, relief evolving to something more akin to annoyance. Determined to hold his irritation in check, he said, "Now you are saying I am a dupe?"

She raised her eyebrows as she looked down at the fireplace to her side. "Well. I cannot believe that an intelligent person would not be having second thoughts."

"Now we've established I am a dupe, and I am not intelligent . . . Perhaps I am not intelligent. That, I can live with."

Her expression was serious, but she said lightly, "Come now, don't be silly."

"But I am silly? Just not intelligent? Besides not being trustworthy, sane, or ethical, that is?"

The moment he saw the hint of a smile, he knew all would be well.

Chapter Twenty-One

Claire stopped before crossing the bedroom threshold, rapped her knuckles thrice on the jamb outlining the open door.

Alice looked up from where she sat playing on the floor, a jointed wooden doll in her hands. Its opaque eyes were topped by thin, finely painted eyebrows, and two cherry-red circles centered each cheek. A stiff, striped green and yellow skirt disguised any legs it might have.

"Claire?"

"Ah! How did you know it was me?" Claire laughed with delight.

"I heard your footsteps on the stairway. I mean, it sounded like yours. Also, you always knock three times."

"You should be an investigator. Oh! And that is why I am here. I have something to show you. You won't believe it, the most amazing luck!" Claire could not help but pause dramatically. "I found Zillah's hidden note."

Alice dropped the doll onto her lap and clapped her hands together. "Truly? Where was it? When did you find it? Was it in the wall where we were searching?"

Claire brought the folded note across the room, took Alice's hand, and put the paper in her palm. "It was in a wall, between the stones. Exactly as you'd remembered. But it was in a different wall. Closer to Raven Heights."

Alice held the thin vellum reverently.

"I was looking at the cliffs, from my bedroom, as I do each

morning. My eyes skimmed across the ruins of an ancient wall, and I realized there could be remnants of more than one single wall. This wall was closer to the sea, and I recalled you had heard the sounds of the waves crashing that day you and Zillah hid it."

Alice ran her fingers along the edges of the note, then handed it back to Claire without unfolding it. "Have you read it? Are you sure it's Zillah's?"

Claire hadn't considered it could be otherwise. "It has to be. It was tucked into the crevices, and it was precisely where you remembered. Five stones high, eight stones right. It has to be Zillah's note. It wasn't signed by her . . . but it absolutely has to be hers."

"What does it say?" Alice barely breathed, staring in Claire's direction.

"It has a name upon it. That is all. Just two words." Claire would never forget those two words. "Do you know the name Whittaker?"

Alice shook her head to signal she did not.

"Benjamin Whittaker." She saw no change in Alice's expression. "Are you sure? That was all it said: Benjamin Whittaker."

Alice frowned with concentration, paused before answering. "No."

Claire had been holding her breath as well; she released it now along with the wishful hope she'd toted in haste to Pelican Inn. She'd been certain this clue would release a snug puzzle piece, that all would drop neatly into the riddle Zillah had created for them.

Neither young lady said anything for a minute. Alice continued to concentrate, or so it seemed, as her sightless eyes turned toward the lighted window and stared unwaveringly.

"I don't recognize that name at all, Claire. Shall we go ask Miss Bethany? I think she has lived here longer than Aunt

Amelia. But we could ask Aunt Amelia as well."

"Miss Bethany is in a . . . a business meeting. With Mr. Randall. I think now would be an unwise time to interrupt."

"Then in the meantime, I have an idea," said Alice. "I think we should go—after we ask Aunt Amelia first—and see Reverend Hinkle."

Claire thought the name somewhat familiar, yet could not place a face to the person. Mrs. Dawson was not a stickler for attending services in the village, so neither did Claire. "Is he the local vicar?"

"Yes. He and his wife have had the vicarage since he was a young man, is what I was told. Which must be ever so long ago, because his voice sounds so old. I am sure the reverend will be able to help us, he knows everyone! Or if he doesn't, he most likely knows all the gossip and news passed on to him by his predecessor. The vicar loves gossip. I've heard the women say he should have been a female."

"That is not very kind." Claire's laugh belied the chastisement in her words.

"I know. But it is the truth." Alice smiled mischievously.

It took a few minutes to locate Aunt Amelia, but she was as unfamiliar with the name on the note as they were.

"Whittaker . . . No, I am afraid I cannot help you," she said again. "Alice, I think that is an astute suggestion of yours, to visit the vicar. That man is a veritable ledger on legs. If anyone alive should know of this Benjamin Whittaker, I would place a wager that our vicar shall."

Both young ladies were about to depart together, to visit the vicar, when Aunt Amelia reminded Alice that she'd promised to help Grace with the shelling of the peas for dinner.

Claire rushed to say, "It's all right, Alice. I shall go posthaste and see the reverend on my own. And I promise to come right back here and tell you what I learn." At Alice's crestfallen look, she added, "Will you take the task of speaking to Miss Bethany as soon as she is available? Ask her if she recognizes the name, and we will compare notes in an hour or so."

Alice nodded fervently and left for the kitchen. Claire received the directions she sought—in addition to unsought ruminations—from Aunt Amelia, then slipped away.

The vicarage was recognizable the moment Claire rounded the bend. It was just as Aunt Amelia's words had painted it: flat, grey stone walls choked in a dense layer of ivy, except where the clinging strands were sharply trimmed to expose the red door, a beacon to visitors in search of an entrance. The only other adornment was five white-framed windows, one on either side of the door, and three marching across the upper story. Aunt Amelia said the cottage reminded her of the wide face of her seafaring cousin Peter, whose wild facial hair covered all but his full red lips and his eyeglass windows. Of course, she elaborated, Peter's beard was not green, and he only had two eyes.

Beyond the small two-story house was visible the peak of a graceful church steeple. A gate in the side garden wall allowed the vicar to go directly from his garden path to the church. Behind the vicarage, a gate gave access to a meadow bordering upon the cemetery. It was a new gate installed by the current vicar and his wife. Aunt Amelia referenced this as the Unnecessary Gate, as the church itself connected to the cemetery, and wasn't that all that was needed? The footpath looping behind the house to the cemetery had been—for all the years she could remember—divided by a stile, but the present vicar and his wife would both be challenged to climb a stile, she declared. A short dumpling with a good heart was how Aunt Amelia described the vicar's wife.

This small church and its yard of gravestones were closer to Raven Heights than it was to the village. Claire had imagined the sounds of the sea as she climbed the hill, and now knew it was not her imagination. The holy ground on its rise was not too distant from the farthest boundary of Raven Heights' vast forested land. She could not help but marvel, once again, why the resting places she'd viewed were always settled on the tops of hills, as if to lay the deceased residents in a position of comfort from whence they could enjoy the local views.

Claire turned to the right to follow the cleanly swept line of bricks to the entry. Three steps ended at the porchless door. Barely had she left the path before the door opened, framing a large man with snowy, wild hair and a trim edging of white beard circling a round face.

"Welcome, child, welcome." Reverend Theophilus Hinkle's smile was as broad as his middle. "And whom have we here?" She could see his curiosity was piqued, to meet a new member of the community.

"Good afternoon, Reverend." Claire curtsied the moment she reached the brick apron surrounding the door. "My name is Claire Temple. I am staying with my uncle at Raven Heights Manor."

"My goodness! I'd not heard that Sir Rudyard had a niece visiting. For how long are you with us?"

Claire did not answer for a long moment. She wasn't sure what to say. If she had her wish, she would live here forever. But she'd never even met her uncle. "I . . . I don't know," she finally stammered.

He waited for her to elaborate.

"My uncle invited me here, but I am told he is not expected to return for perhaps another month or so. That is what Mrs. Dawson has told me. I suppose I shall not know his wishes until he is in residence."

His round eyes made him look like a stuffed owl. "Where are you visiting from? Where do your parents live?"

Claire was not used to such direct questioning from an adult. She blushed, saying, "Nowhere. That is, I do not know where my parents lived prior to their death." He made a sad noise. "I lived at Whiteworth's Boarding School, and Mrs. Cunliffe delivered me here."

"Mrs. Cunliffe?"

"One of the teachers. But she returned that same day to the school." Claire could see he was not yet satisfied with the fact gathering. "And I've yet to meet Uncle."

"This is all too fascinating, and I should like to know more. But where are my manners? Shall you come in and visit?" He opened the door wider.

"I don't think so," she said, standing her ground upon the bricks. "If you do not mind, that is, sir. I have a question, as I've been told you are familiar with all of the families in the area."

His eyes twinkled with anticipation. He twiddled his thumbs, his thick arms circumnavigating his protruding waistline. "How flattering! Though I must modestly admit that it is so. Whom did you have in mind?"

"Did you know the Whittaker family, sir?"

He looked surprised at her question. "Why, now, *that's* a name I haven't heard in many moons. And what leads you to inquire about that family in particular?"

Claire realized she should have expected this question, should have formulated an answer as to why she was inquiring. Could she trust him? If one were to trust a stranger, would not a holy man be the safest to trust? Convinced she was becoming overly fearful due to everyone's warnings, she decided she must trust someone if she were to gain information. Rather than answer, however, she instead asked another question. "I was wondering about a particular Whittaker family member by the name of Benjamin."

He twiddled his thumbs again, his laced fingers resting on

top of his belly. "Yes. I am quite positive there was a male child named Benjamin. Though where the lad fell in the order of the many Whittaker children I could not say with certainty."

"Do they still live in the area?"

"No, child. It has been these many years past, since they left to return to the Midlands."

Her discouragement must have been obvious, because he asked gently, "Is there something I can help you with?"

"I . . . I don't know. That is . . ." She struggled whether to tell him about Zillah's note. It wasn't just a matter of trust; her instincts told her she might be here the remainder of the day once that topic was laid bare. "Is there anything more you can tell me about them?"

"Fine, upstanding community members. Exceedingly fine. Poor in the pocket, but certainly not in the spirit or soul. Theirs was a large family. They lived down the gulley."

Claire looked back the way she'd come, the gentle descent toward the valley. "The gulley?"

He pointed in the same general direction. "One of the first farms as you approach the village from the south." He scratched one of his baby-smooth chins. " 'Twas either the second side road, or the third. I always forget, but that is because I simply look for the huge horse chestnut tree. It is such a magnificent specimen of His handiwork, you cannot possibly miss it." At her blank look, he asked, "Surely you played with the fruit of *Aesculus hippocastanum* as a wee child?"

Claire had no idea what the vicar was referring to.

"And the autumn foliage!" He spread his hands toward heaven. "Glorious, glorious golds. Or should I say *'Soli Deo gloria'*? For His glory."

Claire was not sure what language he spoke. She nodded mutely in agreement.

"I am picturing the second lane now, yes, it was the second, I am quite sure of it. Though if you watch for that tree, as I say, you cannot possibly miss it." His hands returned to their clasped position at his waist.

She cleared her throat. "How long ago did they leave?"

"Oh, gracious. It's been . . . let me think." He looked up at the fluffy clouds floating overhead. Claire wondered if he were asking his question of the angels in heaven . . . or perhaps he was praying, when he suddenly directed his gaze to hers and said, "Twelve years. Yes, I am absolutely sure it was twelve years ago, and I even know the exact month." She thought he swelled with pride, but was not sure it was physically possible his middle could swell any further. "It was April," he stated with certainty. "I recall now that our Ellie had taken sick that winter, at the same time as Granny Whittaker. Fortunately, my Ellie got better as the spring weather arrived. And that was when the Whittakers decided to return to Coventry."

"If I were to go to see the farm . . . in the gully, would the house be occupied by anyone?"

"It is interesting you ask. On top of all of their other troubles, they had a fire. Burned to the ground, the house was. Nothing left standing except the chimney stones."

Claire considered whether a third clue might be found tucked into the stones. As if the man read her mind, he added, "Of course, once it was known the family left, the stones were appropriated by the neighbors for their own uses. Gracious. People are like vultures, aren't they? Preying, when they should be praying." He laughed, a gusty laugh. "My, that was witty on my part. I believe I could use that in a sermon."

Claire had the impression he was anxious to retreat to his study, while the words were still fresh on his tongue and memory. She thanked the gentleman and bade him good day, promising to return on the Tuesday following to have tea with Mrs. Hinkle.

Chapter Twenty-Two

"Tell me more about Captain Henry."

"Captain Henry?" With emphasis on the second word, Bethany Coulter's guarded voice implied *why do you ask*?

"Yes. Tell me why he is so perfect." Malcolm Randall had once again become a regular visitor to Pelican Inn. He perched on a high stool in the kitchen, his large hands wrapped around an oversized porcelain teacup.

"Did I say he was? Perfect?" Bethany stirred her own tea, frowning thoughtfully into her cup.

"You are repeating my words back to me, Miss Coulter. A stalling tactic. Which, by the way, I am familiar with as well as guilty of, so it will not work this morning." Mr. Randall was rewarded with a slow smile as Bethany looked up from her tea and her eyes met his. "All right, perhaps you did not literally say he was perfect, not in so many words. But if he weren't, why would you miss him so?"

A shadow crossed her face. "Yes, I do miss him, that is the truth."

With a twinge of conscience, knowing he pressed her out of selfish jealousy, he offered, "Do you mind my asking?"

"No. Not at all. Why should I?" Her gaze was direct.

"Some ladies would be offended."

"I am not so easily offended, Mr. Rand—"

"Come, Miss. It appears I do nothing but offend you, and on a daily basis."

"Sometimes more often." She grinned, a slight quirk of the lips as she glanced to the side. "Be that as it may, I am not offended, but believe me when I say this subject is a waste of your time and mine. It is done. And I thought you wanted to discuss inventory this morning?"

She opened a well-used ledger book.

"Were you his mistress?" He regretted the blurted question the instant it passed his lips.

He'd overstepped his bounds. But he'd never felt this intensely about a woman, and the mysterious Captain Henry had caused him a sleepless night. Lack of sleep and frustration caused a social error he would not be able to rescind. Certain that Miss Coulter would demand an apology and a departure, he was not a little shocked when she laughed gustily.

"Now, that *is* offensive. However . . ." She smiled, a sad smile. "I suppose the answer would be yes, but it is not what you think."

He was as shocked by her blunt answer as he was by her humoured reaction.

In a matter-of-fact voice, she went on. "But I insist, no more talk of Captain Henry. He shall either return or he shan't." She sipped her tea and flipped the ledger pages to the prior month entries, said no more on the subject.

He chose to follow her lead, lest she throw him out on his ear, as she had every right to do.

A jangling bell broke the fragile silence. "Will you excuse me?" asked Bethany. "That will be Mrs. Violet's niece, with eggs."

"I'll assist you." He began to rise, but she touched his shoulder, pushing him down gently.

"No, please don't bother." Leaning toward him confidentially, she said, "I enjoy her daily visit, and I can manage the basket easily. I'll return shortly."

Mr. Randall watched her go, very aware of the imprint of her hand upon his shoulder, the scent of her hair. He did not move until her skirts whisked around the corner. *I really should leave,* he supposed, rather than sit here idly speculating about the elusive Captain Henry, but he could not resist visiting a while longer with Miss Coulter. In truth, he was not interested in looking at ledger entries. And he was convinced by now that she was not involved in a business relationship with the mysterious captain. It still embarrassed him that he'd reacted so churlishly that day she had first discovered the man was missing.

If not a business relationship, then what nature of relationship existed between Miss Coulter and the captain? It was obvious the man's continued absence saddened her. Of more concern to Malcolm Randall was the possibility that she still had a tendre for the military man. *Why do women love a man in uniform?* he wondered, with a snort.

"Good afternoon, Mr. Randall." Aunt Amelia wandered in to the kitchen. *Wander* was the perfect word to describe the elderly lady, as she was as likely as not to be uncertain which room she'd been heading to, and why.

He was sure she'd heard him snort, but she made no comment, nor any inquiry. He stood and bowed. "Good afternoon, Madam."

"Sit, sit. Drink your tea while it is hot." She tottered to the window. "Where is Bethany?" she asked, as if expecting to see her niece in the kitchen garden.

"She said the eggs have arrived." Slyly, he realized the opportunity, and asked, "Aunt Amelia, has Captain Henry been back to visit since he disappeared the other day?"

"To visit!" She turned around to peer at him. "What an odd thought. He lives here." Reaching for a teacup, she did not see his disquieted look. As she poured her tea, she said, "But no, he has not returned. Not one of us has seen him for . . . How long?

Has it already been two days? Though I am quite sure he'll return soon, as 'tisn't the first time he's been gone for several days, you know."

Mr. Randall straightened with surprise. "Really? I thought she said this was unlike him. This disappearance."

"Nonsense! He goes haring off on a regular basis. Does as he pleases." She smiled. "Don't they all?"

Malcolm spied Miss Coulter's return from the corner of his eye. He hoped she would not think he'd taken advantage of her absence to question her aunt, even if it were so. If he was lucky, Bethany's aunt would not even recall the string of conversation, a trait she had thankfully exhibited often.

"What was that, Aunt?" Miss Coulter set the egg basket down on the closest hutch.

"I was simply answering Mr. Randall's inquiries about Captain Henry. I said it was not the first time he'd deserted you."

Malcolm knew he'd let his petty jealousy push him too far this time, judging by Bethany Coulter's expression. He'd have kicked himself if it were physically possible.

"Mr. Randall, I have a headache. Good day," Miss Coulter said, turning away from him.

He stood and picked up his hat. He said nothing further, angry at himself, and even angrier at the captain. If the man had walked into the kitchen at that precise moment, it was a certainty that Mr. Randall would have dumped all of the fresh eggs upon his military cap.

Aunt Amelia wished him good day as well.

Frustrated with the situation and his boorish behavior, Mr. Randall was not paying attention as he descended the porch steps. Thus, he barely avoided a collision with Grace, who came racing around the corner, taking the steps two at a time.

"Oh! Mr. Randall, I am sorry, sir."

"Grace, do you always race around corners?" His tone was indulgent.

The young miss grinned sheepishly. "But running is ever so much more fun than walking, don't you think, sir?"

He recalled foot races with his brothers, racing to the creek, racing to meals. Had he run by himself for the sheer pleasure of it, as Grace did? No, he thought with disgust, I've probably never done anything that was not in competition with someone. Of course, that reminded him . . .

"Grace, what do you know of Captain Henry?"

"Captain Henry? I don't believe he's returned yet."

He recalled what Aunt Amelia said. "But he has been gone before?"

"Oh, yes." Grace rolled her eyes. "He's very bad. Unfortunately"—she bounded up the remaining steps and stopped to address him from the top of the porch—"the household must go through this cycle every few months. It distresses Miss Bethany no end."

"Every few months?" This triggered a memory: his cousin Dilbert's cyclic disappearances. "Do you suppose he has a drinking problem?"

"I beg pardon?"

Perhaps Grace was unaware of the deadly sins. "Do you know, does he go away to drink?"

"Why ever should he, when he has plenty to drink here?" Grace shrugged and wished him good day as she opened the door to enter the inn.

"Miss Bethany? What's a drinking problem?"

Bethany Coulter set her darning aside. "Why do you ask, Grace?"

Grace plopped onto the cushion next to Miss Coulter. "Today, when he was leaving, Mr. Randall asked me if Captain

Henry had a drinking problem."

"A drinking problem! Why ever would he ask that?"

"I don't know. I told him that Captain Henry goes away a lot."

Bethany laughed with delight. "Ah! Well, sometimes, a man who leaves his family to frequent taverns too often, a man who drinks too much—more than is healthy, to the detriment of his family and well-being—is said to have a problem."

"Then why—" Grace scrunched her face, still confused.

Bethany picked up Grace's hand and squeezed it with a smile. "It is because our Mr. Randall thinks Captain Henry is a man who lives at the inn."

"But . . . why would he . . . ?"

"It's my fault." Bethany chuckled as she returned to her darning. "The man annoyed me, and I failed to point out the mistake to him."

The young lady's eyes were saucers. "You didn't tell him Captain Henry is a dog?" Grace asked in an incredulous squeak.

"No." Bethany couldn't help laughing. "I couldn't. Rather, I didn't." She still chuckled a minute later when Grace left to find Alice.

Chapter Twenty-Three

"Miss Temple!"

Claire heard her name and looked quickly round the village square, but did not see anyone.

"Miss Temple, over here." Reverend Theophilus Hinkle waved from the porch of the apothecary shop. "I'm so glad I saw you just now," he called loudly, taking crab-like steps from side to side as he hastened down the stairs. "Saves me a trip up to the manor. Not that I mind paying social visits, as you know."

Claire moved toward the shop. She smiled and curtsied briefly at his arrival.

"Would you be heading in my direction?" he asked.

She hadn't planned to head precisely in that direction, but avoided an untruth by stating truthfully, "I would be happy to accompany you, Reverend."

Thus began a slow stroll toward the vicarage. Claire was curious to learn why he thought it necessary to pay a visit to the manor, as she'd never seen him there before.

Even if the vicar had no purpose, she could not but help enjoy conversing with him. She loved how he rambled, plus he reminded her of a waddling badger, with the white beard framing his face and wispy white hairs sticking straight out from the sides of his head, above his ears.

"How are you doing today, Miss Temple?" Without waiting for a response, he drew in a great breath and continued. "I was telling my wife about your visit, as we sat by the fire last night—

almost too warm for a fire in the hearth, I had mentioned to her. The trees have not yet set their autumnal colors. That is always the signal for me to begin setting the logs in the fireplace. But the wife has cold feet and cold hands, and we must often be lighting a fire, even if it is not quite autumn."

Claire wondered how he ever framed his sermons in the pulpit, sermons that she heard were surprisingly direct. One would expect the sermons to wander animatedly, resembling his normal conversation. Perhaps this was Mrs. Hinkle's specialty, editing her husband's sermons. "Yes," Claire agreed unnecessarily, "we have had some unseasonably cool nights of late."

The vicar stopped as a butterfly flitted across the path, folding and flashing its wings of gold against a dark brown body. A careful observer would also notice bars of black and white on the forewing, and perhaps a russet smudge or two.

"Striking! When it pauses to rest, one can discern a string of blue pearls outlining the wing." He did not move, and he whispered as if noise would bother the pirouetting butterfly. "Are you familiar with Lady Glanville?"

"Is that the name of the butterfly?" asked Claire.

The reverend laughed gustily. "Heavens, no. This is a Tortoiseshell butterfly. One of my favorites." The butterfly floated across the bushes at the side of the road and the vicar resumed his saunter, Claire following his lead. "If He had not called upon me to care for His flock, I am sure I would have become an entomologist." He stole a glance at Claire. "One who studies butterflies. Insects, rather, but it is the butterfly that fascinates me so."

"Then who is Lady Glanville?" Claire asked, politeness intermingled with curiosity.

"Lady Eleanor Glanville. I heard a story about her from an acquaintance who shares a love of butterflies, never knew her myself. She was born in Gloucestershire, and she pursued her interest in butterflies the remainder of her life. Collected many specimens. Be that as it may, the most fascinating part of her story was that when she died, her will was overturned. I challenge you to imagine why." He had a wide smile upon his face.

Claire had no idea what the connection was between Lady Granville and the butterfly, or where the conversation was going. Or why he had thought to visit the manor, or why his wife suffered from cold feet.

Which did not matter, as he did not linger for an answer.

"Evidently her family was not pleased with the stipulations of her will. They conducted a trial for lunacy, and it was determined that she was indeed insane. Thus the will was overturned. How was she insane, you ask?" (She hadn't.) "Because it was decreed that a sane person could never have pursued butterflies with the passion she demonstrated!"

Claire laughed at the surprise ending. By this time they reached the foot of the small hill where the vicarage perched.

"Where was I?" he asked. "Before we saw that beautiful butterfly?"

"You were sitting by the fire." Claire did not see any sign of recognition on his face. "Telling your wife about my visit . . . ?"

"Ah! Yes, thank you. It was the reason I needed to seek you out, you see. I told Mrs. Hinkle that I'd forgotten to mention to her that you had stopped by the vicarage the other day. When she was gone." He paused as they walked up a slight incline in the road. By the time they reached the top, he was breathing heavily. It took him another minute before he grabbed a breath and continued. "Did I mention that she—Mrs. Hinkle, that is—had gone to check on Mrs. Merriweather, who was due to deliver? Did you know that my wife came just in time to assist? Just in time! They have a fine, robust male child." They paused at the brick pathway to the vicarage.

"I am pleased to know the baby is healthy."

He nodded, his fingers woven together, hands joined at his navel.

Looking at Claire, he suddenly said, "Oh! That reminds me. Since Mrs. Hinkle missed you when you stopped by, she asks that I insist on having you return, and join us for tea and a chat. She is not here now, or I would invite you to visit today."

"Of course. You mentioned Tuesday afternoon?"

"Did I? That is so. I must be repeating myself. Did I already tell you about the Whittakers?"

Claire, still smiling, said, "Yes. When I came to see you—when your wife was at the Merriweather house—you said that the entire Whittaker family had left this area many years ago."

"But that is what I needed to talk to you about! I was telling Mrs. Hinkle that you and I had discussed the Whittakers. I repeated to her what I had said to you, about their difficult times in the valley, and their departure. I told her I'd even remembered the month and the year, because of our Ellie's illness. She agreed, of course. And Ellie has grown to a fine young woman. I don't know if you had heard, but she has married, just this past summer, and moved away. With her husband James, of course." He took out a handkerchief and wiped his sweating brow. "I then told Mrs. Hinkle one additional detail of our conversation. I distinctly recalled that you had inquired about young Benjamin." He sounded pleased with himself. "Isn't that right?"

Claire held her breath. When she realized he was waiting for her to confirm the obvious, she had hardly enough breath to say, "Yes. Yes, that is so."

The vicar nodded with satisfaction. "Yes, I believed I had that correct. Though I could not tell you where in the birthing order Benjamin fell. Fell? Perhaps appeared would be a more appropriate word. Yes. I could not tell you where in the birth order Benjamin appeared. But Mrs. Hinkle knew all of their names. 'Wait. Benjamin, did you say?' she asks me. And I remind her that yes, I did in fact, very clearly recall it was Benjamin you had been most interested in."

Claire feared she would die breathless, waiting for whatever it was he wished to confide.

"And then Mrs. Hinkle exclaims, 'Benjamin! But darling, don't you remember? Benjamin was their youngest. Benjamin did not leave with his parents.' "

Claire stilled, sure she would not ever breathe again. All the air left her body, and she stood still as a pillar, waiting for him to explain.

"She was correct, Miss Temple." He rocked on his heels, smiling.

"Correct about what? Where is he then?" She willed him to finish, wondering how she'd ever found the rambling to be charming.

He lowered his voice, as if sharing a choice piece of gossip. "Benjamin did not return to Coventry with them. Benjamin remained here, with his grandparents."

"Why? Why would they allow their child to stay? Especially their youngest child." Claire was crushed for the little boy. Her father and mother would never have left her behind, if they had remained alive, no matter how destitute they'd become. She was certain of that.

His eyes studied her, read her mind. "They didn't *want* to leave him, Miss Temple. The Whittakers loved all their children. Perhaps they loved Benjamin even more than the others, the Lord forgive them, because he was a frail little thing."

He looked toward the vicarage; faced that direction, ready to take his leave.

"But wait. I don't understand, Vicar. Why did they choose to leave him here? And if so, where is he?"

It was the first time Claire had seen a somber look upon the vicar's face.

"God did not give them a choice, Miss Temple. Benjamin rests with his grandparents." He pointed to the cemetery on the hillside next door. "There."

Chapter Twenty-Four

Twilight nipped at her heels, hurrying her on to Pelican Inn.

She called out to Alice, who sat on the broad, inviting steps of the inn's porch entry. Alice set her doll close to her side, and raised her head to listen for Claire's approaching steps.

Claire stopped at the base of the steps. "One moment, Alice." She surveyed carefully in all directions. The wooden stairs echoed with her swift steps until she was at the same level as Alice. Looking around one more time, satisfied they were alone, she lowered herself to sit next to the young girl.

"Alice, we have a new clue." Breathlessly, Claire began to explain. "The Reverend Hinkle called to me as I left the village. He asked me to accompany him to the vicarage, and I just now left him. What he wanted to share was that he had forgotten to tell Mrs. Hinkle that I had stopped by the other day. And last night, when he recalled to her the details of the visit—my visit to ask if he knew of the Whittakers—you will never guess what she said."

Alice did not guess, but waited with eyes staring wide, her lips slightly open, curved in the shape of a lingering "Oh!"

"Remember how he told me that all the Whittakers left for the Midlands twelve years ago? Well, Mrs. Hinkle reminded him that *Benjamin* Whittaker was the youngest child. And the most amazing circumstance is that Benjamin never left with his parents and his siblings because he—"

"He's here? He's always been here?" Alice's interruption,

which was not typical, told Claire how excited the young girl was.

"No, not here any longer. I mean he is, but it is not as you suspect."

Claire explained, then confided the plan she'd formulated on her way to Pelican Inn.

"I don't know," said Alice. "Shouldn't we wait for Miss Bethany to return from London? She is to return tomorrow."

Claire stood, brushed her skirt with her hands. "I mean to go tonight. Anyway, I would be much too excited to sleep." She descended the stairs, turned, and looked up at Alice, who remained perched higher. "Why is she in London?"

"All I heard from Aunt Amelia was that she has gone to see her bankers." Alice frowned in concentration. "Or . . . was it her solicitor?" She shrugged. "Perhaps both. I can't remember. But she is supposed to be back tomorrow."

Claire hesitated, but only for a matter of seconds. "I am determined to seek the next clue, and I see no reason to wait." She did not add that Bethany would most likely discourage them from the plans Claire had made. Her friend's absence made it easier for Claire's conscience to justify the outing tonight. "This is too exciting. We are about to discover Zillah's next mystery. She has strung a pathway of puzzles for us, knowing she would be gone." Seeing Alice's expression, she added, "I'm sorry. That is insensitive of me. I didn't know her, and in my zeal I forget she gave her life for this game."

"It's not *that* . . ." Alice kneaded her hands together. "If it will help us discover why Zillah died, then I agree it is an important task. Especially if someone did this to her. However . . ." Alice's last phrase hung in the air between them.

Guessing Alice's unspoken thoughts, Claire persisted. "It is not as if we would be putting ourselves in danger. We are simply visiting the cemetery at night."

Alice shuddered.

"Anyway, I must return quickly now, to dine with Mrs. Dawson. You have time to decide whether you'd like to join me." She turned to leave, then spun back. "Why don't we ask Aunt Amelia if you may return with me now, to Raven Heights to dine? Then, we will take candles and explore together afterwards. It will be a fun midnight adventure."

Alice sounded doubtful. "Will Mrs. Dawson allow you to go exploring after dark?"

Claire grinned. "Of course not. That is why it is an adventure."

Alice deliberated. With saddened eyes, she said, "I think I'm afraid to go into the cemetery, Claire."

"Those are just tales meant to scare young children. You and I are older. Think of it as an expedition into the jungles of Africa. We will pretend we are searching for Mr. Coulter." Claire wondered if she attempted to convince Alice only because she herself was a bit hesitant to visit the cemetery at night, alone.

Alice never answered why she was afraid, nor whether she would keep company with Claire. Instead, she offered, "Why don't we send word to Mrs. Dawson that you will dine here, and stay the night with Grace and me? Pelican Inn is not too distant from the vicarage. And I know Aunt Amelia would not mind."

Claire realized the wisdom of the suggestion. There would be less scrutiny of their whereabouts in the midst of the bustling inn, especially with Bethany's absence, as opposed to the quiet manor and Mrs. Dawson's observant blue eyes and sharp-hearing ears.

"That is a perfect idea, Alice."

After darkness fell, the household quieted in stages, until the last footfalls padded down the hallways, and bedroom doors closed solidly. Claire and Alice decided to wait another hour, straining their ears for coughs, or cupboards closing with a deadened muffle.

When all she could hear was Grace's soft snoring, Claire nudged Alice. They dressed as quietly as possible with only the soft milky lantern of the moon. Tiptoeing downstairs, they stayed close to the outside of each step, where it seemed the old wood creaked and complained less.

"What will we be looking for?" Alice asked once they turned the curve in the road that would shield them from any prying eyes at the inn.

"I don't know exactly. But we do know that Zillah wrote that lad's name on the paper she meant for you to find. And we also know that he rests at the cemetery with his grandparents. If we assume they share the same surname, then my plan is to find a stone with the name Whittaker carved on it. Even better if we should discover an individual grave site for Benjamin." An owl hooted nearby and Claire jumped, then chuckled. "It's just an owl."

"I know. Are you nervous?" asked Alice.

"I think my nerves are excited, yes. But it's not fear; at least I don't believe it is."

They walked in silence, two shadows on the road illuminated by the moon.

"What if Benjamin's grandparents have a different name? What if it's not Whittaker?"

Claire kept her eyes on the road. The cloud-shrouded moon gave light enough to see by, barely. There should be no obstacles other than a stray nocturnal creature. "I hadn't thought about that, as we would need to do more investigating. Drat! I wish I had thought to ask the vicar that question. I'm sorry you weren't able to visit him with me. You would have thought to ask the vicar, I am sure." She took Alice's hand and squeezed it.

Claire continued to hold Alice's hand as they approached the hill where the vicarage stood watch over the cemetery grounds. Her other hand gripped the strings of a small canvas bag that draped over her shoulder and hung down her back. She and Alice had packed it earlier, with thick candles and tinder.

There was no need to burn any candles, as the clouds cooperated by thinning enough to allow diffused moonlight upon the landscape. Claire was gratefully thinking that the candles would be unnecessary on this night, when she spied the gnarled oaks upon the hallowed hilltop ahead. The ancient trees spread huge, twisted limbs, practically touching one another like a protective line of sentries with arms reaching, fingers touching, standing guard over the graveyard.

She realized with distress that the gravestones would be difficult to read under the black canopy of trees, especially those chiseled letters worn shallow by time. She should pull a candle or two from the bag before they entered the miniature midnight village.

Claire had no idea where the Whittaker graves would be located within the cemetery, but suspected once she had found the first Whittaker, the family would have clustered their loved ones in close proximity.

She almost faltered in her steps as a thought struck her.

Alice released her hand from Claire's. "What is it?"

"Perhaps this will be where our very first clue comes in. Two rights, and the second left. Most cemeteries I've visited have been laid out in tidy streets and lanes."

"I wonder why Zillah gave us the clues in that particular order. She should have told us about Benjamin's name, and then told us where to go inside the cemetery."

"We'll never know." That was all Claire could think to say in reply. If only Zillah had left a lucid note. Perhaps in her own way that was what she thought she was doing. Unfortunately, realized Claire, once someone leaves the earth, the truth decomposes swiftly, leaving only fossil traces of conjecture and assumptions.

The road flattened at the top of the hill and ran parallel to the iron fence outlining the churchyard. No lights were visible at the vicar's home, nor in the steepled church. It had appeared, at first, that the front gallery of vicarage windows were each lit by a frosty lantern, until one realized it was the moon reflecting its cold light upon the glass panes.

Claire stopped next to the cemetery gate. The moment Alice's walking stick rang against a solid black bar, she sucked in her breath and stopped abruptly.

Claire leaned forward to peer at the closed gate, but could not see evidence of a lock. From the corner of her eye she could see Alice stood frozen.

"Are you all right?"

"I can't do it." Alice hadn't moved.

Claire turned to look at her. "Can't do what?"

"I can't go inside the cemetery with you." Alice's voice was little louder than a whisper. Her cane tapped against another iron bar and she recoiled.

"Why not? It isn't locked, so we can hardly be trespassing."

But Alice shook her head and would not say anything more.

"Can you come with me just inside the gates? A few more steps?" Claire hoped to convince her to come farther once they'd gotten past the entry. "Is it because it is night? And dark?"

Alice smiled, a look of chagrin. "All of my paths are walked in the dark."

"Oh. Of course." Claire felt silly.

"I'm sorry." Alice reached out to touch the fence, pulled her hand back as if frostbitten. As if afraid her fingers would stick to the cold metal, the frozen iron peeling her skin from the bones of her finger, until her hand was nothing more than a skeleton's, like those trapped on the other side.

"Alice, we will be hasty. We're going to find Benjamin's tombstone. And somewhere in the near vicinity—I'm sure of it—there will be another clue. And we'll leave even more quickly than we arrived. I promise."

Claire peered down the moonlit avenue on the other side of the gates. "I know you can't see it, but the churchyard is pleasingly open and clear. Let me describe it to you: The vicarage is just outside the left fenced boundary. Straight ahead, as we enter through the gates, is a wide lane. Comfortably wide, and it appears well graveled. There are cypress trees lining up on each side, with trim hedges beneath. I can see an opening in the hedges, a good walk ahead. That will be a side lane. There's an opening on each side. The clue said two right turns, do you remember? We'll take that first right, and then the next right. And the second left would be the next direction. Can't you see? Zillah knew we would be here, she knew we would find Benjamin's gravestone. It will be easy, you'll see."

Alice hadn't moved from the spot where her feet sent roots into the sacred ground. She shook her head. It was barely conspicuous at first, a movement causing Claire to glance over from the corner of her eye. As Claire watched, Alice continued to turn her head side to side, trancelike.

Claire slung the bag off her shoulder. "Can you hold this side of the bag for me? I need to get a candle."

Alice awoke and held out her hand, and Claire guided it to the top edge of the bag. Still holding the opposite rim, Claire reached in and extracted a fat taper. "Hold a bit longer, I need to find the tinder." She dug until her hand closed upon the tinder box.

Leaving the bag in Alice's hands, Claire knelt and worked methodically to strike a spark. Neither spoke over the sharp metallic scratches. When Claire stood slowly with the lit candle, its watery circle illuminated their two faces, which floated, bodiless.

"I should have thought to bring a lantern," said Claire sotto voce. "If the cemetery is drafty, the candle will be an inconvenience. Here, I can take the bag now."

She reached her free hand for the bag as Alice pulled it toward her own body. "I can keep hold of the bag for you. I don't mind."

"All right. Thank you." Claire waved the candle toward the gate's handle. "Are you ready, then?"

Alice heaved a sigh and shook her head slowly. "No." Again she turned her face toward the cemetery as if she could see through the bars, and said sadly, "I'm sorry, I can't."

"We have to go there, if we're to solve this mystery."

"Please don't go. It isn't safe for us."

Claire meant to go, and nothing would stop her. Except that Alice's next words did.

"There's a ghost lives there."

Claire laughed hesitantly. "Is that all you are worried about? There are no such things as ghosts!"

The little girl took a small step backward. "That's not true."

"Alice, who told you that ghosts are real?"

"Nobody."

"Then see? You don't—"

"I've talked to him."

Claire had a rush of goose bumps marching up her forearm. "Who?"

"The ghost. He told me he lives here, and that I shouldn't be in this graveyard." She turned her head toward the darkened cemetery, sightlessly peering through its bars. "His name is Nicholas. He's young, like me."

Claire did peer through the bars. "Is he there now?"

"I don't know."

"What did Nicholas say to you?"

"He said that there is danger here. He said he didn't want me to return. Ever."

"Was he trying to scare you?"

"I don't think so. He was very nice when we first began talking." Alice frowned. "I think he wished to be my friend. He sounded sad when he told me I had to go away."

Claire tried reasoning. "If he wanted to be your friend, he shouldn't try to scare you away."

Alice shook her head. "I asked him, didn't he want me to come visit with him again, and then he yelled at me."

"I think it was someone playing a mean joke on you. I'm sure it was the voice of a real person. Besides, I doubt that ghosts would even be capable of yelling."

"When I said he yelled, I mean I couldn't hear him yelling in the air, but it was so loud inside my head that my teeth hurt a little. His voice yelled in my head, 'Once you go away, you must never, ever come back, or you'll be hurt.' "

Claire felt another chill run up her arm, starting at her elbows. She ran her free hand over the pimples on her skin. "Perhaps you imagined it." Claire didn't think Alice would have made it up. Alice was honest in a simple, welcome way.

"I didn't." Her shoulders slumped visibly. "It's all right if you don't believe me, but it's the truth."

"I believe you." Claire believed that Alice believed. And that was as much as she could admit to herself. Claire looked around. "I don't see Nicholas, however, so I have to go now. Do you want to wait for me here?"

Alice moaned. "Can't we go somewhere else to solve the mystery?"

"Yes, but first we must find the clues hidden here. I don't know how many clues Zillah left for us. It's like a labyrinth."

"What is a labyrinth?"

"It's a confusing place, like a house with lots of twisting hallways." At Alice's blank look, inspiration struck Claire. "Like the hedge maze. At Raven Heights Manor. When you come to sit at the pond with me, you have to walk through the maze of hedges."

"Ah."

"Think of it as if it were a game. If you take the correct turn, you get to go farther. And you continue to take the correct turns until you reach the summer-house and the pool. But if you don't take the correct turn, what happens?"

Alice did not feel like giggling. With a tremulous grin, she said, "I would run into the hedge. If I didn't have my walking stick with me."

"Exactly!" Claire laughed her encouragement, a hollow sound in the vacuum of the graveyard. "That's how Zillah left her clues. Like a maze. After we find one, we have to go the proper direction to find the next. Else we come to a dead end. If I don't find this clue, we will never know where the next clue lies."

"Like the directions in the first note? About rights and lefts? That's like a maze, too." Alice finished on a soft note, then remained quiet. There was nothing to refute the fact, once she comprehended the analogy of the maze. Still, she looked unhappy.

"I hope you understand. I have to follow up on Zillah's clue about Benjamin. I am sure the next clue must be in the cemetery." Claire noticed the almost indiscernible shivering of Alice's slight body. "I don't hear a ghost inside my head. Do you hear him now?"

"No, but he—"

"So I don't think there's going to be any danger, not for me at least. You wait here. Unless you prefer to return to the inn?"

Alice shook her head no vehemently. "All right. Wait here, and I'll retrieve our next clue, and we'll be back to the inn shortly. You'll see. Would you like—"

Claire had almost asked Alice if the young girl would like a candle lit for herself. How must it be, she wondered for the thousandth time, to live in a land of perpetual darkness? When the sun came up, surely Alice sensed a brightness upon her eyelids? Perhaps a warmth upon her skin, if the clouds allowed it, would be her only way to tell day from night.

"Yes?" Alice was already in twilight as Claire took a step toward the opening in the fence.

"Oh, it was nothing." Candle in one hand, Claire was able to unclasp the gate with the other. "I'll be back as quickly as I can. I promise." As she swung the gate closed behind her, it protested in a loud, slow squeal.

Alice reached out a hand. "Claire." She stood against the opposite side of the iron fence, her small arm pushed between two bars, fingers splayed in the air.

Claire stared at the outstretched hand. Stepping closer, she reached until their fingers touched. Alice slid her fingers up Claire's hand, until she could grasp her friend's hand tightly. "Be safe, Claire," she said in a choked voice. "And hurry."

Chapter Twenty-Five

Claire hadn't any fear whatsoever.

No fear, that is, until Alice had spooked her with mention of a ghost. Nicholas. Who was Nicholas? Could he be another of the Whittaker children?

She shook her head in disgust at herself. She did not believe in ghosts, had never believed in ghosts, so why even speculate on Benjamin's brothers? Surely Alice had overheard the name mentioned some time or another, and it had triggered her imagination. As Claire made an effort to walk heel-to-toe quietly on the gravel, she thought that regardless of where or when Alice had heard the name, wouldn't it be eerie if she found the cluster of Whittaker headstones, and the name Nicholas was carved upon one?

Step by step Claire continued down the central lane of the burial ground. The night made the avenue appear endless, its apex on the moon's horizon. She kept her eye on the small knee-high hedge that neatly bordered both sides of the lane, watching for an opening. The first break in the hedge did denote a side path, where the first row of graves was laid out. Before turning to her right at the intersection, she looked to the left toward the vicarage. Through the far churchyard fence she could barely spy the quiet, dark house.

Aunt Amelia might have thought it looked like her cousin Peter from the front, but there was nothing whimsical to be seen on the darkened planks on this side of the house. Only one attic window relieved the tall walls. Perhaps the original builder did not choose to view a burial site from the parlors and bedrooms.

She looked to the path on her right. If she took this path, and then another right, as the clue commanded, wouldn't that lead her straight back to the fence along the road, from where she'd started? She now doubted whether Zillah's first clue referenced the layout of the cemetery. Still, she would test it. She left the main avenue and started on the lane to her right.

There wasn't much of a path along the row of stones, merely a bumpy, grass-grown trail wide enough for two persons to walk side-by-side. She realized that pallbearers would barely have room to walk with a coffin between them, without trespassing upon the other nearby ancient residents who lay at their feet.

Next right, she said aloud in her head. She could not say why she was hesitant to speak aloud in the silent solitude. Claire willed herself not to think of Nicholas, but the name repeated with every step squished upon the dewy grass. She forced herself to speak aloud—it was more of a murmur. "Are you here, Nicholas?"

Claire gasped. Startled, her breath caught as she came up against a fence. She'd thought it was a person's body at first. Could a ghost have a corporeal manifestation? She willed her heart to slow its hummingbird pace. She'd been so intently studying the ground for the next break in the sequence of stones, for the next path to the right. Instead, she reached the end of this row, and the boundaries of the churchyard blocked her path.

There was no second right turn, or she'd missed it. She retraced her steps to the main alley, carefully scrutinizing each space between the crooked headstones, wondering whether she'd missed a small side pathway. But she hadn't. She stood at the main cemetery crossroad again and raised the candle as she considered.

Returning to the front of the churchyard, she soon saw Alice's silhouette patiently standing not too far away, outside the fence.

"It's me, Alice. I'm back."

"Did you find it?" The relief in Alice's voice was tinged with excitement.

"No." Claire stood opposite Alice, still within the cemetery grounds. "The direction clue didn't work. At least, I don't think so. I followed the path carefully, and I'm quite certain I didn't miss any turns." Claire looked down the lane between the rows of graves. "But maybe we should come back when it's light." She found it difficult to hide the disappointment in her voice.

Perhaps, she considered, *coming back in the morning's daylight would make Alice more comfortable.*

"Would you wish to accompany me on my search here? If we came back to the cemetery in the morning, that is?"

Alice aimed her sightless gaze at the ground. "I can't. I'm sorry." She looked up to clarify. "I mean, I'll come back here with you. As far as the gate. I just can't go inside, Claire. But I'm safe here. I feel it."

"All right." Claire was about to blow out her candle, when she took one last look back. At the end of the peaceful alley of sleeping spirits she thought she could make out the cross bars of the iron fence at the far boundary. "Alice, I think this cemetery is not so large. I should like to try one more plan."

"What is it?"

"I'm going to take my candle once more and see if I can make out the names on the gravestones. It shouldn't take me long to go up and down each row quickly. And if the families are grouped together, as I suspect they will be, then the Whittakers will be located near one another as well." She spoke quickly, her decision made, beginning already to turn toward the graves. "I'll be as fast as I can. If I cannot read the names in this light, to show me where the youngest Whittaker was buried, then we shall return tomorrow."

"I'll be waiting here."

Claire hesitated, but made herself ask, "Have you heard from Nicholas?"

"No. But Nicholas lives inside the cemetery. I don't think I can hear him from outside the gates."

Claire's candle wavered, as did her determination, and she wished she had not asked. "I'm going now."

The gravel avenue crunched with her quick steps back to the first intersection. Turning again to the right at the first hedge opening, she skimmed along the first row of gravestones, her candle held low as she passed each waist-high tablet. Claire was grateful that the crooked stones were at least lined up in rows, albeit haphazardly.

"Joseph Foley," she read aloud. "Jeremiah Foley. Albert Foley."

As she'd suspected, there was a methodical layout. Whether Joseph was Jeremiah's father, son, or brother, she did not care. If she'd had time, she would have read the dates, trying to discern the relationships. But no time for that now. She continued reading the names, focusing now on only the last names, until she reached the iron fence at the end of the row.

Rather than reverse her steps past the same slabs, she turned left to squeeze past the shrubbery that poked through the iron fence. Thus she snaked around to the row behind. Her thought was that if she made her way along this row back toward the center, she would have traversed two rows on the right half. On the opposite side she would continue in similar figure-eight fashion, to navigate the churchyard in one pass, using a minimum of steps. She read the names aloud, moving confidently and methodically.

More Foleys, and here a few Sadlers sprinkled among them. Had a Foley daughter married into the Sadler family? She found herself distractedly fascinated.

Returning to the central lane, Claire next moved to the graves on the left side, quickly skimming the first two rows. More Sadlers now dominated the surrounding turf. And then a brief shock: Coulter! Claire bent forward to read the entire stone. Phoebe Coulter was a thirty-nine-year-old woman, beloved wife and mother, etc.

"We did not live happily ever after,
but we lived happily in short bliss."

She stepped back and stood staring a few moments. The top of the stone was rounded in three shallow scallops, colorless marble rainbows. In the center arch was an angel with short curly hair and a puffy baby face with round, blank eyes. For no reason she could explain, it gave Claire comfort that they had not given Phoebe Coulter a macabre sculpture such as a skull. Claire watched for more Coulters but never saw another.

Thus she continued, covering row upon row in the dark cemetery. If Alice could see, she would have spied a solitary flame flitting in oval paths like a forest fairy, back and forth in the darkness, at gravestone height.

There were more lanes than Claire had anticipated, but she made good progress moving alertly past the weathered gravestones, despite the uneven ground. Once or twice she tripped upon an exposed tree root, tightening her grip upon the fat candle in her fist as she caught her balance.

The next time she reached the central avenue dividing the churchyard, Claire looked toward the rear boundary. She was quickly nearing the final third of the cemetery, by her guess. She could not help sighing, as she'd had no success yet. There would be no reason to return on the morrow if these last lanes yielded no Whittakers. Though she read the stones tonight by the imperfect light of candle and moon, she knew she had not missed any names thus far. The majority had been fairly well chiseled and well preserved. A very few were not legible on the weathered stones, but they looked to be short names, none of a length of characters to be Whittaker, nor in particular Benjamin Whittaker. And of the remaining faint names, there had yet been a sprinkling of enough recognizable letters to eliminate the name she searched for.

Only two rows of graves remained. The burial sites in this area appeared newer, each stone upright and barely weathered, as opposed to the ancient mausoleums guarding the rear of the churchyard, in a death march along the iron fence.

While the stones may have been brighter, it was darker in these last rows due to the ancient oak trees. Their serpentine roots exposed along the ground were a mirror image of the gnarled limbs overhead. Claire had to step carefully, slowing her fruitless search.

She held her candle low, squinting at the first headstone: Cromblehome. Keeping the candle at the same height, she crept to the next: Basset. Each of the remaining graves held a different last name. She did not think she'd already encountered any of these names, but could no longer be sure.

What was Nicholas's last name? she wondered, then superstitiously wished she had not thought of the young man's name, not even in her head.

She hurried to the opposite side. She recognized a name, Littleton, she was most certain she'd read earlier, toward the front of the grounds. Why would this Littleton—Claire read the first name: Louisa. Why had Louisa Littleton been buried away from her family? This touched Claire with sadness, no matter the reason, as she pictured the young girl alone. She moved the candle lower to read the dates, swiping the flame from left to right; birth to death, subtracted one date from the other. Ah,

Louisa Littleton died at the age of eighty-two. Claire moved on, feeling happier for Miss Littleton.

Her happiness was short-lived, however, as her consternation increased with each remaining stone. She walked reverently to the last grave: Ainsworth. Not Whittaker. There were no Whittakers in this churchyard, not a single one.

Claire straightened, putting a hand to massage the small area of her stiff back. She was finished; she would not return. If she'd seen no Whittaker graves tonight, she would certainly not expect to see a piece of paper lying haphazardly on the ground in the morning. Zillah would not have laid a page out in the open where it could be blown randomly around the churchyard like a bleached leaf.

Where is the next clue, Zillah? She picked her steps across the bones of oak trees exposed upon the surface. And why did you point us to Benjamin Whittaker?

It was time to join Alice.

She had barely started back when her pondering gave her pause. What was it that Reverend Hinkle had said? He'd corroborated the existence of Benjamin, had pointed to this very assemblage of permanent residents.

She recalled Reverend Hinkle's words, "Benjamin rests with his grandparents."

The vicar had then turned his portly body and reached across to point a pudgy finger to the cemetery. This cemetery.

Somehow she'd missed it. Benjamin's, and his grandparents as well. Of course, their name might not be Whittaker, if their daughter had married a Whittaker man. So it may be just Benjamin's grave she missed. Her enthusiasm renewed, she decided she must return in the morning for one last try. She would scour the graveyard once more, from the front gate to the rear fence bordering the ancient vaults.

The vaults! She turned around and squinted in the awful

dark. The ancient sentinels with their ornate carvings and bizarre architecture often entombed entire families. She hadn't thought to look at the mausoleums. Logic had argued that the poverty-stricken Whittakers could not have afforded a family tomb. She recalled the vicar had described the family as "poor in the pocket."

Still . . . perhaps generations earlier, the family had been better off, when the first massive crypts were built.

It would only take another minute—surely three at the most—to peruse the dozen or so large structures. Once more she traversed exposed roots, making her way to the far left corner, to the first vault. The ground was damp with decayed leaves that never received the drying rays of the sun.

With her hand held higher this time, to read the first arched entrance in the dark, she had to be careful not to tilt the candle, else she would have hot wax drip upon her. A trio of narrow, pointed lancet openings imitated a doll-size medieval church. Gargoyles leered at her, perched on projecting cornerstone ledges, as she reached up her arm to see the name carved on the tall, middle arch's keystone: *Marsden.*

The next tomb was a miniature Greek temple. Four caryatid columns gracefully held a wide stone gable with large letters as pretentious as the monument itself. *Oddelow* was boldly, deeply etched from one side to the other, using up every inch of the lintel.

Claire would be disheartened not to find the name she'd hoped to discover, but the tombs themselves were certainly fascinating. She smiled to think that she was in a cemetery, admiring family crests by the wane light of the moon.

The third vault—she was not quite halfway down the row—was, of course, of an entirely different architecture. Simple and boxy, it wore decades of scars, and the grey stone was weathered to near illegibility. Except on the capstone above its flat entry. *Whittaker*, she read upon its lintel.

Chapter Twenty-Six

Whittaker. The name was unmistakable. On a flat-roofed vault that was twice the width of the others. She'd almost missed it while studying the intricate urns at each of its corners. A simple Etruscan wreath of stone leaves rose from the center of its roof.

With renewed energy, Claire meticulously explored every inch of the tomb's front exterior, looking for a hidden nook. Holding the candle in one hand, she used the other to smooth her palm and fingers across the old surface, feeling for loose stones, certain she would find a hiding spot with the next clue neatly folded and tucked away from the elements. She spent several minutes perusing the surface, in particular the stones edging its dungeon-like grilled entry.

Zillah! How had you ever found this desolate spot? Claire moved back and forth, careful to scan every area within reach. Though the crypt was taller than she, her logic was that Zillah would only have hidden a clue within her own reach. Not knowing how tall the other young lady had been, Claire hoped her guess was accurate. Next, she circled around to the left wall.

As she rubbed her hand over the surface, holding the candle close to the wall, she thought about Zillah. Claire wished she'd known her. Not just to have a friend her own age, but to have an exceptional friend with such an adventurous imagination. Every word said in memory of Zillah had been kind, lauding her love of mysteries, her enjoyment of each day with playful enthusiasm. Claire felt tears ready to spill, in mourning for the young woman she'd never known.

Swiping the heel of her wrist across her wet eyes, she squinted through tears around the rear corner, at the ground behind the tomb. If she'd been Zillah, she would have found a niche on this back wall, where there was barely room enough to squeeze between the tomb and the nearby iron rails of the cemetery's fence. She didn't like the idea of stepping into that dark crevice, but it made sense as a hiding spot. Claire raised the candle in front of her, swallowed, and squeezed into the narrow space.

In less time than expected, she breathed more deeply as she moved from the back wall to the remaining side wall. Relief mixed with mild disappointment, though she was still hopeful that she was close to success.

Cautiously, lest the hot wax drip down her arm, she moved the light methodically over every imperfection on the right exterior wall. There were no crevices large enough to hold a note. Her probing touch found no loose stones.

This brought her back to the front of the monument, where she shook her head in bafflement. She'd been sure she was on the cusp of discovery. The final clue should have been scratching her palm by now. She'd already envisioned herself moving backward from the cold rock monument, hastening away from the shadowy churchyard to share the clue with Alice.

Claire stepped back and stared, considering. The only spot she hadn't touched was the iron grate that stood as a door into the tomb. But the mesh of iron rods were widely spaced, like a moat gate, and it was obvious nothing was hanging or hidden on their surface. She moved to the grilled door to peer into its dungeon, but it was too dark to see the floor behind. In frustration she smacked a fist against the flat ribbon of the cross bars. The iron hummed with an echoing metallic ring, and astonished Claire as it budged the tiniest bit in response.

She immediately swung her candle to shine its light along the edge of the portal where a lock might have hung, but none was exposed. She nudged the gate softly this time, and watched in amazement as it swung further inward. She was doubly shocked there was no whining squeal of rusted ironwork. The doorway was now open almost enough for her to squeeze through. She hesitated, her breath coming quick, her heart a tribal drum, as if she attended her own sacrifice. It was ever so tempting to explore the four walls inside.

She reached her candle around the grilled gate, lighting the miniature cavern, her feet anchored safely outside. *If I wait for daylight to explore the interior,* she thought, *I shall still need artificial lighting.* Having come this far, Claire swung the gate a little wider and did step inside. The enclosure was not claustrophobic, not yet. From the entry to the back wall was perhaps six steps, and side to side even longer; it looked twice as wide as it was deep, twelve steps at the least. To her dismay she was reliant upon the candle alone, as the moonlight, like Alice, had refused to follow her into the dark cave.

With a sense of déjà vu, she hoped she would not have to spend as much time exploring each of the four interior walls as she'd already wasted on the exterior.

Holding the candle high, she turned to survey the crypt.

The back wall glinted faintly in the flickering light of her candle. Stepping closer, she saw the squares of veined marble, stacked in rows from the height of her knees up to the roughly masoned ceiling. Other than a few feet of stone to either side of the layout of squares, this wall was a mirror-like surface of stacked tombs.

Each polished marble square had a name and date etched upon its glassy surface. Aha—this would be where she would discover the elusive Benjamin, at last. Hurriedly, she scanned each row, moving side to side with her candle, beginning with the lowest row. Mimicking her earlier graveyard quest, she methodically snaked from the end of the first row up to the second. Every square held a Whittaker, and she could now see from the dates why the outside of the structure appeared ancient.

As she reached the top two rows, most of the faces of stone were blank. Either they would no longer reveal their occupants—their faces unreadable, forever sealed with unknown, undocumented Whittakers within—or they were still empty, their closed mouths waiting to be fed more Whittaker bones. But according to the vicar, the last Whittaker had departed. The tomb would never be entered again.

But someone had. They'd entered it recently, and at least once, for the hinges to open so quietly and smoothly.

And then she saw it. The crypt on the far right of the mausoleum, in the second row down from the top. Benjamin Whittaker was carved on one long, single line, with dates below the name. Dates confirming that a very young child rested in a casket behind the solid panel, a child whose life had ended not long after it had begun. Claire placed her free hand beneath the carving. "Hello, little Benjamin," she said in gentle voice, and bowed her head for a handful of moments in respectful silence.

Now an expert at waving the candle with one hand and exploring stone walls with the other, she moved to examine the rough paving of the wall to the right of Benjamin's resting slot. She felt something at the same time her candle picked out the anomaly.

It was too solid to be folded parchment. Not believing her heart could beat any faster, she peered closely, careful not to set her hair on fire. There, set into the wall, outlining the marble tile, was a metal lever. Claire tried pushing and pulling, then stopped when she felt a draft of cooler air.

The candle light showed a darker line of shadow to her right, where a thin faux layer of masonry had swung forward to reveal a hidden passage.

A passage to where? There was only an empty field on the other side of the iron fence she had squeezed by when she had efficiently walked the perimeter of the tomb. And she'd seen no sign of a doorway on the outside of the rear mausoleum wall.

With a disoriented feeling she shifted her flame to light the passage entry, and understood. At the same instant she both guessed and witnessed it: a stairway led down into the earth below the tomb.

She shook her head, telling herself silently that she could not do it. She could go no farther. Her body shook in agreement to her denial of any bravery. But her feet did not heed, and they stepped forward to stand upon the top step. It was no darker in the descending chute, after all, than it had been in the tomb's interior.

The candle in her hand was still thick, not even close to a stub; she decided to descend a bit farther. Halfway down the dry dirt steps, she regretted with vexation the extra candles and tinder box left behind with Alice. And the reminder of Alice made her pause. How long had Claire been gone? It might be selfish to continue. Though, one could justify that Alice most likely had no idea how vast the cemetery grounds were, and might not even expect her back this quickly. Claire bit her lower lip as she deliberated. She was so close to the hidden discovery. Surely it did not make sense to come this close and then return to this very spot the next day. Additionally, it was so dark in here, the morrow's daylight would not assist her once she plunged into the underground.

Having rationalized to her own satisfaction, she moved forward, treading carefully as she descended the worn steps.

The stairway angled steeply into the earth, but the earthen artery was not stifling, to her surprise. There was enough headroom to testify that its builders must have been much taller than she.

Once Claire reached the floor, her candle revealed to her an arrow-straight tunnel. She had hoped to discover a dead-end chamber at the bottom of the steps, the next clue awaiting her. But of course, she reasoned with chagrin, nothing tonight had been as straightforward as one might wish. It would have been too unlike Zillah at this point to provide her sleuths with a piece of parchment lying helpfully in the middle of the earthen floor.

Claire moved her candle from left to right. The walls appeared to be dry. The tunnel's flooring was, thankfully, flat and level. And the headroom was still quite adequate, which she was even more thankful for. She could not bear to have proceeded on her own by crouching within a low, claustrophobic burrow. Even now, she must not acknowledge the tons of heavy earth above her head.

The air here below was colder, with no hint of the draft she'd noted earlier at the first opening of the hidden panel. She took a breath of the still air, then placed one foot tentatively in front of the other. She patted her side, feeling for the bag of candles that had hung at her side the entire walk from Pelican Inn, before she remembered again that the canvas bag no longer hung from her shoulder, but sat uselessly outside the churchyard gates with Alice. Why hadn't she brought the lightweight bag inside the churchyard grounds with her? It did no good for Alice. Without the security of knowing she had fresh candles and tinder, Claire wondered how it would be to find her way back to the stairs in pitch blackness, but forced herself to abandon that thought at once. So far it was simply a straight, level tunnel, thus there was no reason to think the unthinkable, and it was silly to make up problems and add to the anxiety she struggled to ignore.

She focused her attention instead on the tunnel walls on either side. They were somewhat smooth, and could therefore hide no clues. She glanced at the floor of the walkway constantly as she moved ahead, not only to avoid stumbling, but also to look for any clues tucked along the rounded edge where walls met the tunnel's base. Not forgetting the high tunnel ceiling above, she waved the candle up high occasionally, in case Zillah had scratched the next clue on the ceiling. This made her grin as she realized that without something to stand upon, Zillah—unless she was at least seven feet tall—could never have scribbled on the ceiling. For that matter, how had Zillah ever even discovered this tunnel? Or the passageway lever next to Benjamin, or the Whittaker crypt? It was so ludicrously coincidental. None of it made any sense.

Almost immediately, her right hand brushed across an open space. She stopped and stepped back to illuminate the smaller opening. Both arms stretched straight as a sleepwalker's, she waved the candle as she groped the air to determine whether it was a false turn into a dead end of stone. It was not. It was a true fork in the tunnel.

Claire stopped to consider. Whichever way she took, she must be extremely careful to be able to retrace her steps.

Still she stood indecisive, until realizing Zillah had given her the answer. A right turn, another right, and then the second left. It hadn't referred to the cemetery lanes after all. It must apply to this tunnel deep beneath the ground.

A distinct current of air wafted from the branch on the right. "Two right turns," whispered Claire, shuddering at the soft echo wafting in the closed space.

Finding no rock wall to block her path, her feet shuffled forward down the right branch, her fingers stretched ahead. Claire hesitated, looking over her shoulder. She disliked leaving the main tunnel behind. But the faint light she carried was enough to give a slight illumination to this branch. Placing her hand again on the wall to her right, afraid she would miss the next small opening in the dark, she continued forward. *Just one more right,* she said to herself, and then the second left. The walls began a slight curve back toward the left, to parallel the original tunnel, but the two never did rejoin.

As she slowly ambled, she considered where the conduit might be leading her. Her initial descent into the crypt's passage had aimed toward the cemetery's rear boundary. Considering this tunnel path veered a bit to the right, then curved to continue in the original linear line, she should now be heading even farther from the cemetery's front gate, angling farther away from the road to the village. So . . . What lay in this direction, beyond the farthest ornamental ironwork?

The sea. And the manor cliffs of Raven Heights.

Very soon the tunnel exited into a surprisingly sized cavern. About twelve feet in each direction, her first thought was a root cellar, but then she laughed a short, abrupt laugh that echoed around her. A root cellar accessed via a cemetery? With a hidden handle to access the vicar's turnips and carrots? Hardly likely.

From the back of her mind bubbled a recollection. She saw Roman reclining lazily—insolently, more likely—by the dolphin fountain. "Buried treasure" was the phrase Roman had used that morning, telling Alice of illegal goods hidden beneath a blanket of sand on the beach. *Or caves,* he had said, to keep the goods dry, above water level, and to preserve the contraband at cooler temperatures. Her eyes did not focus on this cave, but on the caves Roman had described. She remembered he had said that tunnels and cliff caves were part of the smugglers' web. Secretive places where barrels could be hauled up and safely stored.

Certainly, she'd discovered a former storage room used by pirates ages ago. This tunnel would end high above the sea, in a hole on the face of a cliff, where no one would notice a barrel slithering up, hoisted in a sling of ropes. Alice had been mesmerized by Roman's tales. How unfortunate she could not explore this room with Claire.

Claire decided she would bring Alice to experience this amazing site tomorrow, if the enticement could outweigh the little girl's fear of imaginary ghosts. They could even invite Roman and Vitus along, making a ghoulish picnic of the adventure. Surely Roman would be amazed to find surviving evidence of an actual smuggler's den.

Had her own ancestors been smugglers? Was Raven Heights built with pirates' gold? The idea fascinated Claire as she realized they may have hauled their barrels up by the secretive light of the moon, up the cliff's side and into the mouth of a tunnel, a tunnel that ended in the cemetery, where no one would ever suspect a cache of barrels stored beneath an ancient crypt.

As she paced from one edge of the room to the other, scanning the floor, she spied no telltale signs of what the illicit goods had been, no glass shards or maroon stains from remnants of wine bottles; no dried remnants of tobacco leaves. She could not remember what other items Roman had mentioned as profitable.

On the opposite wall loomed two darker holes. Approaching closer with her candle, she discovered each small archway was three or four feet wide. She slowly moved the candle forward to ascertain their depth.

They might only be smaller storage chambers, to separate some specific goods from those in the larger storage room. But it seemed more likely, Claire realized with an unsettling combination of excitement and dread, that the tunnel would continue, and lead to the sea cliff. Else, her theory of a pirate's conduit for goods was incorrect, as well her assumption that Zillah was leading her to the next branch of tunnels in this buried maze.

Two choices, so of course she must take the rightmost, to

satisfy the legacy of the clue. She thrust her candled arm into the interior of the opening on the right, to shed light upon its size. The walls and floor appeared even more smoothly finished than the tunnel she had exited from. The ceiling would almost brush the top of her head, but she would not need to stoop, so she stepped gingerly into the entry and moved forward.

This second tunnel began an almost imperceptible upward slope. And she was able to traverse it much more quickly, due to its improved surface. She imagined she smelt the faint brine of the sea. If she continued to ascend, and if her hunch was accurate, she should eventually drop into the water, assuming this tunnel continued in its current direction to the face of the cliffs. It was impossible, though, to detect direction in the dark underground with absolute conviction.

She had hardly navigated this slightly inclined branch, her left hand now groping along the wall, before she almost fell into an empty space on her left. She yanked her free hand back lest this narrow dark crevice prove to be a nest for spiders. Stopping, she thrust the candle to probe into the vertical fissure. It did not appear to continue angling upward. It looked flat and narrow. Too narrow for comfort.

Mentally, Claire reviewed her expedition thus far. From the tunnel's straight entrance, she had taken the first small branch to the right, prior to finding the storage chamber. Once in the storage chamber, she'd chosen the right exit of the two on its back wall.

She was currently walking that smooth tunnel with its upward slope. By her reckoning, she must therefore ignore this first left and take the next. Shuddering, it was easy to convince herself she should not squeeze into this rift in the cavern wall, barely enough for a body as slight as hers. Her imaginary pirate would never fit his cutlassed girth into this fissure.

She wondered if the next opening on her left would reveal a

similar constrictive gash in the wall hiding her clue and ending tonight's search, or whether the next left would be her exit to the precipice. Either would be a relief.

Ignoring this opening, Claire drifted forward in the inhospitable dark, a cocoon of light floating along. Occasional tight spaces triggered an inexplicable panic of claustrophobia as the height or the width of the tunnel would suddenly narrow. But she kept breathing steadily, and she was soon rewarded as the pathway opened up to its earlier generous dimensions. She must also keep an eye on the ceiling. Several times she stooped just in time to avoid jagged rocks that had not been smoothed away.

There were changes in this section, convincing her she approached closer to the sea. The tunnel walls glistened slightly and felt moist to the touch as she trailed her hand along the surface, which was still rock-hard. And she detected a distinct draft of cooler air. She glanced down and noted that the floor of the tunnel reflected the new dampness, like packed sand left as a wave recedes.

The dank walls and the slight breeze might also signify a crevice leading from tree roots above. She thought she could hear faint dripping sounds, the tiny splash of a water droplet in a muddy hole along the tunnel's floor, echoing like distant music.

She remembered a tale from when she was young. She'd listened with fascination as a traveler had told her parents of his visit to a faraway land, a land where monks in saffron-colored robes filed past a giant Buddha statue lying on its side. Along the length of the reclining mammoth effigy, which filled the length and height of the temple, were gold coin bowls of different depths and circumferences. As coins were dropped in each of the Buddha's offering bowls in succession by the faithful who filed past, a melody rang: musical rain drops.

Claire screamed as something dropped onto her head. Like

Alice, she had an unreasonable fear of spiders, and she swiped a hand through her hair. It was only water, where a blob now lay matted on her scalp. A second cold drip plopped from the center of the ceiling, and she moved to one side, lest it extinguish her candle flame. The thought of traversing back to the entrance in total darkness panicked her; Claire deliberated returning toward the crypt's dry entrance posthaste.

Her thoughts raced with other threats. She saw in her mind the gate she'd left ajar. What if a late caretaker should notice and close the gate or, worse, lock it? Her heart began to hammer, its beat reflecting in her dry throat.

Her desire to turn back struggled with her more immediate desire, which was weighted by her instinctive belief that she must be near the end of this tunnel, and of her journey. Her anticipation of fresh air ahead made her decision. The need to breathe, even if it meant balancing at the edge of a sea cave. Thus she blanketed her dread and hurried her steps along the smooth floor.

Her eyes were becoming accustomed to the dimness, she realized with wonder. Or . . . Was it becoming lighter in the cave? Claire squinted; it was in fact a bit lighter ahead. As she felt her way forward, wishing it to not be her imagination, hope became her lantern, growing steadily. The cave walls glittered in response to a higher level of light. Rounding a corner, the abrupt shaft of light frightened her.

A beam of moonlight pierced the ceiling fissure from above, throwing its spirit spotlight onto the tunnel floor. She stood in the cool light, staring into the miniscule crack several feet above her head. It meant she was near the surface, about to leave this underground grave at last. But Claire found herself hesitant to leave the welcoming light, instead allowing it to cleanse her in the dank cave. There was no warmth to the light. If this was all the stingy moon could offer her, it was enough.

Standing hypnotized in the soft light would not help her escape. Should clouds blanket the moon, the cave would plunge into total darkness again, with only her flickering candle to light her way. With a strong reluctance, Claire moved forward, returning to a Styxian river of darkness.

She was not surprised to see another fork in the tunnel, hopefully the last. Without hesitation she hurried into this second left branch, thus fulfilling Zillah's prophecy.

Chapter Twenty-Seven

The dim moonlight lay behind her, and Claire's eyes had to re-accustom themselves to the sparser candlelight. This branch had a displeasing odor, wafting on the slightest of breezes, but it was not the salty tang of sea air. Perhaps it was the stagnant pools collected by damp walls dripping ceaselessly onto the floor, but she found it more cloying than the smell of mud.

Before her adjustment to a lower luminescence became complete, she was shocked to find herself tripping upon an obstacle lying in the center of the tunnel, which sent her flying blindly forward. Claire grasped the candle tightly as she fell. She could only reach out to brace herself with one hand, her knuckles painfully scraping the rock wall. She dropped to her knees, the heel of her palm painfully bruised on the hard flooring, her knees throbbing with the impact.

Melted candle wax dribbled painfully onto the knuckle of her thumb. She cried out but did not release her hold on the candle. Claire panted loudly, waveringly, trying to keep the tears at bay. She concentrated on inhaling and exhaling until her heartbeat returned to normal. She still had light. She still had light, she repeated to the beat of her thumping heart.

She got to her feet unsteadily and turned to investigate what had caused her stumble.

A small, dark mound blocked the tunnel path. It appeared to be discarded clothing. Or a small animal. Claire stepped closer. She squatted, but thought better of it and stood so that she might escape more quickly should it be an animal, should it still be alive. Her candle was stretched forward on a stiff arm, as far in front of her body as possible, while she leaned back and away. The bundle had not moved, had not made a sound. Claire crept gingerly a step or two toward it. The candlelight wavered as she held her breath. She gradually leaned another few inches forward from the waist, her arm trembling as she held the candle closer.

It was an animal. Claire recoiled, but it did not attack her. She waited patiently another full minute, imagining that it moved with each undulation of her flame. When the creature still hadn't inched any farther, she nudged it with her toe. No response.

Once more she placed the toe of her half boot against the dark fur. She grimaced as she hesitantly rolled the animal over. It remained as motionless as before. The decay of the small body would explain the sweet, fetid odor. Feeling safer, she squatted again, brought the candle nearer. And gasped.

Claire recognized the smallest of the recent litter belonging to the gardener, Jacoby. The undersized puppy that Vitus had chosen to take home. But something was wrong. She held the candle much closer, careful not to singe the fur surrounding the glazed, moistless eyes. The dead puppy's head was queerly flat. Only then did she see the large rock next to its tiny body. She glanced up. Was there another break in the earth, invisible to her in the dark ceiling, but wide enough for a small curious puppy to fall through? Had it tumbled into the tunnel through an opening in the ground and hit its head? With dawning revulsion, she knew that was not what had happened to the unfortunate animal. Someone had smashed the rock deliberately on the small dog's head.

This was Vitus's puppy, and he had not even mentioned it had gone missing. That turned her insides cold.

Alice perceived Vitus as kind; she'd said so with assurance. And Claire had yet to see unkindness overtly manifested in the silent younger brother. Yet Bethany had known him longer, and her recent warning echoed in Claire's head, even as Claire remembered suspecting that Vitus—dark, brooding Vitus—had patiently befriended Alice in order to discern how much the young girl knew of Zillah's death.

To kill a small animal required a meanness that was disturbing. A puppy could not be threatening; it was impossible for a sane person to begin to imagine what pleasure could be found in destroying a small animal that could not escape or defend itself. Claire felt sick.

As well, she found it shameful to admit to herself that she had recently felt an attraction to Vitus.

When she'd first come to Raven Heights, Roman had been her charming confidant. She demurred in the face of his audacious flirting, even as she found it flattering. What innocent orphan would not find the un-asked-for attention welcoming? Claire had never known the compliments of a man, the sensuous whispering tickle in her ear when he leaned in so closely his shoulder touched hers.

Yet over the weeks of her stay at her uncle's home, she found it more enticing to covertly observe Vitus. At first it was sympathy, as he quietly took Roman's barbs with what she assumed was helplessness. Slowly, she came to admire his stoic aloofness, his commendable choice to ignore without disdain or rancor. And she studied his eyes when she could do so without being caught. He had intelligent eyes, framed in his dark face by darker lashes. Sometimes, she would watch him as the threesome sat near the fountain, as he studied the fish flashing in the sun-dappled water. Then his eyes would look up with no warning, directly at her, and she would glance away with a blush. Fortunately, this seemed to escape Roman's notice, else the elder brother would surely recede into his pouting display. Roman began to seem wearily transparent, the more his brother became opaquely mysterious.

Claire shook her head in the dark tunnel. She could not possibly be attracted to someone capable of bludgeoning an animal. And though she had believed Roman to be the bully, based on his browbeating of his brother, that intimidation paled in comparison to this heinous act. She refused to ponder any longer on Vitus, if he could have fooled her so well. She stared at the dark, matted fur of the puppy, where blood had stained its skull as it lay dying.

The puppy had not even been born while Zillah was still alive, so it was not the puppy Zillah wanted her to find. Claire vowed to hastily complete this night's work, though the lighthearted adventure had taken a dismal turn.

In the dark corner behind the puppy was another . . . crevice? Junction? The poor little thing had been so close to escaping its fate, if it could just have crawled through the narrow opening, where a person would be hard pressed, literally, to fit. As Claire stood with her candle, the light caught a glimmer in the tight space. Caches of gold still on her mind, she stepped over the dead puppy's body as she moved inquisitively closer to the opening.

The glint reflected a brass-buckled belt. What an odd space to stuff a change of clothing. Now she could pick out a pair of shoes, dark trousers—Claire screamed when she saw the exposed bone connecting the hem of the pants to the shoes.

She stepped away, gingerly stepped back over the puppy and moved along the tunnel until the smell was not so strong, not sure she could ever wholly erase the smell that was now an inseparable part of the imprinted memory.

How long would it take a body to reach this state, in the cool underground of the tunnel? If exposed to vermin and beetles

. . . She willed herself not to gag. This must have been the smell the puppy was investigating when caught in the act.

It was not Zillah stuffed so callously into the crevice; they had found Zillah's body. And these clothes were masculine. She knew it wasn't the child Benjamin Whittaker. Claire knew no other young males connected with this dark game. Was this nameless victim the reason Zillah led her here? To a murdered victim, not to a golden trove, nor to another clue?

There would be no remaining clues, she now knew. Zillah must have discovered the secret of the dead person, must have known his death was no accident. But why not immediately tell someone what she'd found, why leave cryptic clues about something as serious as a murder? Even for someone who loved games and puzzles, this made no sense.

Claire's brow wrinkled as she tested different scenarios. Zillah had been here and left at least once, to have written the directions. Vitus knew, at least after the fact, that the directions had been given to Alice in a note. He need not have translated the foreign words correctly for Claire and Alice, unless confident the connection would never be made to tie the words to the cemetery vault.

Suicide must now be eliminated, for why come here, then exit to leave clues, if her original plan had been to creep along the maze only to throw herself over the open ledge into the surging water? A suicide note would have served the purpose better than elusive hints.

Zillah must have spied Vitus entering the hallowed entrance, to know that it was here. At first she might have thought the hidden caves a lark, until she happened to discover the murdered body too late to save herself. However, unless she had foreseen her own death in the dark tunnel, why leave clues at all with the caveat "unless she never came back"? At some point, the situation must have become bleak, else the timeline did not make sense to Claire.

Claire stared ahead into the darkness, unable to banish Zillah's image from her mind, even though she had no idea what the young woman looked like. In her mind's eye Zillah was the same height as her, faceless, as all Claire could picture was a slim body lying face-down in the water, lifting with each swelling of the sea, and dropping into the abyss between the waves, long dark tresses spreading about her head like curling octopus tentacles.

Claire was sure she now heard the sound of waves breaking not too far from where she stood, their dull reverberation felt through the rock, the thunder of rolling waves touching her hearing and rhythmically receding into silence.

After they'd pulled Zillah's cold body to shore, they would have assumed her head had cracked upon the rocks below. But Claire now knew Zillah had already been dead, before the bloodless body had been dropped from the cliff opening above. She made herself glance toward the puppy again, and the large blood-stained rock near its head. Claire suspected, with gagging horror, that Vitus had done the same to Zillah, when she came here the last night of her life. It could have been this same lifeless rock that spilled the life from Zillah.

Clair knew this, as she knew she would be next. Wasn't this why Vitus had insisted she memorize the turnings in the twisting tunnel? To trap her at this same spot, where she followed his directions as faithfully as the little puppy had followed him, until Vitus became bored and lured to the excitement of cruel violence? She turned wildly around, expecting to feel her own skull being smashed in by a rock. She had to return to Alice. Now. Her breathing was painful, and her near-sobs audible, reverberating from the wet walls.

It was then she heard the echo.

Chapter Twenty-Eight

"Claire?"

The deep male voice reverberated through the chambers. Was it Vitus? She strained to hear the timbre; Vitus's voice was deeper than Roman's, but the cave added a resonance that was difficult to pierce.

Please, please, please, let it be Roman. As much as Roman could annoy her, she'd never wanted to see him so badly.

But of course it could not be the older brother come to her rescue, as Roman could never guess she was here. It was Vitus who'd made sure she memorized the twisting directions, who knew these tunnels well. Vitus knew exactly where he wanted to lead her, as surely as a shepherd herds the trusting sheep on the day they are destined for slaughter.

Claire was not even sure which direction the call came from. It might have come drifting to her from the unexplored darkness ahead. But it could also be coming from the tunnels behind and bouncing off the cave walls in front of her. One thing she was sure of: unless the echoes came from ahead, her pursuer blocked the way back to the crypt, effectively trapping her. Claire forced herself to breathe deeply and concentrate, scrutinizing her options. If he approached from the mausoleum entry, she might have time to quickly duck back, this instant, to the last fork and hide in the alternate tunnel. Prior to that was the storage cellar, which must surely be more distant than the approaching visitor.

She did not want to go forward toward the cliff. It would be too convenient should he plan to push her over the edge, to the teeth of the rocks below. But could she be any more helpless at the cliff than standing here, an exposed bug in the light of her flame? She brought the candle to her mouth, puckering her lips to blow out the light. Found she could not do it. She must wait to know whether her pursuer carried a candle or a lantern, because if so she would be exposed the same whether she ditched her small source of light or chose to keep it.

She looked around wildly. The passageway was wider along this stretch where the puppy lay. The damp walls curved bell-like, outward from the narrow ceiling toward the floor, in the hint of a pyramidal shape.

If her seeker had no light, and if she extinguished hers, she might hunch down along the ground where it met the slanting wall, and thus have the slightest chance of elusion. If he should amble on past without seeing her huddling, she could race back to the crypt entry. Race was not the correct word. If she had no light, she'd be groping blindly as she hurried along, arms stretching ahead to avoid a concussive collision with a rock wall, hands scrambling along the sides to find the tunnel branchings on her reversed path.

"Claire?" The caves echoed: *Claire. Claire.* "Are you here?" the voice rumbled loudly, closer.

She squinted furiously in both directions. Still she saw no light, not even a dim glow signaling the pending approach of a lighted assailant. Was it possible he traversed the passages without a light? With that realization, Claire made her decision. She blew out her candle and pressed herself against the cold rightmost wall, hugging it as she slithered down to the floor, to wedge herself into the damp space where the wall angled out to meet the floor. Crouching down, she hoped to avoid groping hands that might be tracing the walls at chest height.

As the caller came closer, she tried desperately to breathe without making a sound. If only she could discern for certain whose voice called. But the hollow tunnel continued to distort and bounce the words back to her, its owner unrecognizable. And to add to the dizzying confusion, her heartbeat drummed too loudly in her ears.

"Claire?" There was a pause as the speaker waited for a response. Then, in a concerned voice, he added, "I've come to help you, Claire."

She was afraid to answer. Claire might pray it was Roman who came to her rescue, but feared with a bitterness it was Vitus who stalked her. Had Vitus given the same directions to Zillah, driving her toward a point in the cave where there were no further openings? A place where no one could hear her beg for mercy? A place where no one could hear her screams?

She heard soft footsteps approaching. The steps were slow and cautious, intermingled with an occasional musical drip of water. A thump confused her, until she suspected it was her pursuer tripping over the small dog's body. That was the only warning she had that the person was frighteningly close to where she stretched quietly prone. She had an instinct to curl into a defensive position, to pull her knees to her chest, but forced herself to remain prostrate and vulnerable. A shoe scuffed the floor as it passed her head. She closed her eyes, afraid to look. She bit her lip as she held her breath, so that she would not whimper in anticipation of a rock descending heavily to crush her head.

Miraculously, the steps moved past her. They began to recede in the tunnel ahead.

"Claire, can you hear me?"

It was Roman! Her tense shoulders slumped in relief and she opened her eyes though it made no difference. "Roman!" she cried, stifling a sob.

"I'm here, Claire. Where are you?"

She heard the panicked relief in his voice.

"I'm here, Roman. Don't leave me in the dark. Please. I'm behind you." Her voice did break this time. She thought she heard an echoing clink of metal on the rock floor. Then she detected his shadow passing her, creeping slowly in the other direction, and she reached out blindly for his leg. "I'm here. On the floor." Her hand grazed his calf. When he halted, she moved her hand up to his knee as she struggled to sit.

Roman grabbed her hand on his knee, clasped it tightly with both of his. "Claire." He sobbed her name. "Thank goodness I found you. Thank goodness." He drew her up and hugged her fiercely. He held her close, his face buried in her neck. His whisper was more of a moan. "I thought I'd lost you. I thought I was too late, Claire."

Chapter Twenty-Nine

"Did you see Alice?"

He released her from his smothering embrace, one hand still protectively upon her shoulder in the dark. "Alice? Where? Is she safe?"

"Yes. But I thought you would have—She was outside the cemetery gates. She said she would wait for me."

"That's odd. I didn't see her."

When Claire inhaled with a worried gasp, he squeezed her shoulder. "Don't worry. I was hurrying, and it was dark. You know how quiet she can be. I'm sure I simply missed her small form blending in with the shrubbery along the fence. We will go to her together, and put her mind at ease. And yours. At the entry gate, you said?"

"That's where I left her. But I don't know how you could have entered the cemetery without practically stepping over her. Unless . . ."

"Unless what?"

"Is there another way out? Did you come from another entrance?"

He paused, pondered for several seconds. "If there is another entrance, I'm not aware of it. Why would you think that?"

She laughed hollowly. "It's nothing, just my imagination. I was thinking that if this were a smuggler's cave, there might be an exit near the coastline." She crossed her arms, rubbing her hands on her upper arms for warmth. "It's cold in here. Do you suppose we are below Raven Heights Manor?"

Again Roman paused, as if looking around in the pitch blackness would reveal true north. "We must be. You have an excellent sense of direction, even in the dark."

"No, I'm totally confused now that I've taken these turns. Speaking of the dark, I don't suppose you brought a light of any sort? I had a candle, but . . ." Should she admit she was hiding from Vitus? "I have no way to relight it."

"I do have a lantern. Let me fetch it. I set it down up ahead, when I heard you." She felt his hand drop from her shoulder. "Wait," he said. His hand slid down her arm, took her smaller hand in his. "On second thought, come with me. It's over here." He tugged her toward what she thought of as the cliffside direction. "I find myself unable to risk losing you again in the dark. It's just a few steps this way."

Taking small steps, she followed on his heels about ten feet along the tunnel, to the spot where he'd turned when she first called to him. The toe of his boot rang tinnily against a metallic object, and he bent to retrieve a lamp.

Before releasing her hand, he said, "Your hands feel like ice. We must get you out of this damp tunnel as soon as possible."

She listened as Roman tinkered with the lantern, and it was with relief she had to close her eyes against the sudden brightness of the flame.

She opened her eyes gradually, meeting his eyes over the warm amber light. "Why were you traversing the tunnels in the dark, if you had a lantern with you?"

"I thought I heard echoes ahead of me, but I couldn't be sure whether it was you or . . . Someone else." Neither of them had yet to say his brother's name aloud. "I extinguished it a couple of minutes before I found you. And what of your candle? Shall we light it as well?"

Claire glanced behind to where she'd huddled near the floor

to hide, but it was too dark outside the lantern's ring of light to see where she'd left her candle. "No. I don't think that's necessary, as we have your lantern now."

Looking back at Roman, she found him staring at her, and she returned his gaze unabashedly. The bright light of the lantern was as welcome to her as the sunshine breaking through the clouds after a dark, thundering night, and she was not willing to be the first to leave its warm cocoon.

"How did you—" Claire began.

"Why did you—" Roman said at the same time.

They both laughed briefly, nervously.

"You first," said Claire with a crooked smile.

"No. After you. Please." His eyes were warm in the golden light.

"Roman, why are you here? If you didn't see Alice, how did you know I was here? And how on earth did you find me in this tunnel?"

Roman laughed. "One question at a time. I told you once that I often walk the cliffs at night. I had this instinct, Claire. I won't admit to following you. I haven't," he promised at her alarmed look, touching her arm reassuringly. "I have not been skulking after you everywhere you go. But I do believe we have an affinity between us. Tonight you were on my mind more than usual. I saw a light in the cemetery. Of course I had no idea it was you. I saw the light moving toward the rear of the cemetery, and then I lost its track. When I made my way through the graveyard, the gate to one of the mausoleums was ajar. And I saw the cavern stairs. I heard someone up ahead of me and doused my lantern, thinking it might be . . . someone I did not want to make my presence known to."

Claire listened attentively, wondering if Vitus was also lurking in the cavern, but all she could hear were the distant drops of water, echoing hollowly. Making a forlorn sound: *doip.*

"And what of you?"

"What?" Claire had been staring at the dark tunnel ahead.

"What brought you here?" asked Roman. "I can't begin to imagine how you came to be at the cemetery."

"I was following Zillah's instructions." She saw him tense.

"Zillah? What instructions are you talking about?"

"Zillah left a . . . a note." There was no reason to bring Alice's name into the explanation, lest they should both be chastised for their silly quest. "The note said which way to turn at each junction of the tunnel."

"Do you have it with you?" Roman's voice was intense. "Can I see it?"

"It no longer exists. Do you suppose she was in here? She must have been. And how did you know which turns to take once you entered the tunnel?"

"What do you mean it no longer exists? What did you do with it, Claire?" He sounded angry. "It could be evidence."

"*I* didn't do *anything* with it," she said in a defensive tone matching his in volume. "Why should you suppose I disposed of it willy-nilly? If you want to know where it is, ask your brother."

Even in the semi-darkness, Claire saw the pallor of his skin, the pained expression.

She wondered if it was time to tell him the worst of her discoveries. Instead, she blurted out, "He threw the note onto the bonfire, that day you came upon us by Jacoby's cottage."

Roman looked confused, or perhaps thinking furiously, his brow furrowed. "That makes sense. Of course he would destroy it." He looked at her, as if knowing they were both coming to the same conclusion. "You asked how I knew which turns to take. I also had a copy of those same instructions, only mine did not come from Zillah. I found them on the floor of the wardrobe, under a small rug." He was studying her reaction as he added, "In my brother's bedroom."

This did not surprise Claire, but she had to ask, "What made you think to look in his bedroom?"

"Not for a map, I can tell you that. But I had a feeling he's been hiding something. Ever since Zillah's death."

"But why didn't you confide in me? You knew that Alice and I were trying to discover clues about Zillah's whereabouts that night."

"But I hardly knew you. More importantly . . ." He paused. "I did not know how close you'd become to my brother. I didn't know if I could trust you with that information."

Claire felt herself blush in the dark. With a taste of guilt, she knew he was right. She'd been attracted to the tall, silent Vitus from the first moment they'd met in the gardens. Even as he'd annoyed her. She touched her palm in wonder, remembering the sting of the nettle, and how the reddish weals had smarted for hours. So long ago. In contrast, tonight she was numb to any feeling.

Roman reached out to Claire, his hand protectively on her shoulder. "I was afraid I'd be too late." He moved his warm hand up to massage her neck as he said, "Vitus was not in his room tonight." He pulled her closer, mindful of the lantern held to the side. "Oh, Claire, I could not lose you like I lost Zillah."

Claire knew a sudden stabbing of fear. Vitus knew that Alice was the original keeper of Zillah's clue. He had come upon Claire and Alice by the bonfire, had reprimanded Alice for retaining the paper. And now Alice should have been at the cemetery gate. She and Roman must find Alice, ensure the little girl was protected, before Vitus could harm her.

She pulled back from his hug. "Roman! I found something. A body." She shivered in his arms. "It's disgusting. What kind of person would do such a thing?"

Roman moved his hands to her upper arms, held her the

slightest bit away from his body. "Are you going to tell anyone?"

"What do you mean? I realize he's your brother, but—Roman! How can we not?" Claire searched his face, wondering if he was still planning to protect his younger brother. His blue eyes looked darker in the tunnel, probably because the pupils dilated to compensate for the low visibility.

"I wish you'd had a different answer, Claire. I really do." Now his eyes looked near-black, his pupils two large midnight coins. "Because it means I have to kill you."

Claire, in shock, backed up until the opposite wall pressed wetly against her shoulder blade. In panic, she looked toward the crevice, and decided to bluff. "Because of the death of a small dog? You are teasing me. That is not funny, Roman."

She thought for a moment he bought the mistake, as he lifted his lantern toward the small puppy's body lying several feet behind them. She could see his eyes squinting, deciding whether she'd seen the other body in the crevice behind. Seconds stretched to hours until he turned back to her.

"Very clever, Claire. But I think we both know what you saw."

"I saw nothing! That is what I shall say. I promise, I won't breathe a word of it. Not to any soul."

"Claire, Claire." He looked sincerely saddened. "I could have lived with your suspecting Vitus of Zillah's death. Rather, *you* could have lived. Because it could never be proven, after all this time. I just wish I'd removed the second body, but I couldn't allow more tell-tale flotsam—or was she jetsam?—to be found floating on the morning's tide. Yes, I should have disposed of it months ago. But I hesitated. I thought if the body were further decomposed, the bullet wound might not be visible. Or maybe they can always tell. I don't really know. Regardless, the last time I glanced in at him, he was still identifiable as himself, and the mortal wound was still obvious. Too soon for me to throw him over the cliff into the sea."

She could hear her father's voice: *One of the two men always lies.* Too late, she knew Roman was the liar.

"But I never guessed," he spat with bitterness, "that witch Zillah would leave clues so easy to trace."

In desperation, Claire must take his side, must prove her support. "I can help you dispose of it! We can toss the remainder into the sea. Or, what if we bury it tonight?" She felt ill, discussing a dead human being like yesterday's decaying manure, or the turning of compost. "No one will know. Maybe you didn't trust Zillah to tell about the body, but you know you can trust me." She sounded hysterical to her own ears.

"Why, Claire, you could have assisted me in my life of crime. You are a clever girl."

They both knew Claire was only pleading for her life.

"Regardless," he said, looking again toward the creviced sepulchre, "Zillah never even knew about this body."

"Then why . . . ?" Claire missed a major thread. "Why did she have to die?"

"She saw the storage room." He shrugged. "I had no choice."

"But I saw it, too. There was nothing in it."

"Not tonight. It's empty, yet it was chock-full when Zillah spied upon me. Overflowing with very, very valuable goods. Most of it smuggled." He looked at Claire. "Much of it stolen."

"You stole it? Were you smuggling as well as thieving?"

"It is easy for you to judge, living up at the manor. But I don't plan on living the same modest life as my father and every other farmer in this district. I deserve more, and I plan to take what I deserve."

She chose not to contradict his impression that she had lived a privileged life. Instead, she said, "And so that you could live the life you claim you deserve, she had to die?"

"I would have been hanged had it been learnt."

Claire ignored his rationalization. "Whose body is that?"

"What a morbid question. Do you wish to see it up close? I can show—"

"No!"

"I met him in the cave that night. As I was retracing my steps back to the entrance. He told me he'd seen Zillah enter and asked had I seen her. I'm sure he supposed we were having a harmless liaison. But I knew when her body washed up, he would be able to connect me to the incident. I couldn't let him live after he knew that."

He won't let me live, either. She knew with certainty that she would be Roman's next victim. His last? A terrible thought struck her at once: Alice might be vulnerable.

"You realize Alice will not be able to identify you this night. Don't hurt her. Leave her alone."

"Maybe."

"Roman, please. She knows nothing. I dragged her along with me to see the cemetery at night. She would not even come inside the gates. If you did not see her, I'm sure she is already home and asleep. She knows nothing about these tunnels. Or this tomb. She could never find it in a hundred years. Your secret dies with me."

He began talking to himself in a monotone, as if he'd heard nothing of what she'd said. "Shall they find *your* body? I haven't decided. I thought I would have all night to decide, you see, but not if Alice goes tattling that you are still in the cemetery. I have less time than I thought I would." He sounded mildly annoyed.

Unfortunately for Claire, this meant he would soon be tiring of their conversation.

"I could carry you to the cliff cave and drop you into the sea. That's what I did with Zillah. I killed her here, right where we are standing. Then I carried her to the mouth of the cave. They say people who are unconscious are heavy. But she was light.

Surprisingly light, like a hollow-boned sparrow."

Claire had more questions. Part of her screamed that it did not matter, none of it mattered, should her brain and her body die tonight. But she thought of it as her last demand, her last sustenance, before her execution.

"Who is that?" She pointed.

Roman's voice was dulled by boredom. "Are you thinking to postpone your death by engaging me in these useless questions?"

"No," she said truthfully. "You owe me this much, Roman." He snorted in ridicule, but she persisted. "Why did he come here the night you killed Zillah?"

"He said he'd come to say goodbye. Before he left for Africa."

The realization twisted in her stomach like a knife. *"You killed Calden Coulter?"*

He shrugged in the semidarkness but chose not to answer her accusation.

"Oh, my God," she cried aloud. "Bethany will be devastated."

"I don't think so. For how is she to learn about her father? Not from you."

Through this entire nightmare, Claire had been brave. Now she found tears running uncontrollably down her face as she thought of Bethany. "I still don't understand. Why was Calden Coulter saying goodbye to you?"

He laughed noiselessly, his mouth twisted in derision by the light of the lantern. "Not to me. To his wife."

"But Bethany's mother—Ah, yes." Bethany remembered the single Coulter stone she'd read earlier but could not remember the woman's Christian name. It seemed like a memory from weeks ago. It could not possibly have been within the last hour.

But then the name did come to her. "Phoebe. Phoebe Coulter." She remembered the short verse carved below the young woman's name, and recalled the words aloud: *"We did not live happily ever after.*"

"What's that?"

"It was written on her tombstone."

"Well, maybe now they will, now that they are together ever after. Thanks to me." His laugh was arrogant. Claire should have slapped him.

"To think," she said in reverent quiet, "that husband and wife are buried so near one another, without either of them knowing."

"You don't know what they are cognizant of in the afterlife. Perhaps they do know that their bodies lie close to one another."

"I hope so."

His eyes glittered in the dark. "But you will know all about the afterlife, won't you? Very soon."

If only she could keep him talking until she figured out an escape. "I have more questions about Zillah."

What could she do without a candle? If she could grab his lantern, he would catch her quickly if she ran with it. Perhaps if she smashed it against the cavern wall. Then they would both be in the dark. But Roman knew these corridors much better than she.

Still, it might be her only chance.

Suddenly he grabbed her upper arm, too tightly. She'd waited too long.

"Roman! Wait!" She heard the begging in her voice, the desperation.

He was able to set the lantern down and straighten again without releasing his manacle-like grip. "I'm sorry, Claire. I liked you. You know that, don't you?" He stroked her hair gently, tucked a loose strand behind her ear. This delicate affection was more frightening to her than the tight grasp his other hand retained on her arm. "But, regretfully, we've already wasted too much time, and Alice may be going to find help soon, so . . ."

Claire watched as his hand dropped from her hair and moved to his pocket. Everything was happening in slow motion. She thought of Alice and Bethany. She saw Mrs. Dawson and Mr. Randall. Her friends were in a silent panorama, smiling at her as they slid by. Even Grace and Mr. Tully smiled and waved to the beat of blood pounding in her head, blocking out all other sounds.

If Roman said anything else, she could not hear it, as she was trapped in her own world where each second stretched agonizingly, pregnant with the last memories of life.

Claire saw the glint of lantern light on steel. She squeezed her eyes shut.

Chapter Thirty

Roman jerked suddenly, like a fish on an invisible line. Claire stared at the knife in his hand as he dropped in slow motion to his knees, and then fell forward.

She looked up to see a dark figure emerge into the faint light and take his place. Vitus stood breathing heavily, a large rock in his right fist. Her eyes dropped quickly to Roman's head. The light hair was already beginning to mat with dark blood.

"Vitus." Her voice shook, and the little light there was began to dim. Claire did not think the cave could become any darker, and yet it did. She reached out a hand to steady herself, and felt the wall spinning under her hand. As she began to slump, Vitus caught her.

"Don't faint on me, Miss Temple." She heard the order given through a fog. "We've got to get out before he awakens. I don't know how hard I hit him."

She felt his strong arms supporting her, willed her muscles to respond, but they felt as limp as seaweed.

"I'm so sorry." Claire felt her eyes fill with tears. She couldn't look his way, her face burned with shame. "I thought you were the murderer. I was afraid of you."

"Shhh, don't think about it now. Let's go. You've had a nasty shock. And Alice is worried about you."

"Is Alice all right?"

"She's fine, but she's frightened. It was Alice who came and found me."

"Where did she find you? Roman said you were not in your room tonight."

Vitus shook his head, his face grim. "I don't know why he said that, because it wasn't true. Alice came to the house. She can confirm that for you. She said you'd gone into the cemetery and she was afraid you were in danger. We rode back—she wouldn't hear of staying behind, and held tightly to me—as swiftly as we could."

"But how did she know I was in danger?"

"She said after you'd entered the cemetery, she heard someone approaching. She stepped behind a large tree and waited. She heard the cemetery gate creak open and the other person's steps faded away. She hurried to find me."

"Then she didn't know it was Roman?"

"No, neither of us did. All she could tell me was that it sounded like the heavier tread of a man." Vitus picked up the knife where it lay close to Roman.

"I kept him talking." Claire shuddered as she looked down at Roman's still figure. "Vitus, he killed Zillah. He told me."

He nodded. "I'd begun to suspect that. I didn't know why he was pointing suspicion to me. Something's come between us these last few years. Roman had started acting strangely."

"He's been smuggling. And dealing in stolen goods as well. Zillah discovered it by accident. He said that's why he killed her. There's another exit at the cliff's edge. He said he killed her and then he threw her body down into the sea." She turned suddenly, to stare back in the direction Vitus had entered from. "That's not all. He left another dead body hidden in these tunnels."

"Another body? Do you know whose it is?"

She reached for the kitchen table with one hand as she began to crumple, her other hand clutching her stomach. Folding in half, she grabbed the edge, gripping it tightly, her knuckles white. Mr. Randall, hastily at her side, caught her by the waist should she faint.

Bethany turned to him and clung for support, like a vine being ripped from its safe trellis by violent gusts. He brought one hand up to cup her head against his shoulder, his other shielding her against him as she shuddered with loud sobs.

Claire stood by helplessly, abashed to be in the party responsible for bearing the news on Bethany's return. Thus they finalized Calden Coulter's existence, knowing his footsteps of adventure would now end abruptly at a tombstone. She turned her glance to Vitus, who reached to take her hand, signaling by his touch that she'd had no choice. She had no smile to silently thank him, but gently pressed his fingers that wrapped around hers.

EPILOGUE

In the days following the service for Bethany's father, the friends continued to gather in the kitchen at Pelican Inn. They could have comfortably sat in one of the larger parlors, but like Claire, everyone gravitated to the warm, busy kitchen.

The group—Bethany, Malcolm Randall, Aunt Amelia, Grace and Alice, Vitus and Claire—continued to find peace in one another's company, talking through the events of the last week, helping one another heal. They reanalyzed most of the past six months, and even earlier memories, while Zillah was still with them. Their gatherings reminded Claire of the Christmastide holidays, but it was now the sad event of death that brought all together, rather than a joyous birth.

She noticed no one spoke of Roman, who had been found alive, unconscious, and taken into custody the night Vitus had rescued her.

Claire had replayed that night in her head so many times, it became a macabre play she could not stop attending. If Vitus had not arrived when he did—if, and if; these what-if scenes must end as well, or she would never have another full night's sleep. She must put the horror behind her. The fact was that Vitus had not only arrived in time, an impossible feat in itself, but miraculously made his way through the labyrinth to her.

She looked up at Vitus, who stood by her side, leaning against the counter. His hand was entwined with hers, but he was looking at Mr. Randall, the two of them deeply engaged in conversation. The two men had become fast friends in the short time they'd known one another.

When the cups and the tea kettle appeared, Mr. Randall moved across the room to assist Bethany, and Claire had Vitus's attention. "Vitus, I've been meaning to ask you: that night, how did you know where in the cemetery to find me?"

"Alice told me." He nodded toward the young girl, who was helping Grace stack round lemon-iced biscuits on small decorative plates.

"I know she told you I was at the cemetery, but how did you know I was in that mausoleum?" Claire knew he could not have had time to search each headstone as she had, peering for a particular Whittaker.

"She was extremely specific in her directions. She told me you would be inside the Whittaker crypt, at the very back of the cemetery. In fact, she told me it would be the third tomb from the left."

Claire looked down at the kitchen floor without seeing it, picturing that night, and how the far boundary of the cemetery was invisible, overshadowed with trees. Impossible for a blind girl to know. "But she never even entered the cemetery. I went alone."

She didn't see his shrug, but it was obvious in his voice as he said, "I don't know. You'll have to ask her."

Claire looked back at Vitus. "And once inside the tunnel?" She could see herself taking the first artery off the main tunnel, a minor branch one would not assume to follow. She visualized the two exits on the rear wall of the storage chamber, equal in size. "However did you know which turns to take? Oh, I know. You recalled the directions provided by Zillah."

At his look of surprise, she knew he had not made the connection himself. "I hadn't thought of that in my panic. But I do remember the clue now. The one we burnt."

Claire chose not to correct the "we" in his statement.

"Alice knew, Claire. Her instructions were so precise. But you say she never entered the cemetery?" Vitus squinted, recalling to memory that night. "It was too far to the vaults for her to see you in the dark, even if she had sight. How was that possible?"

Claire nodded thoughtfully in agreement. "Exactly. How was it possible?"

When Alice finished preparing the plates, she followed with her cane as Grace and Bethany brought the delicacies to the table.

"Alice," asked Claire when they'd all been seated, with Alice between herself and Vitus, "Did you follow me inside the cemetery? That night?" she added unnecessarily, when Alice had not answered.

Alice acted as if she struggled to find the memory. "No," she said, drawing the syllable out, sounding in doubt.

"Then how did you know where to send Vitus? How did you know I was in the mausoleum?"

Alice blushed. "Oh. I forgot. I guess I did go inside the graveyard."

"But . . . You were so adamant about not stepping foot past the gate."

Alice changed the subject. "Did I tell you that Vitus put a halter on his horse, but we didn't even put on a saddle? I've never ridden bareback on a horse before. I held on tight to Vitus, and he said I wouldn't fall off."

Vitus smiled a lopsided grin. "Yes. She was quite the brave horsewoman."

Claire turned the subject right back. "And Vitus said you knew exactly which turns he was to take down inside the tunnel. Had you remembered Zillah's clue?"

Alice held the lemony biscuit close to her mouth, about to

take a bite. Instead, she put it down. She hesitated before saying, "I wanted to tell you the truth, but I didn't think you would believe me. And I don't want you to think I'm a fibber."

Claire put a hand on Alice's arm. "I promise you that I shall always believe you. You are the heroine who helped us solve Zillah's murder. Zillah would have been so proud of you."

Alice looked down in embarrassment, but Claire saw the smile that Alice tried to hide.

"Thank you. But I don't want the credit if someone else should have it."

Claire was surprised. "And whom would that be?"

"Nicholas told me."

While Claire made an effort to keep her expression neutral, her forearms tightened with sudden tingling bumps. *Surely this could not be the same Nicholas Alice had been afraid of.*

"I told Vitus that after you were there I heard someone approaching, a man's footsteps, and the gate creaking," said Alice. "But the truth is I left the moment you went back into the cemetery. I didn't want to leave you because I said I would wait for you. But Nicholas was upset, and he was yelling at me again. I was outside the gates, but I could still hear him. He told me that I had to go and find someone to help you as fast as I could go. I left to get Vitus."

Claire felt the chilling pinpoints spread to the flesh of her legs. "I see." But she did not.

"Then, when I returned with Vitus, Nicholas told me where Vitus could find you. And I waited at the gate. I was sad, though, because Nicholas said he had to tell me goodbye. Forever," Alice said in heavy-heartedness. "He told me his mamma and his poppa were waiting for him."

Again Claire wondered if Nicholas was a real boy, unbeknownst to blind Alice.

"Did he say where his parents were?"

"No. He just said he was supposed to be with them a long time ago. They were waiting for him, but he stayed behind to watch Zillah first. He told me Zillah used to visit the graveyard, and she always brought flowers to put on the forgotten graves." Alice took a bite of her biscuit before continuing. "But now he can go find them. He was so excited, he made me happy too."

"Let's take some flowers, like Zillah did, for Nicholas and his mother and father." Claire put her hand on Alice's silver-blond head. "Would you like that?"

Alice nodded. "Can we go today? And how will we know where to put them?"

"If we don't see a stone with Nicholas's name, we can put them under a nice tree. But . . . are you sure you're willing to go inside the gate?"

"Yes. He said it's safe for me now in the cemetery." She turned her attention to her biscuit.

Claire looked at Vitus. They studied one another above the young girl's head, not knowing what else to say to her story.

After tea was finished, Alice asked, "Claire? Can I take Nicholas some seashells, instead of flowers? I think boys like seashells better."

"That's a wonderful idea. I think Mrs. Dawson will agree it should be safe now for us to walk down the path to the beach."

Claire did not know who had sent word to Mrs. Dawson that night, but the moment Claire was brought home to Raven Heights, Mrs. Dawson had rushed out and almost stumbled down the porch in her haste.

"My dear! My dearest." Tears ran down her face as she enveloped Claire in her arms.

Ashamed to make eye contact, Claire was glad to bury her face in the woman's shoulder. "I am so sorry. I should never have been out at midnight. I should never have gone near the cliff. And I should not have pursued this mystery." Now Claire was crying as well. "I have no right to ask your forgiveness. And my uncle shall be so displeased."

Mrs. Dawson pulled away, her crying abruptly ended. "That is absurd. We shall never mention this to your uncle!"

Claire stopped crying as well, her wet eyes wide in disbelief. "I can't lie to him. I cannot be dishonest."

Mrs. Dawson pursed her lips together. "Of course not. Of course, you are right. So how shall we frame it to him?" Her large blue eyes were bright. "Claire, don't you worry. I know your uncle too well. He will be so happy just to know you are finally here. And that you are safe. He will be so proud that you young people solved the mystery of Zillah's death." In a hushed tone, she added, "And the disappearance of Mr. Calden Coulter." Her head drooped as if the sadness inside it was just too heavy to bear.

"I shall understand if he should not want me to stay at Raven Heights, if he should—"

"Nonsense! He will do no such thing. You have become special to me, and part of this family. I shall not allow it! I do have my own independent income, you know. Or perhaps you do not know. Nevertheless, child, I promise you: if he throws you out, then he shall lose both his niece and his cousin. And his housekeeper, ha! For you and I shall set up in comfort in a respectable cottage. All on our own. And crowded with your Uncle Myles's paintings in every nook and cranny, to keep us company." This was accompanied by the tinkling laugh Claire had grown to love.

"Thank you, Mrs. Dawson." Claire hugged her. "For everything."

Returning her thoughts to the present, Claire pushed her chair back and stood.

"Shall we go?" she said to Alice, who scooted her chair back as well and felt for her cane.

"I'll join you both. That is, if you don't mind." Vitus rose from his seat.

Claire's smile was the only answer of encouragement he needed.

The three of them left Grace and Aunt Amelia sitting at the table, where Grace was showing the older woman the scarf she had been working on.

Captain Henry sprawled on his side near the open hearth, his long, smooth velvet ear draped down his face. One of his eyes slanted open beneath his droopy brow to study them aristocratically, then closed in contentment.

They passed by Bethany and Mr. Randall, who were carrying their plates and cups to be washed. They saw him lean intimately toward Miss Coulter, speaking in a low voice.

And if the three hadn't headed straight out the door, they would have heard Malcolm Randall say, "I want to stay forever with you, Miss Bethany Coulter. And I promise I'm good for more than just cooking and financial backing." He kissed her cheek and whispered, "I can even help you straighten all the doilies every morning, after those pesky guests leave."

ABOUT THE AUTHOR

Sharol Louise and her husband live in the Pacific Northwest, where her psyche was born. However, her body was born in downtown Los Angeles, so it took about twenty-five years for the two to catch up.

As a youngster, she thought people were referring to the dictionary when they said "the good book," as she grew up in the library reading Edgar Rice Burroughs, Mary Stewart, and Sir Arthur Conan Doyle.

A former docent with The Seattle Public Library, Sharol is passionate about libraries, and has visited over 150 libraries across the United States.

She's been known to miss her bus stop when engrossed in a novel and wishes that her books may do the same for you.

This is Sharol's fourth book for Five Star Publishing.